Praise for Margaret Irwin

'One of Britain's most accomplished historical novelists.
Her love and respect for the past shines through every page'
Sarah Dunant, author of *Sacred Hearts*

'Accomplished, fluent, graceful, picturesque and
very readable'
Times Literary Supplement

'Kind, courageous and fertile; it mingles history and
romance with such spirit'
The Observer

'Beautifully and evocatively written, this is historical
writing at its best'
Historical Novels Review

'Margaret Irwin's books have an unsurpassed colour
and gusto'
The Times

'Splendidly retold . . . the strange drama in this writer's
skilful hands has a strong romantic appeal'
Daily Telegraph

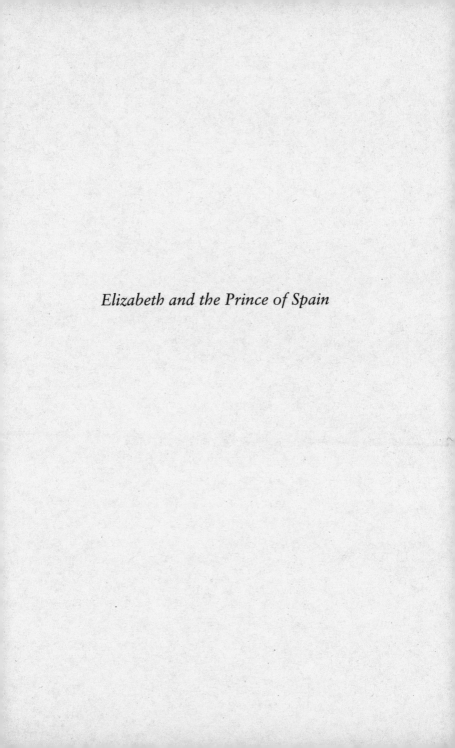

Elizabeth and the Prince of Spain

MARGARET IRWIN (1889–1969) was a master of historical fiction, blending meticulous research with real storytelling flair to create some of the twentieth century's best-loved and most widely acclaimed novels, including *The Galliard* and *Young Bess*.

By Margaret Irwin

The Galliard
Young Bess
Elizabeth, Captive Princess
Elizabeth and the Prince of Spain

Elizabeth and the Prince of Spain

MARGARET IRWIN

Allison & Busby Limited
12 Fitzroy Mews
London W1T 6DW
www.allisonandbusby.com

First published in Great Britain in 1953.
This paperback edition published by Allison & Busby in 2013.

A CIP catalogue record for this book is available from
the British Library.

10 9 8 7 6 5 4 3 2

ISBN 978-0-7490-1262-5

Typeset in 10.5/15 pt Sabon by
Terry Shannon

The paper used for this Allison & Busby publication
has been produced from trees that have been legally sourced
from well-managed and credibly certified forests.

Printed and bound by
CPI Group (UK) Ltd, Croydon, CR0 4YY

Elizabeth and the Prince of Spain

PRELUDE: THE BOY

'My father has fought bulls singlehanded in the arena,' said the boy. 'He is brave as a lion. He has never been defeated. He is the Conqueror of the World. How could he be conquered – by a pirate fleet of heathen Moors?'

'The East is Europe's worst danger,' said a dry voice in dusty answer.

'It *was*. But my grandfather drove all the Moors out of Spain after they'd ruled and ravaged here for seven hundred years. And he was not half as great a man as my father.'

'No, but his wife was,' the tutor muttered, all but sniggered, and covered it with a hasty cough, his precise tone at once correct again. 'My Prince, it is not the heathen who have conquered the Holy Roman Emperor, the "Invincible Emperor". It is the winds and the waves of the sea. Listen to the storm raging even now against this tower.'

He stooped eagerly forward, his sharp nose peaked against the light, his black-sleeved arm swooped to draw back the heavy curtain and in a dramatic gesture pushed aside a wooden shutter.

Outside the small panes of glass a jagged landscape leaped into shape against a frantic sky. Those were not the Guadarrama range that Prince Philip knew, but the mountains of hell.

'Look at the lightning,' insisted the tutor, a stiff man but now curiously gloating, as many a peaceable man will do in a scene of violence in which he need take no part. 'Hear the rain flailing down on the stones of the courtyard far below. *These* are the enemy who conquered the Emperor Charles V at Algiers, smashed his great ships to splinters against the rocks, blew his tents away like dandelion clocks on the seashore.'

Something chilled his enjoyment in his descriptive powers. He turned from the window and saw his Prince looking at him. Philip said coldly, 'The storms show the wrath of heaven. It is God who directs the winds and waves. "He spoke and His enemies were scattered." Do you tell me that God fought for the Moors against the Emperor my father?'

Another flash, a long rending crash tore the sky across as he spoke.

'This is blasphemy,' said the boy. 'God himself denies it.'

Dr. Siliceo hastily snapped the shutter to again and pulled the curtain over it, shutting out the enormous scene from the stuffy glittering little room. Candle flames in the draught, which even glass, wood and tapestry could not suppress, winked against the silver figure writhing on the crucifix, flickered over the livid blood-pink and blue in a Flemish picture.

'Certainly,' said Dr. Siliceo severely, 'it is blasphemy for Your Highness to deny victory to your illustrious father. That is exactly what I was explaining. You must write and tell him that you understand his defeat was caused by no human agency; it was by the command not of God but of the Devil.'

As so often, Philip felt himself rebuked without quite knowing why. 'I will write,' he said heavily.

Yes, he must write. Yet again.

Pen, paper and ink. More and more paper, more and more

ink, yet another pen. He was always doing it. 'He fights and I write,' Philip muttered. It was all he could do, while his father fought battles, risked his life in them. 'Emperors don't get killed in battle,' Charles V had often scoffed to those who tried to restrain him, but he had very nearly disproved it this time. His wretched troops had been mowed down in a surprise attack in the drenching night, some had broken and fled; the whole army might well have been totally destroyed if the Emperor had not seized his sword and rushed into the front ranks, rallying them by his courage alone to drive their attackers back into Algiers.

If only Philip had been there at his side! But he would have been no use; only an added responsibility and anxiety to his father. His common sense saw it clearly though bitterly.

One day he would be a full-grown man, he would be a great soldier like his father; he would have more and bigger ships than any in the world, and his armadas would avenge this defeat suffered by the armadas of Spain.

Yet the hope of doing what his father had failed to do lay heavy as lead upon his spirit. Lethargy fell on him like sleep; he longed to sleep, to die, and never to be called upon to prove himself as great a man – no, greater even, than his father. 'Let me alone for I am not better than my fathers.'

'Let me alone,' he said aloud. That of course could not be taken literally. Dr. Siliceo retired to a corner of the room and bent his head over a book, low, lower, as his breathing grew louder. *He* could sleep.

To sleep, to die, to lie for ever carved in marble like the beautiful young Prince Juan on his tomb at Avila, who had never had to live to be King of Spain but had died instead at sixteen. Philip would not be afraid to die. But to live; to take over the mastery of more than half the world; to make swift decisions in the heat of action; to break the power of his arrogant nobles and then seem to make friends with them, while always distrusting them; to trust no one, depend on no one, to listen to advice and take none of it – yes, Philip was afraid to live. How could he ever do it all?

He was small, he was not very clever, and two great Kings would hem him in on either side, his father's lifelong rivals, older than his father and much bigger, two crafty wicked giants, but his father had outwitted and defeated them, outrun them in the race for the Empire. They were Henry VIII of England, huge as a bull, with a bull's brutal inimical stare, in the full flush of his career of murderous matrimony; and the sly 'Foxnose,' François I of France, also well over six feet, whom his father had conquered and captured in battle and held as his prisoner for two years in Madrid. The French would never forgive it, watched always for the chance to attack Spain with every ally they could muster, even the heathen Moors.

Yes, the Very Christian King of France had actually joined forces with the fanatic enemies of Christ, with the Sultan, Soliman the Magnificent, and his slave-born sea-captain Barbarossa the Red-beard, and helped them to build up this pirate fleet at Algiers with the Moors who had been driven out of Spain. From that ancient port on the North African shore they raided the seaports of Spain, destroyed Spanish shipping and trade, and drove the wretched coast-dwellers further and further inland to the safety of the mountains.

'Three things from which no man is safe,' said the old

Moorish proverb. 'Time, the sea and the Sultan.' And now the sea and the Sultan had defeated his father, and no man was safe. No man was safe until he was dead.

The boy laid down his pen on the blank sheet of paper and stared at the tortured figure on the crucifix. Yes, even He was safe in spite of His sufferings, since there had been nothing more to do but suffer unto death.

He rose and walked to the window, making no sound even when he drew back the curtain and the shutter. No lightning now pierced the dreadful night; nothing could be seen. Yet he saw something, the pale glimmer of a face framed in a nun's coif, and it was looking at him.

It could not be; the tower rose sheer from the rock, no one could be there, floating in space fifty feet above the ground. He was seeing a vision, a nun's face. Relief surged over him in an engulfing wave; God had sent him the answer to all his fears and doubts of himself in the world; He meant him to renounce the world and become a monk.

The nun's lips were moving; speaking to him; he could hear no word through the thick glass, nor could he do so, if the window were open, against the roar of the tempest. Yet he knew what she was saying to him, dead contrary to his thought. 'Go back,' she said, 'back to all you have to do.'

'I have not the strength.'

'You will have all the strength you can bear.'

'How *can* I do it all?' But he knew her answer even as her face drifted into darkness. 'As it comes. One thing at a time.'

At this time he could write a letter of condolence to his father.

He shut out the now empty darkness and stood remembering where he had seen that face before. A few months ago at Avila he had stared with the curiosity of a boy at a young woman who some years before had run away from home to become a Carmelite nun, and now proposed to reform the Order and bring it back to its ancient austerity. She was mad, some people said, others that she was a witch; she had visions, or else she was tempted by the Devil; she was a hopeless invalid, paralysed at times, unable to move hand or foot; yet when she prayed, her body sometimes floated up into the air. Her family had complained of her and now her convent was doing so, her confessor had ordered her to make rude gestures of repudiation when visited by beatific visions; she had been warned by the Church, even threatened by the Holy Office of the Inquisition.

Philip stood so still that Dr. Siliceo blinked, sat up, stood up.

'Your Highness requires—'

'Nothing. Yes. What is the name of that nun – the "ecstatic" who is causing trouble at Avila?'

'Teresa of Avila,' replied Siliceo; 'a tiresome woman. Why does your Highness ask?'

Philip did not answer. A little shakily he went back to his desk.

The tutor repeated drowsily, 'A very tiresome woman. Her Superior has told me that she prays for suffering. That is doubtless a way of ensuring that one's prayer shall be granted.' His chuckle rustled like a dead leaf across the room, but there was no sign that his pupil had heard him. Philip was writing. Siliceo took up his book, but his eyelids dipped lower, lower, then flicked open on the desk inlaid with gold and mother-of-pearl, at the jewelled quill scratching at the paper, and the smooth flaxen head ducked over it like a fledgling chicken's bending to peck. A good-looking boy, drowsed the tutor comfortably, perhaps not so good a scholar as one would expect from a pupil of his, but every inch a Prince, especially on horseback where you didn't see how few the inches were; silver fair, his veins showed the blue blood, pure of any taint of the Moor, a rarity prized among the proudest Spanish families, and prized above all by Siliceo, who believed passionately in racial purity and preached that not only all infidel Moors and Jews should be expelled from Spain, as had been done, but all those also who had been converted to Christianity, and even all who had ever had a Moor or Jew, however far back, in their ancestry. Conversion could be feigned; the only sure test was pure Spanish blood.

But Prince Philip, alas, had more of Flemish blood. Siliceo had been engaged to correct that error; the boy had grown into a typical well-bred Castilian, respectable (outwardly at least), grave, reserved, and austere in manner, even more a Spaniard than many who were pure bred, since so much conscious effort went into being it – 'a *converted* Spaniard,' Siliceo chuckled to himself in malicious somnolence. So contrary is even the best regulated mind, particularly when half asleep, that he felt almost peevish at his success. Well, he had trained the Prince to be a gentleman, which was more than his father, the Holy Roman Emperor Charles V, that gross Fleming, could ever be. 'These Hapsburgs!' he muttered on a faint snore that startled him awake. At that instant an eyelid flicked open for a second in his mind; could training be carried a shade too far? That small figure before him, grimly plodding away at his squeaky quill, was a strange silent boy; it was most unlike him to speak even as much as he had spoken just now.

Something there was in him that seemed to check his imagination, his motive power; just as the uproarious rejoicings at his birth had been checked, broken off by his father's command and the whole Court ordered into mourning, sackcloth and penance, when the appalling news reached Spain that the Holy City of Rome was being sacked, and by the Christian troops of the Holy Roman Emperor himself. Outrage, murder and ruin, more horrible even than that wrought long ago by the heathen Goths, ravaged and all but destroyed Rome. It was the most shocking conquest in history, also the unluckiest, for every man who had taken active part in it was said to have met since then a violent or disgusting death.

The Emperor Charles himself was not there; it was not his doing, as he had frequently explained, but that of the other fellows, the subordinates who had let the men get out of hand; slack discipline, starvation rations, they had caused the rot.

True, he had ordered the march on Rome, but he was never one jot the worse for it; his appetites were as huge as ever, whether for food and drink, for bouts of boisterous jollity or an equally unrestrained melancholy; for more power over at least half of the Old and all the New World which, as fast as it went on being discovered, had long ago been decreed by the Borgia Pope to belong to Spain 'to all eternity.'

Unabated, unsated, the old ruffian appeared to savour every moment of his invincible career, for all that he talked at times of his need to 'make his soul' and repent of his sins – but never with any mention among them of the Sack of Rome. In spite even of that, his luck had held, till now.

But it had been no good omen for his son, born in that hour

of hideous victory over the Pope and his Church, to be the Very Catholic King of Spain; to have the high festival at his birth turned into bitter penance, as if he were doomed to an inheritance of guilt. Was the boy indeed haunted by a sense of guilt and need of atonement?

He was. But what haunted Philip was the fear of not behaving himself correctly in public, and every moment of his life was public, every natural function had to be conducted as a solemn ritual. Even at four years old, when he was breeched, it was a religious rite as well as a gorgeous ceremony; he had been perched high up on a mule and led across a vast plain where rocks as big as houses lay tumbled on top of each other in the burning sunlight; he came to red walls that reached up to the sky, and was told this was Avila, and shown the tombs of Torquemada the Grand Inquisitor, and the handsome marble youth who like himself had been Prince of Spain. He had been taken out of the quivering heat into a cold dim chapel where psalms were chanted round him, and long black-robed nuns took off his baby petticoats, touching him with unaccustomed hands, some podgy and clammy, some knuckly and sharp, but all strange; they put on his new manly breeches and black Court dress. Then he had to stand and face a long procession of lords and ladies and clergy, and then a vast cheering crowd below the stone balcony where trumpets blared in his ears and heralds shouted, proclaiming him the Prince of Spain. Very tired, bewildered, half deafened, frightened, he did not flinch, he bowed when told to, he behaved perfectly.

So he did even when he had been naughty and his mother, that serene beauty who seemed to him the Queen of Heaven, whipped him in front of her Court ladies and they shed tears at such cruelty to the tiny fair princeling. But Philip had not cried before the ladies when he was four. He had not cried when two years ago his mother died, and he had to lead her funeral procession out from the gaunt rock city of Toledo down through Spain, riding day after day across the vast tablelands of Castile and La Mancha and Andalusia, down towards Granada, down into the tomb of her grandparents Ferdinand and Isabella. There they lay at Granada, where they had forced the last surrender of the Moors; and there she, young and lovely, now must lie. The great vault was opened, her coffin lowered into it before the weeping multitudes; but Philip did not cry.

And he did not cry now when he was alone, and fourteen, though his whole world lay shattered before him, and his father, the Invincible Emperor, had been conquered by his enemies. No, *not* by them, never that. What was it old Siliceo had said, now blinking like a sleepy black cat in his corner, so little did he care? 'By no human agency,' echoed young Philip in a whisper, staring at the devils that his father found so amusing in that picture by Hieronymus Bosch. Birds swallowed men, toads danced with women, a lean thoughtful face looked out dispassionately on them all, wearing a pink hat, and on its brim yet more devils. The colours were like torn flesh, but unreal. Nowhere on earth could one see pink so violent, so vile, so virulent.

'No human agency,' repeated Philip; and was answered by the wind that flapped the edges of the heavy curtains, rattled the shutters of the turret room in the alcazar that towered defiantly on its rock above the Castilian plain.

The room became filled with the patient persistence of the

boy in proving to himself that the heathen hordes had not conquered yet again, that it was not the infidels' fleet who had defeated his father's ships at Algiers, but 'all the elements that had conspired against Your Majesty's prudence and greatness.'

BOOK I: THE PRINCE

CHAPTER ONE

1554

'I am going, not to a marriage feast, but to a fight,' said the young man.

'And what else is marriage?' grunted his father.

The young man stamped his feet down into his new silver-laced boots while the tailor reverently pulled them up higher and the trunk hose of white kid lower, till they fitted skin-tight round the slim and shapely legs, except for a wrinkle near the knee. The shaggy old man huddled by the window at a table that was covered with the inner mechanisms of a quantity of clocks, flicked up a red eyelid to scrutinize his son's legs. 'The hose are too long,' he said, 'or rather,' with a wheezy chuckle, 'the legs are too short.'

'An inch off just here,' the tailor whispered to his second-in-command. The legs tautened as if to stretch themselves, they balanced momentarily on the tips of the toes, striving for an unavailing instant to deny the sombre truth uttered by his father.

If only he were a few inches taller! It was important that he was a small man, because it was so important that he should be a great one. His father was old and ill and seemed at times half childish in his frantic preoccupation with his clocks, trying to make them all keep exactly the same time; although he knew well he should now concentrate on eternity and have done with time, and was threatening to retire to a monastery and do so. Yet his father, the Emperor Charles V, was still by far the greatest man in the world, and he would bequeath to him the greatest task that any man could undertake; nothing less than that he, his son Prince Philip, should be master of it.

'For it must come to that,' his father had always told him; 'it is One World now. One faith, one rule, and one man to support it,' so the Emperor had told the solemn boy whose pouting under-lip had mimicked his own in the effort to look portentously important; and he said it again now to the sadly conscientious young man who at his command was trying on before him the wedding garments that were an inch too long.

But this time he varied his formula. 'It is *your* world now,' said the thick guttural voice. 'It is *you* who have got to make and keep it one, under Spanish domination everywhere, for that is coming, mark you – it must come, in spite of those damned Lutheran princes stabbing me in the back from my own land of Germany. Luther – Luther – why did I ever let him live? I had him in the palm of my hand' – his fist shot out (and a startled tailor toppled over backwards on his heels), the gnarled fingers struggled to spread out, but had to twist up again – 'and I let him go!'

'Why did you, sir?' Prince Philip's question was almost an accusation.

'God knows! His safe-conduct I suppose. I'd promised him that. Machiavelli was a sound statesman; a prince who breaks his word is stronger than he who keeps it, no doubt that's true. But even an Emperor must think of his soul – sometimes.' The Emperor paused to consider this paradox, then rejected it.

'But no, I know why I did it. I said, "We'll keep this little monk, he may be useful to us some day." A handy weapon against the Papacy, I thought. There have always been heresies in plenty, and one could always stamp them out in time. But I wasn't in time. Luther's been dead for years, but he's still infecting the world. This plague of heresy is spreading like the Black Death, and what will be the end of it all? The death of society, of the civilized world, that's what heresy will bring. It is an international conspiracy to destroy government in every country, to bring one revolution after another, to divide nations, even families against themselves. It exalts treason into a virtue. Men will betray their country to be true to their "ideas" – ideas of what? That Judas Iscariot is a saint, for he betrayed his Master.'

And this was what Philip had to fight, as fiercely as ever his father had done, in hand-to-hand combat, or even the Cid himself, the hero of Spain, against the infidel. The infidel was again the enemy. The heathen Moor, or heretic English, there was nothing to choose between them, except that the latter were the more dangerous since they still pretended to the name of Christians.

His father's rivals, the two crafty wicked giants that he had dreaded as a boy, had been dead seven years, but their work went on. France was again at war with Spain, as bitterly her enemy as when François I had allied himself with the heathen Sultan and his pirate fleet.

And England, for whom Henry VIII had opened the door into heresy – opened it only ajar, since he had intended to keep the doctrine, and the profits, of the Catholic Church, while ejecting the Pope and monasteries – England had kicked the door wide open, and all through the reign of Henry's son

Edward had had heresy imposed by the law of the land. But now for the last year Edward was dead and his elder sister Mary was Queen, and Philip must go to England to marry her and help her bring back the country to the Church of Rome. It would be difficult, dangerous. The law would be now on the side of the Church, but a great part of the people were still against it; still more were against Mary's Spanish marriage. Protests had been openly made in Parliament and even by Mary's devotedly Catholic Chancellor, Bishop Gardiner; last winter the Spanish Ambassadors for the marriage negotiations had been snowballed by Londoners, who concealed stones in their snowballs; and early this last spring there had been a large-scale revolt headed by young Thomas Wyatt, of a most respectable family of diplomats and public servants, a revolt which had surged in civil warfare through the London streets right up to the Queen's palace and all but succeeded in overthrowing her government. Yet Wyatt had been executed, declaring to the end that he was no traitor since he had fought only for 'true religion'. A very pretty example of the high-minded treason his father was inveighing against, considered Philip, and tried to say so, but the Emperor only mumbled, 'Hey, what's that? Wyatt? You needn't worry. That business was well squashed, I saw to that. Executions in plenty. England's been made safe enough for you to go there for weeks past.'

And he lolled out a bright green tongue that slipped and fell sideways in his mouth. It never failed to startle his son's nervous susceptibilities, though Philip knew that it was only fresh leaf that his father sucked to promote saliva in his fever-cracked mouth. But every time it licked out at him like a lop-sided lizard he wished that his father, in spite of or perhaps even instead of being the conqueror and master of the world, were just an ordinary father. Why should he take more than a dozen clocks to pieces all at once? One or two might be reasonable, even three or four might be excused – but fourteen, perhaps fifteen! It was, like everything to do with his father, extravagant, disproportionate, positively gluttonous.

'*How* many clocks, sir, have you disintegrated there?'

'Why – all there are in the palace,' replied the Emperor in a voice surprisingly mild at the irrational demand. 'Time is important, you know, and you will find it so. Be sure that you keep time on your side.'

'Tick tock, tick tock' they all agreed, for at last he had put them together. They began to strike, some deep and sonorous as a church bell, some tinkling and thin as a child's rattle, some playing fragments of tune, some striking hammers, some slow, some fast, but all measuring out the time, one, two, three, four, on and on to the full number of eleven. 'There!' shouted the Emperor through their discordant din, snatching off his horn-rimmed spectacles and flinging himself back in his chair, an exhausted bear in all his furs, hot though the day was. But presently a smile like Jove's smoothed and expanded his rutted, forward-thrusting face. 'There, at last! They are all striking together at the same time.'

But not all. One, the smallest, came cheeping in at the very end, like a belated chicken out of its egg. The Emperor thrust his enormous jaw at it.

'But in any case,' said Philip's precise, slightly disdainful tones, as he pulled his new round globular watch out of the pocket of his discarded coat, 'it is not the right time.'

He could have bitten his tongue out as he heard his own words, but it was too late.

'What's that? Not the right time? These lazy rogues, these muddlers, bunglers—' and the Emperor Charles roared to his servants to bring again the exact time by the Cathedral clock; would not speak again till he had heard it; would not finish the portentous warnings of this farewell interview; but put on his owlish spectacles anew, and set to work in grim silence to regulate them all over again.

An ordinary father would not have done that. But none of Philip's family were ordinary.

He squared the slight shoulders on which the burden of Hercules was doomed to roll; he looked over the bowed backs and busy fingers of the tailors crawling round his legs, fitting on the wedding garments that were to be his armour for the Crusade that he must lead for Spain, the Empire of the world, and the one true Church to bind it together. And then he looked at the grey silhouette of his father's sunken head against the window, and beyond it the jagged outline of rocky hills, bare and tawny as a lion's skin in the harsh sunlight, that was his home. Yes, one – or other – of them must marry Mary of England. And why not the other?

A tinkling chime went up from one of the clocks. The rest followed in ragged chorus. The spell was broken; they were free to speak. Philip resumed the clothes he had been wearing, dismissed the tailors, collected his words.

'As Your Majesty was betrothed to Mary over thirty years ago –' he began, then gulped and started again rather more hurriedly. 'If the marriage were arranged for Your Majesty, that would be the best course.'

'I am over fifty-four and too old,' grunted the father.

'I am under twenty-seven and too young,' said the son.

'As the prospective bride is thirty-eight, she seems tolerably balanced between the two of us. But not in reality. For no one would call you young for your age – you are quite ten years ahead of them. But I, alas, am at least twenty years older than my age, a crippled wreck whose only wish is to leave the world and become a monk.'

But he was still the reigning Emperor, and knew there could be no gainsaying his commands. He thrust out his underhung jaw, fringed with sparse grey beard like the stubble of dead gorse on a wintry cliff, as he passed sentence on his son. Philip stood condemned.

His indigestible veneration for his father rose in his throat. Not for the first time he was tempted to disgorge it. It had suffered a rude shock in his boyhood when he had learned that the Emperor had been defeated by the Moorish fleet at Algiers. The discovery that no man, not even his father, was almighty, remained a guilty secret within Philip's breast, to be shunned even in this moment when he longed to remind himself, yes, and his father of it; to tell him that his hero-worship had once been shaken; that his father's very presence acted as a dead weight, crushing, paralysing him; that though no man could want the adventure of going into a hostile, heretic and semi-barbarian land to marry a prim old maid nearly a dozen years older than himself, yet he could almost welcome it, since it would at least remove him from his father's influence.

Only once before had he left Spain, and that was to go into his father's country of Flanders, where that influence had been ten times stronger and more all-pervading than in Spain. For the Emperor had never ceased to be a foreigner in Spain, while in Flanders he was adored as a native hero, and what was more a good fellow of the first water, or rather vintage.

Philip's visit to Flanders had been a lamentable failure.

At least in England he would be free of that influence, though it did not make him the less indignant at being sent there. He bowed ceremoniously and said, 'As an entirely obedient son, I have no other will but yours, and therefore leave it to Your Majesty to act as you think best.' He added under his breath, 'Not my will but my father's.'

'Are you seeing yourself as Jesus Christ?' demanded Charles on a spurt of laughter that blew the leaf out of his mouth, and he had to replenish it with another from a bowl of water on the table. But he felt a trifle worried. His eyes, enlarged by the globular horn-rimmed spectacles, scrutinized the pale, stiff young man before him as though he were part of the mechanism of his clocks. There could be nothing wrong with the mechanism. The Spaniards, a race as stubborn and untameable as their cruelly barren land, were taking him to their hearts ('if they have any,' he snorted) as they had never taken himself. Yet, unlike so many heirs to the throne, Philip never attempted to set himself up in rivalry to his father, he was indeed entirely devoted to him and did everything his father told him. Not too good a boy either; even at fourteen he had needed watching with the women, aha! and the sly young dog had shown his sensuality by coupling his demands for Titian's religious pictures with discreetly worded requests for 'poesies,' as he called the Master's voluptuous paintings of naked females with respectably mythological names. And now as a young man, for all his public decorum, he took his private pleasures, but perhaps too private; he could never really lose himself in a debauch, and that was partly why he had been so unpopular in Flanders; the old Fleming his father found in this a trace of satisfaction. He had to bear the weight of the world, but he had not let it cramp him unduly; he had taken his pleasures with Flemish grossness and fairly openly, though not flagrantly; but Philip with all his appetites had no gusto, perhaps not much guts. He had won a prize in the tourneys in Flanders, but it was his affectionate aunts who had been the judges. He certainly did not care for war and fighting, though he had his own sort of courage; put him to the tortures of the damned and it would be his pride to pretend he felt nothing. He could stand anything; but would he move? A rock could stand; but the ruler of the world had to be a deal more than a still, carved face in a marble block. There was after all something wrong with this boy; he had never been one.

And into his mind, as though it had passed there from Philip's, there flashed the unwilling memory of his crushing defeat at Algiers, and the stilted dispassionate letter of condolence that his son of fourteen had written to him. He had hoped that damned dull tutor had dictated it, but no, the construction was too bad; it was clearly Philip's work, and clear proof he never was a boy. He shook off the memory, which often before he had shared with his son; though neither of them had ever spoken of it. It gave an edge to his annoyance with Philip for so obviously being about to do what he was told, and think himself a martyr for it. It was unfortunate that others thought the same; the Bishop of Pampeluna had actually compared him to Isaac, sacrificed by his father Abraham. That must have pleased Philip. It was time he learned how lucky he was.

The shrewd screwed-up eyes peered over their spectacles. The green tongue shot out to strike again. 'Fortune is a strumpet,' he chuckled; 'she keeps her favours for the young.'

'Mary Tudor is the last gift one would expect from a strumpet,' came in slow answer as the young man turned from his father; in no impatient movement, for it was his pride to be patient, but with the deliberate determination of acceptance.

Something deeply, sluggishly inert in his nature welcomed the chance to be heroic through acceptance rather than action, suffering rather than adventure.

Heroically he turned again and strode back towards the table, kicking shreds and snippets of stuff shed by the tailors out of his way, as if to spurn the pleasures he was leaving of his life in Spain. Bare and bright the sunlit scene rose outside the window; a lizard flashed emerald across the white wall of the courtyard below, and some young men riding past on their way to the tiltyards were singing an old song of how they had returned from hunting to find their vineyard stripped by the Moors, and there would be no wine for them. Seven centuries of Spain lay in that song, but to Philip it was too familiar for him to have noticed before; only now, as he heard it jigging away into the distance, he thought that he would not hear it in England.

The Emperor divined the self-pity in his gaze and remarked in affectionate exasperation, 'Take another text to yourself for comfort; it is your father's good pleasure to give you the kingdom.'

'A kingdom whose people rose in arms to prevent my coming! A kingdom whose angry Parliament refuses me even the title of King, and has shorn away every vestige of power from my position as the Queen's Consort.'

'You'll get it back in the night-time,' Charles told him with cheerful ribaldry. 'What more powerful position could you hold than that? A young man in bed with an old maid must be a boor or impotent if he fails to get all he wants from her. You are neither. Win her to you, and she'll do her best to get her councillors to give you all we want. Kings don't count for much now in England. Henry VIII did, but he was a giant, and even he was careful to keep on the right side of the people. But now it's the councillors who rule the country – and rule the Queen too. You'll have to win *them* over – not so easy.' He pushed his horn-rimmed spectacles up high on his wrinkled forehead and leaned back in his chair, talking with greedy enjoyment, lisping sometimes and mumbling often, almost inaudibly, yet greedily savouring his own sound advice, blinking in amused memory of the little scenes it called up of that strange, that incredible country that he had once visited for a fortnight when he was a youth.

'Drink English beer, and praise it. It's bitter, but better than their wine, since Henry sold the monasteries and lost their vineyards. Talk to people as human beings, not as abstractions. Look them in the face, don't squint sideways at their boots, it makes them think you've something to conceal, and so you have, your shyness, but they'll never guess that. So look straight at their eyes. Smile, and when any Englishman tells a story, laugh. It's always meant to be funny. But be serious when you talk of sport. Don't forget Henry was the best shot of his day, and I'm told they still speak wistfully of their bluff King Hal; he might chop off your head, but was equally likely to clap you on the back and call you a useful fellow with the longbow or the tennis racket. Make love to the women with discretion. The English do not make kind cuckolds.

'And don't let our women go with their husbands. They'll

make more mischief than any soldiers. Send them home, send them to Flanders, send them to hell. But don't, as you value your peace, your hoped-for crown, your very life, don't let them meet the Englishwomen!

'If you do all this cleverly, you'll be crowned King in Westminster Abbey in three months and, what's far more important, you'll be shipping English troops to Flanders to fight with us against the French.'

At last Philip had a chance to speak.

'England should do so for her own sake. France will invade her from Scotland as soon as the Dauphin is old enough to marry the little Queen of Scots.'

'That confounded brat!' exploded Charles, spitting yet another leaf across the table. 'King Henry swore when she was a baby in arms that she was the most dangerous person in Europe. And here she is just ten years old and the King of France vowing to support her claim to the English throne and so unite it to the French!'

'Queen of Scotland, England, France,' murmured Philip. 'A combination strong enough to overbalance Spain.'

'If it happened – but it won't. We'll break it, for we'll be in first with England. That wretched little northerly island muffled in her sea-fogs right away from Europe, she's always been able to tip over the balance here. All my life and my father's, we have had to woo England. They say we Hapsburgs do not need to fight – we marry instead. And we married England long before you were born, when my poor aunt, Katherine of Aragon, wedded King Henry VIII and then could only succeed in rearing Mary Tudor. It was her one *faux pas* and she paid for it, but look how we've all paid for it! That florid, exorbitant, terrible fellow, Henry, upset everything, divorcing Katherine and bringing the Reformation into England unawares – brought it in like an imp in a bottle to work his divorce and re-marriage. But it wouldn't go back into the bottle, it rose and swelled into a gigantic genie, beyond his control.

'But now, in you, Spain has her best chance to win a real grip on England.'

'No better chance,' said Philip deliberately, and looking his father in the eyes as he had been told to do, 'than when Your Majesty was betrothed to Mary Tudor.'

The Emperor looked back at his son in irritation. It was more than tactless to remind him that he also had had the opportunity to knit the two countries together, when as a youth he had been betrothed to Mary Tudor, a little girl with long fair hair of which her father had been inordinately proud.

It had been a brief settlement, almost momentary; and the moment had passed, the betrothal had been cancelled, and the two countries had floated apart like ships that passed in the night.

'Leave it,' said the old man tersely. 'You'll never make me twenty again.'

'Nor Mary five. But,' said Philip chivalrously, 'I will undertake my poor, deserted aunt.'

His father floundered. Humour from Philip was apt to be unexpected, it threw you off your balance. Charles talked on in his rapid guttural, trying to recover it. 'What's that, you jackanapes? Your aunt? Drop it, you puppy. She's not your aunt, though her mother was mine. But Henry could never bear me to call him "Uncle", – I had to change it to "Brother". So be careful. You've offended her enough already, never writing to her until at last the poor woman had to do it first. What woman can bear that? Having to write the first letter, send the first portrait. And now you're putting off going to England again and again though I told you weeks ago that you'd damage your prestige if you dilly-dallied.'

He stared, startled. For the first time in their lives he had caught sight of a cold gleam of anger in the eyes that he had ordered to look into his; they were so looking, and the Emperor rather wished they were not doing so. For the first time it struck him that perhaps he did not know altogether what this self-contained young man was like, or might become.

'I am going,' said Philip, 'to fulfil your obligation, your father's, and your grandfather's. I am the fourth generation to woo an English alliance. To do so, I am abandoning not only my pleasure in my faithful mistress of many years' standing, but my duty towards my all but affianced bride. We have already settled a large dowry on the Princess of Portugal which will also have to be abandoned, as a bribe to buy her off, and is therefore a dead loss. My own loss will be a wife near me in blood and talking my language, sharing my way of thought, in order to go to a strange country that is seething with hate of Spain, religion and civilization, and marry an old maid with whom I cannot exchange a word, except in languages foreign to us both. I grant you that my future wife has shown consideration for me in begging me to bring my own cooks and physicians. But it is an uncomfortable hint at the likely danger of poison. I see no occasion for reproach.'

The Emperor decided to change the subject rapidly, and introduce the stimulus of a mild flick of jealousy. Philip had frequently shown an inclination to covet something only when someone else wanted it or was likely to acquire it.

Eyeing his son astutely, he told him, 'Well, if you wait much longer, the English Cardinal, that fellow Reginald Pole, will get there first. I have had the devil of a time holding him back as it is. Take care he doesn't cut you out. Ha ha! He's as much of an old maid as she is, and two of a feather might get together. They've done so already in letters, and *he* doesn't wait for her to write first. Their mothers planned their marriage at one time – Lord, what mothers won't do!'

'Sir, he's a Cardinal—'

'He's a Plantagenet. He's a better right to the English throne than she has. That's why all his family were executed by Henry nearly twenty years ago. What's that – a Cardinal? That's nothing. He could get dispensation, he's never taken priest's orders. But in any case he'll be even more dangerous as her Father-in-God than as her husband, stirring up the Devil's own mischief through pure religion.'

'*Pure* religion? Does that mean he's tainted with reform?'

'Oh no, he's right as rain,' his father assured him testily. 'You'll never find *him* charged with heresy. My fears are all the other way, that he'll be too rigid. I don't trust him, he's too sincere.'

Philip understood this surprising statement very well. 'You think he'll want the English nobles to give back their Church property?'

'Exactly. As if the greedy robbers would give up their spoils after near a score of years! The Queen hopes for it, of course, she's a woman. But he's a Churchman and ought to understand. No, he mustn't set foot in England till he brings firm assurance from Rome that it's the right of every

Englishman to keep what he has stolen. The Pope understands that. But the Pope's not Pole.'

'Nor a Plantagenet.'

'The plant of the Devil! Spiritual pride, beware it. But allied with family pride, beware it doubly. Especially in England.'

'Even with the Tudors?' There was more than a shade of contempt in Philip's tone.

'Especially with the Tudors. They've no shadow of right to the throne – except that their grandfather killed the Plantagenet Richard III and picked his crown out of a thornbush. That makes 'em prickly.'

'Is this Plantagenet, Pole, ambitious?'

'No, oh no, I wish he were. He'd be safer if one could buy him off. No, he's a nice fellow, a good fellow, but he *will* talk Christianity. He's even done it to the Pope. He'll do it –' the Emperor's wheezy laughter choked him for a moment – 'to the English Bishops! Imagine what trouble *that* will lead him into!"

'I can imagine it very clearly,' said Philip grimly.

'Yes, the English clergy are in a ticklish position, both religious and matrimonial. They've changed themselves three times over in the last half-dozen years. First, Catholic though not Roman in the last years of my Uncle Henry, and all the clergy celibate, not a wife for any one of 'em, not even for his precious Archbishop Cranmer, who helped him to divorce my Aunt Katherine and marry Ann Bullen and then helped him to un-marry and behead her – but, oh no, never a wife for his useful dog Cranmer, though he'd smuggled one over from Germany in a box, they say. Well, there they are, all of 'em as good as gold and celibate as bullocks, and then under little Edward they all turn black Protestant and rush into matrimony like the rats of Norway that fling themselves in droves into the sea and get drowned. That's England all over – no restraint. One day, no parson's wives, only an occasional modest mistress tucked away decently in the pantry, all very right and proper, and on the morrow the whole country swarms with parsons' wives, pert and prim, fat and slim, messing up their husband's work, meddling with the parish, setting it all by the ears, and then in a few months it's crawling with parsons' brats and the next year double the number. King Henry always said the reason against the clergy marrying was that they'd breed like rabbits, and so they did, right on until last summer, when the poor boy Edward dies, Mary becomes Queen, and hey presto all the wives have gone to earth with their litters, and once again the clergy is celibate, Catholic, and Roman too this time. All this talk has made my throat as dry as the Sierra,' he suddenly accused his son. 'Where's the sherry?'

He reached for the flagon. 'Ah that's better. Sherry – "Caesaris – the wine of Caesar!" Well what's good enough for Julius Caesar is good enough for me. And now for God's sake let me go to dinner. The pleasures of love, especially in holy wedlock, are apt to be grossly over-rated, but it is impossible to exaggerate the pleasures of the table.'

The grandees of Spain entered and hauled him out of his chair, supported his crippled feet, all but carried his painful tottering frame to dinner. He sat and crammed his mouth and belly with food, poured rivers of the wine of Cadiz and the Rhine down his wry neck, and rolled his parched tongue against his palate to let the heady coolness linger on it as long as possible. The sound of his steady chumping was interspersed with the occasional gulp of a belch, but there was none of his ambling mumbling lisping talk, for his mouth was far too fully occupied. To Charles one thing at a time.

His appetites were huge, and even now in his sick old age his digestion almost matched them. He had always found gluttony the safest vice. Vast meals appeased the craving of his senses, made him satisfied, satiated, stupefied, able to relinquish slightly the clutch of his conscious mind on the problems that beset the master of the world – a world shattered and disordered, with the old order crumbling into decay.

But here on the table was order still, unquestioned, established, sacred, each course following the other in harmony unalterable as the stars in their courses; the beef after the broth, the coney and capon after the carp, the swan after the stork, the peacock after the partridge, the venison after the veal, the perfect progress of one savoury flavour after another leading up to the voluptuous chorus of crowded sweets, grapes and apricots and peaches in tarts and fritters and garnished custards, hypocras and cream of almonds, translucent jellies quivering in the towering shapes of the gods on Mount Olympus, treading on rosy clouds with sugared violets in their saffron-shredded hair.

There he sat cloying his palate, cramming his appetite, mercifully dulling his senses, releasing him from his long, taut task of living.

Was life then but a craving to find death? But he had no need to ask it, knowing the answer lay in his longing to lay down his crown, to leave this vast glittering hall and its crowds of nobles, superb yet subservient, who handed him each fresh dish on bended knee; and to put on the single coarse robe of a monk in the monastery of Yuste, sleep in a bare cell, and never come out into the world again.

Even an Emperor must think of his soul sometimes, he had said; but it was not true, it was not possible, it was not even right, while on the business of being an Emperor. One thing at a time. Statecraft must come before soulcraft, Machiavelli had put it down in black and white, but all sound statesmen had known and acted on it long before. He had kept his word and spared Luther's life – and look what had come of it!

What if, in sparing Luther, he had launched the world in revolution for centuries to come?

He had done it for reasons of State; but he would have felt far more guilty if he had done it just because it was the right thing for him to do. The State must come before the individual soul.

Yet Christ had shown that the individual soul mattered above all else. So how could one be a Christian and a statesman – let alone an Emperor?

One could not, that was the answer; and he had only a little time left to make his soul before he died. He would pray continually, have masses said for him unceasingly, he would do penance, fast – the heaped dishes swam before his blurred eyes, and his sated yet insatiable appetite made an agonized protest against that latest resolve. But would his state of health permit it? Surely his Confessor would feel bound to grant him a dispensation from fast-days. And a serpent whispered in his mind, 'Yes, surely the Emperor's confessor –'

He drowned the whisper in yet another enormous tankard, now of golden Rhenish wine from his Fatherland. A fig for Julius Caesar and his colony of Spain – this was better than all the wines from Cadiz and Jerez! But in that instant's clarity that comes before intoxication, another doubt floated to the surface of his clogged and wearied mind. How was it that in this, their final private interview, he had forgotten to impress on his son, more urgently than ever before, that the chief danger awaiting him in England lay in that enigmatic young woman, not yet twenty-one, the focus if not indeed the cause of the revolution this past spring in England, the half-sister of Philip's bride-to-be, King Henry's red-headed bastard by Ann Bullen (and as much a bitch, he'd swear, as her mother), the Lady Elizabeth Tudor?

CHAPTER TWO

Prince Philip rode out across the sun-dazzled square at Valladolid in his armour of new clothes; crimson velvet, silver lace fringe were all to the taste of the gaudy English. His escort of a thousand horsemen glittered around him, his bodyguard of three hundred in the red and yellow livery of Aragon, with his Teuton Guard close behind, and the highest grandees of Spain, each followed by his retinue. Chief among them, at the Prince's right hand, rode the Duke of Alva at the head of a troop so perfectly disciplined that even Philip tautened his already rigid bearing under the eagle eye of the greatest soldier of his day. Alva was silent, austere, yet magnetic; men and even fate seemed compelled to obey that narrow face and the portentously lengthy prong of his greying beard. Charles had warned his son against his hero-worship of the great General; Alva, he said, was a greybeard from birth; there was too much caution in his courage, and no panache; worse, he needed watching, he was secretly ambitious, a sanctimonious hypocrite who looked like a prophet but didn't lose sight of the profit.

Philip was well used to disillusionment; his father had warned him against all his advisers, even his only real friend, the Portuguese Ruy Gomez da Silva, whose smooth dark profile was now jogging along on his left side. Ruy had been

Philip's unofficial guardian since his childhood, for he was ten years older. He had lately been made Secretary of State and promised the title of Prince of Eboli because the Emperor, though he would not go so far as to trust him, or anyone else, declared that he was at least a foreigner and therefore cleverer than any Spaniard could be. He was even clever enough to be no taller than his young Prince.

They rode out of the capital of Old Castile, past the stone gateway of San Gregorio's College for poor friars, founded by Philip's great-grandmother, whose royal arms were encrusted among its fantastic carving. A less happy reminder of Isabella the Catholic was the end of the little mean street where her devoted servant, Christopher Columbus, having brought to her country a new Empire of fabulous wealth, had died in miserable poverty less than fifty years ago.

Both places were too familiar for Philip to notice, except to wonder when he would see these landmarks of his birthplace again. He rode on towards Tordesillas and Benevente, making a detour down the frontier of Portugal to pay a parting visit to his grandmother. This was the way he would have ridden to meet the Princess of Portugal if only he had succeeded in remaining betrothed to her.

And this was the way he had ridden ten years ago when he was sixteen, towards another Princess of Portugal, Dona Maria Manoela, his first wife, a year younger than himself. Then, as now, he had set out from Valladolid, but not as now through the roar of cheering crowds and the choking white dust raised by a thousand horsemen; and then, but not as now, he had been on fire with curiosity to look on the unknown face of his bride.

It had been autumn on that earlier journey, and the peasants, trampling the grapes in the vintage tubs, their bare legs purple to the knee with the juice, had scarcely turned their heads to look at the little company of travellers with the slight fair boy in their midst, dressed so inconspicuously in a plain hunting-suit. For Philip had then ridden incognito, accompanied only by Ruy Gomez da Silva and a few of his servants. Etiquette forbade his meeting Dona Manoela while on her bridal journey to him, so he went secretly and in disguise to follow her sumptuous procession all the way into his country.

That earlier journey seemed more real than the one he was riding now. He could never smell roses, nor for that matter the whiff of sweat and garlic from a shouting crowd of peasants – as he was smelling it now, mechanically lowering his head from time to time in answer to the cheering – without remembering how he had gone down into the thick of just such a crowd as this and let himself be jostled and his nose and ears affronted no less than his dignity, while he hung about with a suffocating gauze mask over his face, and his feet in the dirt of the Badajoz streets, to catch the first sight of his future wife. He had waited a full hour before there appeared at a window high above him in the deep blue night a slight figure in a silver dress like the slip of the new moon. It had only been for an instant before she vanished, but it had been enough to make him continue to follow her, still in these uncomfortable and undignified conditions; until at last at Salamanca, among a host of grave old people, she stood before him face to face, with pink autumn roses in her hands, and the delicate eyebrows in her round baby face arching high at her first sight of him.

They joined hands and danced; they kissed and came together; for a little time, a year and a little more, the world was their playground and they the only people in it. Suddenly the idyll was over; she lay dead; and he had the rest of his life to remember the curve of her plump cheek, the pout of her lips, like a rosebud opening in the sun. Had she ever known how much he loved her? She could not have done so, for he had been too young to show it, she to know it.

Her childish ghost laughed and chattered in his heart as he rode on to Tordesillas, to meet a living lady who had been a ghost for nearly fifty years. His father's mother, Dona Juana of Castile, was still the nominal Sovereign of Spain, though her wits had fled from her half a century ago, distracted by grief for her handsome faithless husband, Philip of Hapsburg. When at last his death killed her jealousy – of his women, of his boon companions in hunting and drinking, even of his dogs – he had left her with but one clear purpose in her frantic mind, to keep his body in her constant sight. She had borne it embalmed in a coffin over the mountains, travelling only by night for four months, until at last at Tordesillas it found rest in Christian burial. But she never found rest.

She stared through her straggling hair at the fair young man, who flinched under the terrible intent gaze of the crone who had once been the most beautiful of the daughters of Ferdinand and Isabella.

'Who is this young man? Prince Philip, you say? Ah, I remember, he was christened after my husband, but he's not grown into as big and fine a man as Philippe le Bel of Burgundy. You came here lately with your bride, my granddaughter, a sweet child, such a silly mouth. She will grow as plump as a partridge. Where is she now?'

'Madam, she died nine years ago. I am going now to wed another bride.'

'Oh, then you *are* like my Philip. But like all other men too. No man can be faithful, to the living or the dead. You danced with her before me. It was a pretty sight. You are a good dancer. So now she lies still, and you are going to dance with another. Dance, dance, my pretty young man. But one day you will lie still too.'

'Madam, I know it. I think often of death.'

'Then you are a fool. Death is not for you – yet. You will cause many deaths before you come to it; the deaths of those you love and who love you.'

'Of those you love.' His father had warned him that at his early age he must for his health's sake moderate his passion for his bride; he had not done so, and the result had been, not his ill health, but her death in childbed.

He had no need to hide his emotion. His Stoic role would mean nothing in those clouded eyes that saw only what lay beneath. He choked back his pride and said, 'Madam, I am your grandson. I am heir to my father's throne and yours. I shall rule over more dominions than any single man has governed since Charlemagne. I pray you, Madam my grandmother, do not lay a curse on me.'

She laughed, a harsh and desolate sound. 'Who spoke of curses? I speak only of what I see. I see a pretty young man who thinks of death.'

Her mind seemed to clear suddenly for a space. She understood that he was going to England to marry the Queen, she even recollected that Mary was the daughter of her youngest sister Katherine of Aragon, who, poor child, had had to be despatched to that remote island in the Northern seas. And Juana herself with her husband had once visited it when they were sailing from Zeeland to Spain, though only because the frightful gales of mid-winter had driven their ship on to its shores.

People said it was that storm, raging and bellowing for two whole days and nights, that had wrecked Juana's wits. But at the time she had been the only calm person on board; indeed, as she crouched, clasping her husband's knees, her wild eyes had shone on his face in peace and joy that so soon the black waters would swallow them and they would go to death together for always.

But the sea had cheated her. The sea had brought them to England and into a forced alliance with that country and its first Tudor sovereign, the cunning upstart adventurer, Henry VIII's father, who had tricked Juana's husband and dared woo Juana when he was dead.

'Those slant-eyed Tudors,' she murmured to her grandson, 'they are not strong, but they make themselves so by guile. Watch them as you would watch the smiling beguiling sea, the cruel treacherous sea. Be careful of the seas round England. They are her strongest allies. But most of all beware of love, which is fiercer than the winds, more cruel than the waves. Love and hate are only the two sides of the same coin, and the coin rings false. All your life, hate will smoulder and whisper its dark way through your love.'

She was a witch, everyone said so, Philip reminded himself as he stumbled out into the sunlight and the glad company of a thousand men. Only her blood and her position, the highest in the land, the Queen of this land, had saved her all these years from being burnt as a witch by the Inquisition. For that Holy Office had first been instituted against the crime of witchcraft, and only later worked against heresy, which at this moment, by comparison, seemed an almost venial sin.

He stood still a moment by a fountain that splashed its cool drops on his hands, and smoothed out his face into the blank mask of icy decorum necessary to a Spanish Prince. A birdlike glance from Ruy Gomez's black eyes did not see that there had been anything disturbing in the interview.

They rode on to Benevente, where his son Don Carlos met him to say goodbye, a boy of nine, excitable and nervous, with a big head and rather humped back and sad eager eyes, who was apt to make Philip depressed and uneasy. Dona Manoela had been Philip's first cousin twice over by both parents, almost as near in blood as if she were his sister; medical critics had considered the marriage not only premature but unhealthy. Philip glanced in furtive anxiety at the queer little boy who had caused the death of his mother; one shoulder was a little higher, one leg a little longer than the other, and his spurts of courage and initiative, of kindness and even of precocious intelligence often seemed uncoordinated, out of focus. That might be natural at his age; so might be his frantic rages and savage impulses of childish nastiness or cruelty.

Philip reminded himself that the Emperor liked the lad and thought he often showed promise of a bright and original wit. But surely Carlos should already be thinking of himself as a man, instead of calling himself 'the little one' in a way any ordinary boy would despise as babyish. Flashes of eccentric cleverness might please an old man who was himself apt to be eccentric, and could afford to be so since he was exceptional, but they didn't clear Philip's mind of the suspicion that in general Carlos was backward. How would he shape when he had to take his place in his turn as master of the world?

Carlos himself had no doubts on the matter; he told Philip

various plans of what he should do when he became 'Imperator Mundi', and then, ingenuously, 'But it's Your Highness who'll be that when my grandfather dies. Perhaps I could go out to the New World and be Emperor of the West instead. I should like to see Red Indians.'

'I shall die, too, some day,' said Philip.

'Then I'll be Emperor of both worlds,' said Carlos, and added with a friendly goblin grin, 'but I hope you will not die yet.'

Yes, there was good in the boy, he had affectionate though childish impulses. He cried that he could not go to England with his father, which was unreasonable; he laughed with delight in the pageants given in his father's honour, the flaming torches leaping against the night; he shrieked at the fireworks and the towering elephants made of painted cardboard, moved by men on horseback inside them. Most of the adults were equally childish; the chroniclers exhausted their adjectives in describing these gorgeous marvels and scarcely noticed a first performance of a first play with comic interludes by a young writer called Lope de Rueda. Philip yawned at the arguments of shepherds and shepherdesses interrupted by a Ruffian, a Fool and a Negress; he listened doubtfully when Ruy Gomez declared this to be a new form of art in which Spain might lead the world; there could not, he thought, be art in crude native forms like plays, written to amuse a mixed crowd mostly of simple folk. He preferred the bull fights, scarlet and black and gold scintillating in the white June dust, but he did not like his 'little one's' unrestrained yelps of joy every time a horse was gored or a man stood within an inch of death.

He embraced the boy goodbye, repressing his instinctive

distaste in having to do so, and thankful that there was no further member of his uncomfortable family for him to see.

His son was an oddity who might become a monstrosity; his father was a hero, but extraordinary; his father's mother was mad. Philip's craving to prove himself ordinary, the only entirely rational and balanced member of his family, had been shown by his choice of his mistress, Dona Isobel de Osorio, when he was only fifteen. By now she had provided him with five children and the settled, rather stuffy peace of an affectionate but unemotional matrimonial household of many years' standing. Dona Isobel always spoke of their union as marriage in the eyes of God, which to Philip were not equal to those of the law; to her friends it was more like their silver wedding, and as middle-class as it was middle-aged. There had never been anything in it of the passion he had felt in his legal marriage to Dona Manoela.

He rode on towards his next marriage, attended rich banquets, listened to long speeches, watched stately processions in the dark churches that opened like tombs out of the white heat. At the holy city of Santiago he met the English Ambassadors. They struck the critical Spaniards as being gentlemen, or at any rate the Earl of Bedford did, though they wore far too many fancy buttons, and in the Earl of Bedford's case every one of them did its duty. Philip entrusted them with a million gold ducats without any sign of unease, though he knew it would cause another financial crisis in Spain. The Lords Bedford and Fitzwalter hastened to write a favourable report of his affable manners, and attended mass with him in the Cathedral, greatly, they declared, to their edification, and did not hear the Spaniards' comment that 'they need it badly enough.'

At last he reached Corunna, where a hundred ships awaited him, and six thousand soldiers who were to protect him against the French and go on to join the Emperor's forces in Flanders. Lancers from Guipuzcoa waved and tossed their lances in welcome to him so that the air seemed full of lightning, and the thunder of the drums rolled along the coast until it was drowned by salutes fired from the muskets and big guns, so loud and long that the chroniclers declared 'the human race has never witnessed such a discharge as this, nor ever will again.' His ship, *The Holy Ghost,* was covered with carved gold and crimson damask and heraldic pennons. Three hundred sailors clad in scarlet were to man this one vessel alone; they climbed the rigging and did acrobatic exercises there, three hundred monkeys in scarlet coats, to amuse him while he waited for a favourable breeze.

On Thursday evening the 12th of July the sea was like silk and the air held its breath, and the captains grumbled that they might be held up here for a month.

Philip walked on the shore with Ruy Gomez and discussed the news brought by a ship that had drifted into Corunna that day from England. Queen Mary was already waiting for him at Winchester, also with a thousand gentlemen, and what was more, with two thousand horses for the Spaniards – most unnecessary, complained Philip, when they were shipping all the horses they needed, but it was too late to alter it now. 'The English Master of Horse will probably lead them into his own stables,' was Ruy Gomez's unkind comment.

The Queen was evidently determined to make unheard-of preparations for her bridegroom. 'To make up, I suppose, for the only really important preparation which she should have made months ago.'

'And that is, Your Highness?'

'Why, to cut off the head of her young sister Elizabeth. Hasn't our Ambassador been urging our demand for this ever since the rising this spring to put her on the throne? And all Renard could do was to get Mary to put her in the Tower for a couple of months – and then let her out!'

'But she is under close guard at Woodstock – as safe as any prison.'

'And what prison would ever make her safe, as long as she is alive? Her red head is the potential head for all the rebels and heretics in the country. It should be lopped off.'

Ruy Gomez felt some alarm; his ten years' greater age and experience, a cool and balanced judgment, and moreover his birth and upbringing in a perfectly ordinary family, had made him apt to feel his young friend unpredictable. Certainly Philip was not prone to be rash or sudden in action, but who knew what he might be if he thought himself personally insulted? But he guessed hopefully that the Prince, alone with his friend as etiquette scarcely ever permitted him to be, was enjoying the rare luxury of letting go his temper. Philip was grumbling, quite naturally, that the English Queen could hardly blame him for not rushing to her with the haste of an ardent lover when she persisted in keeping alive 'that devil's brat to stir up rebellion against me.'

'It might have caused a worse rebellion to behead her,' Gomez said; 'Renard himself seems now to be coming round to that opinion. She has won over many of the people. And some of the nobles too, even old fogies who went to cross-examine her in the Tower, and instead fell head over heels in love with her.'

He watched the effect of this, hoping it would intrigue

Philip, sufficiently anyway to prevent him demanding as a wedding present the Princess's head on a plate immediately he landed in England. But Philip, kicking at a stranded jellyfish, which made a mess on his shoe, only snarled at the low tastes of the English who could set up as a heroine 'a wanton who was smirched in her early teens by her uncle.'

'Her step-uncle, Highness. And it is a moot point if the smirching were actual or only to her reputation. In either case it has rendered her as wary, subtle and alert as a rat that, having once escaped the trap, will know how to elude – or attack – any future adversaries.'

A contemptuous smile gleamed in the Prince's light grey eyes. 'And you think she may attempt to bite *me*?'

Ruy Gomez laughed outright. 'Is Your Highness too high to be bitten by a woman save in the way of kindness?'

Only Ruy could dare thus far, and Philip had always delighted in it when he chaffed him; but Ruy could never feel certain that it was still safe to do so. It added spice to his teasing; he glanced in some anxiety at his young friend's face – though he knew that if it had ceased to be safe, he would see nothing in that face to tell him so. But this time all was well, for Philip was laughing too.

'No, for I can see how dangerous she is, and indeed would be even if dead.' He remembered the little Queen of Scots, even as a baby 'the most dangerous person in Europe.' Elizabeth's death would make that child the future Queen of France, and also the unquestioned heir to England, until he could provide another.

It was a perverse fate for a young man, both susceptible and attractive in his fashion, that he had to marry an elderly virgin in order to strengthen his fight against two charming girls, one twenty years old, the other ten, rivals to each other, enemies to the might of Spain.

Thinking of those two who were his foes, and of the one who must be his ally, he murmured sadly, 'You at least are fortunate. You are wedded to a bride so young that the contract forbade consummation for two years, and now one of them has already passed.'

'Several more may do so before I get back from first England and then Flanders.'

'I hope your Anna will not have grown too tall for you,' said Philip with a spice of malice, but hastened to add with his accustomed courtesy, 'When I saw her at the wedding, I thought her very striking for her age, and', he added, again on the plaintive note, 'likely to become beautiful perhaps, in an unusual way.'

Ruy knew that Philip was most dangerous when he seemed most vulnerable. Self-pity and envy of another's more fortunate lot were the last things to be encouraged in him. He deliberately made his voice casual and dispassionate as he answered, 'She might have become so, Your Highness, if she were not also – well, as you have just said, "striking"! And literally. She has fought a duel with a page in her father's house "to defend the honour of Castile" against some silly jeer, and the boy by accident ran her through the eye. She will always now have to wear a black patch over it, which is naturally a great disfigurement.'

Philip was not deceived by his friend's apparent indifference. Other men he knew had already begun just lately to show themselves far from indifferent to the future Princess of Eboli, in spite of the black patch. Why had Ruy not told him of it before, he asked himself, but not aloud, and turned the question over suspiciously in his mind. What a termagant the girl must be! He felt amused at old Ruy, so placid and reasonable, hoping to tame her, and doubted that he had the necessary qualities. The corollary, of course, was that Philip might himself possess them. With that his discontent surged back over him; Ruy would mate with his tall dark spitfire, a young eagle, blinded though she was in one eye, while he himself must go and marry a poor old tame goose.

He fought down his envy. Ruy was his greatest friend. He would always do his best for him. He turned and smiled at his friend, who drew a deep breath but still felt a little cold as Philip spoke.

'You will conquer your duellist. But do not let her fight a duel with you. Next time it might be her husband who would become blind.'

They walked on along the shore, stepping carefully to avoid the pools of sea water turned to rosy flame in the sunset light. Ruy wished they had not spoken of Anna. He hastened to speak instead of Queen Mary, of her goodness of heart, her simplicity, which Renard had said made her seem much younger than her years. She was good to the poor – Philip yawned. She had been called Merciful Mary – Philip frowned. She had no right to be merciful to her enemies, and therefore his. And Ruy could tell no stories of her. As a young girl there had been wild romantic schemes to rescue her from her cruel father, to steal her away in a boat some moonless night. But she had only bungled it and stayed at home.

Next morning there was a slight wind from the south; the many-coloured ships weighed anchor and spread their towering sails to the breeze, careening before it, dipping and curtseying, as they bore Prince Philip out to sea, northwards to England, with the July sunlight sparkling on the waves.

But the sailors muttered that it was Friday the 13th.

And when they landed in England it was raining.

CHAPTER THREE

How it rained! It would never stop. It came sluicing down, not from clouds carved into torrential shapes that might break up into splinters to reveal an arrow's point of blue beyond the grey, but from a flat sheet of lead that could give no hope of change for the morrow. Their horses squelched and splashed through the mud, the rain stung his face, ran down the back of his neck, down his nose and legs, into his gloves, seeped through his clothes sewn with diamonds, even through the cloak of thick red felt provided to protect their splendour.

His father had been conquered by the sea. Was he to be conquered by the rain? He longed to admit defeat, to turn tail and ride back to Southampton and his ships, draw anchor and sail back towards the sun. But all he did was to stop at the ancient Hospital of St. Cross outside Winchester to be welcomed by kind old gentlemen in mulberry robes who helped him to change out of his black velvet and silver, now looking and feeling like a drowned rat's skin, and into black trimmed with gold, and under-garments of white and gold.

Almost at once they too were clinging damply to him as he rode on again in dismal state through the West Gate of Winchester, through obsequiously bowing and kneeling aldermen, and sulky townsfolk huddled together in suspicious silence and a smell of wet sheep, up to a small host of Bishops that towered like archangels in their mitres and spreading copes on the steps of the Cathedral, but kept as far back as they could in the shelter of the doorway. Not till he and his suite had attended the Cathedral service of rejoicing in his safe arrival, with a particularly long-drawn-out chant of the Te Deum, was Philip free to go on and lodge in the Dean's House, to peel off his wet clothes yet again, and warm his icy legs before a log fire (in July!), to dine comfortably at leisure and in privacy and then, just as he was going to bed about ten o'clock, be sent for to his first interview with his future bride. Her maiden status had to be protected by lodging across the way at the Bishop's Castle, so he was told to come 'secretly,' with only a very few of his gentlemen in attendance. They looked at him in some anxiety, but he gave no sign that his composure was in the smallest degree ruffled by having to dress all over again and sally forth once more into the night, this time on foot.

He put on silver and gold embroidery and the white kid trunks he had tried on before his father – how little the Emperor knew what he was now going through on his behalf! With his chosen grandees he went out into the thick darkness and the Bishop's garden, the torches sputtering ahead of them, their beautifully shod feet slopping through the mud, and the trees dripping down on their heads in the long tunnels of the pleached alleys, the wet leaves shuddering and whispering as they brushed them; until they saw the gleam of lighted windows on the black waters of the moat and went round it to a little back door, up a private stair. It led straight into the Queen's private apartment, or rather a long gallery where several people were standing, and one small figure was moving restlessly up and down, jewels glittering at every turn.

As the door opened she came quickly towards it, hardly giving time to the two torch-bearers who had to precede her. She kissed her hand in the odd English fashion before she held it out to Philip and he, remembering his instructions in another still odder English fashion, kissed her on her lips; dry, rather hard, they met his uncertainly, eagerly. There were no men in England of sufficient rank for her to give even the formal kiss; of any other she had evidently no experience. She was shy and timid as a young girl, and in her heart that was what she was; but he saw a middle-aged woman, whose intent gaze was appealing to him, not as her political ally and partner, but as her sovereign and lover.

He had come, not to a wedding feast but to a fight. But the Queen had come, not to an arranged alliance, but to a love affair. 'These Tudors!' he thought, would nothing, not even a mixture of Spanish blood, teach them manners? Mary's mother had been Katherine of Aragon, of the bluest blood of Spain. But her father had been Harry Tudor, from a line of Welsh adventurers, who had rid himself of one wife after another in his sentimental lust to find himself perfectly married.

A damp chill crept into his heart as his bride's thin hand moved in his; was it holding his, clutching his, saying to his, 'Till death do us part'?

He tried to make his hand answer hers; 'Only remember your manners,' his limp touch told her. 'This is a marriage of convenience; it is bad manners to try and make it a romance; to tell me so plainly that you are a virtuous virgin starving for love; to remind me that I am young and you are old.'

But she was gallantly recovering from her embarrassment;

she became gracious, cordial to his suite, even gay; he noticed that her skin was fair and very clear. Her rather thin hair had lights in it like a sandy kitten's where it had not gone grey. She must have been very pretty, even piquante.

But her little round face and pointed chin which had for so long kept their youthful shape in solitary retirement, as the faces of nuns stay young because there is no worldly stress to make them old, had been suddenly drawn into hollows and sagging folds in this last half year of agonizing action and suspense. Her ungrateful country had rebelled against her marriage to this young man and so had delayed his coming month after month, tearing her empty heart in pieces; and some thought he would never come at all.

And now he was here beside her, he was holding her hand, speaking grave, slow, often incomprehensible courtesies (she had not expected him to speak English, but why should his French be so bad?) – but he had come, he had come at last, the miracle had happened, and she could not be so much older than she had been last August, not as much as a year ago (already she was forgetting what had happened in that year) when she had ridden to London to be Queen, triumphant over all her enemies, and dear Jane Dormer had said she looked as though she were in her twenties. Yes, and even the playwright John Heywood, who had not seen her since her eighteenth birthday, said she had not changed a jot from then, when he had written a birthday ode to her 'lively face' that was like a 'lamp of joy'. If it had been so then, how much more reason had it to be so now!

And so it was. But it was a lamp that gave no spark to her bridegroom's feelings. With a disapproving mind and sinking heart, Philip watched his bride falling in love with him; and knew that others were watching it. As his grandees were presented to her and kneeled to kiss her hand, he could hear all the things they did not say, would not say till afterwards when he was out of hearing.

'The Queen is a saint, a dear, a really nice little woman; she dresses very badly.'

'The Queen is elderly and has no eyebrows.'

'The Queen already begins to make love to her young bridegroom.'

As for the English, the Lord Admiral Howard was already playing the bluff sailor, making jokes that Philip could not understand, but he could see all the English understanding them and laughing, the men boisterously, the women (only a few, and so old – why were they all so old?) shyly and titteringly; he could guess the gist of them and did not care for it.

He suggested that as his gentlemen had been presented to the Queen, he should now be presented to the rest of her ladies who were in the apartment adjoining the gallery. Mary agreed, not very brightly, and was determined to accompany him. They went in together, a resolute little pair, and there were all the English ladies, some of them far too tall, and all showing too much leg, some in black stockings, as they curtseyed. Two by two, they were led forward to him. He stood there cap in hand, and kissed each on the lips as she passed, 'in order', it was translated, 'not to violate the custom of the country.' And in most cases it brought him no better satisfaction than that, but not in all; and to Mary no satisfaction at all.

So when the ceremony was over and he had pointed out to her in his careful halting French that it was getting very late and high time they should both go to bed and get a good night's rest before their public meeting and marriage tomorrow, she took him firmly by the hand and led him back to the gallery and the funny little canopy in front of all the candles (were they arranged so that he should not see her too clearly with her back to the light?) for another chat in her bad Spanish, in his bad English, in their bad French, about the weather, about his journey, about her little dog. But he thought of an unknown young woman of whom no one dared speak, though he suspected that many others were also thinking of her.

The most ominous factor in this official gathering was the absence of the Queen's sister and presumptive heir to the throne. Philip, not a fanciful man, felt that absent figure as an uneasy presence in the minds of all these English who smiled at him with large white teeth and watchful eyes; behind those eyes lurked the image of the Lady Elizabeth, whether as a sinister shadow or an anxiously concealed hope.

There was the Chancellor, old Bishop Gardiner, now installed again in his See of Winchester after years of prison under King Edward's Protestant régime; he had been demanding Elizabeth's death as furiously as one might guess from his fierce black eyebrows, but had now had to follow the Emperor's new policy of appeasement; Philip would like to know his true opinion of it.

Also that of the Lord Admiral Howard, who had had to take Elizabeth to the Tower only this spring, with an armed force, since she had refused to budge on pretext of illness; and they had taken a long time to get there, on the same pretext. What did Howard really think, or know, of his great-niece's probable part in Wyatt's rebellion? Had he secretly sympathized, wished for its success, and his great-niece on the throne? In any case Philip felt it would be pleasant to relieve the boredom, which ached in his every limb, by giving that jocose jackass a twinge of discomfort in his turn, and see how he would be able to hee-haw it off.

So in casual talk with him he asked after the health of Howard's great-niece; he had heard it had caused her, and him, some trouble. His polite inquiry was translated in a rather lower voice than the rest of the conversation, but it reached the Queen's ears and he saw her face pucker and turn pale. Lord Howard on the other hand went beetroot-coloured under his tan as he hastily assured the Prince that none of his family's health gave him any cause for anxiety. His evasion of Elizabeth's name was more significant than any mention of it; it was as though they were all afraid to call up a spirit by naming it.

'What sort of spirit?' he asked Renard in a low tone as they walked to a window to see if the rain were lessening, and his dapper Ambassador opened his mouth in a sudden round O, plucked nervously at his two little tufts of beard, and replied unexpectedly, 'A spirit full of enchantment.'

An alluring description! Yet Renard, too, had always urged her death. Was this intended as a warning? But he could not ask further. Mary wanted to know if he would like the window open, and indeed it was stiflingly airless and muggy, he put up a hand to his damp forehead and firmly held back his jaws from cracking open in a huge yawn.

At last he got away, but he had to learn to say 'Good-night, my lords and ladies' in English, and had to come back to her to learn the uncouth words over again before he could say them to the ladies in the next room, where the giggling was like a gaggle of geese, and some old lady called de Clarencieux thanked God that she had lived to see this day, though she wished she could have brought him a more beautiful wife; and the Queen herself, still more embarrassingly, expressed her gratitude to him for taking anyone so old and ugly.

No language could express his feelings, or evasion of feeling, after that; he said good-night and wished it were goodbye; he staggered out again into the dark and heard the drops pattering on the moat, and the chimes of the Cathedral clock strike midnight as he fumbled through the dripping vegetation; and fell on his bed while Ruy Gomez peeled off his gold-embroidered white kid trunks and praised Mary's fresh complexion and charmingly friendly manner, and then spoilt it when he tactlessly agreed that Mary seemed older than they had been informed, and brightly suggested that if dressed in Spanish fashions she might not look so old and flabby, or was she scraggy? But Philip was past caring. He fell down, down into blessed sleep and forgetfulness, down, down, down, till so late next morning that he was all but late for his wedding.

And then he had to get up and try on two more gorgeous suits sent him as a present from the Queen, one all white covered with pearl and gold and those everlasting diamond buttons, the other all crimson, both all wrong; and visit her publicly in the cruel grey English daylight in her white satin robe and scarlet shoes, still more wrong; with fifty ladies round her and not one of them pretty; and all the Ambassadors and Envoys Extraordinary to give their welcome.

But the one who was absent gave a greater triumph than any present; the French Ambassador, de Noailles, and his gleaming sardonic teeth in the midst of his black beard were not there to grin discomfiture on the proceeding; no, the discomfiture was that of de Noailles, who had never been invited, since Spain was at war with his country – 'and so will England be, as result of this marriage, in a matter of weeks, or at any rate months,' declared the more optimistic of the Spanish prophets and the more pessimistic of the English. And the French Ambassador had to remain at home, gloomily spewing out his ill-natured garbled accounts of the wedding at second-hand from all the anti-Spanish spies he could rake up, for his reports to his master King Henri II of France and his flat-faced Italian wife, Catherine de Medici, who was growing fatter and fatter and must be bursting like the frog in the fable with rage at this clever counter-stroke of Spain in marrying the English Mary, against their blow in betrothing the little Scottish Mary to their son the Dauphin of France. Now France's project to claim England through her was forestalled. Spain had taken over England first. That, to Philip, was the real significance of this tremendous ceremony in the ancient Cathedral of Winchester. 'Check to the King of France' was the whole point of this move, of his stately progress with Mary up the aisle in time to the sacred music. 'France has failed,' it pealed out in triumph in his ears, 'failed to annex England in the name of Mary Queen of Scots. But open your gates, ye everlasting doors, and the King of Glory shall come in. Who is the King of Glory? The Lord of Hosts, Philip of Spain, he is the King of Glory. He has annexed England for Spain and the Empire of the World.'

If Mary could actually bear him a son, that would set Heaven's final seal of approval on the match. But even if she did not, and were to die in childbed (she did not look at all strong, he considered, as they approached the altar), then he as her widower could still make a claim to this country. The Church would support it against the bastard Elizabeth. His bride must understand this sacred purport of their marriage.

Her dry little hand lay in his like a withered leaf, her thin lips moved in silent prayer, her short-sighted eyes, blank and blind in rapture, were fixed alternately upon the crucifix and on the plain gold ring on which she had insisted 'because maids were so married in old times.'

To her, the marriage had another purport. She heard the music throb, boys' voices soar in angelic ecstasy; Stephen Gardiner, her father's old friend, now again Lord Bishop of Winchester, rolled out the sonorous Latin phrases; the incense burners wafted their blue spiced clouds through the damp heavy air, little bells pricked it, tingling, and the congregation sank on their knees; the old times had come again and all the right and ancient ways of serving God through His one true Church and His Viceroy the Pope; all just as it had been in her father's day, when he had gone to mass with her mother, and herself as a little girl holding their hands; all just as it had been then, and was now so again, while she held the hand of a young man as fair as an angel, who was, unbelievably, her husband; all just as it would be now for ever in this happy land, freed by her at last from guilt, and grateful to her, for ever and ever.

There followed a feast where Philip wondered heavily if even his father's Gargantuan appetite could cope with half the dishes served him. The massive sideboard behind his head creaked under its weight of gold plate; a marble fountain on it whispered and tittered, and a clock more than half his size thumped its loud ticking into his ears. Incomprehensible voices shrilled higher, grew gruffer, all but shouted as the wine went round and round. Heralds blared a piercing blast on their long glittering trumpets and proclaimed him King of Naples. This was a happy surprise arranged by his father so that he should not be a mere Prince beside the Queen his wife; but even so he took a lower seat than she and was given only silver plate where she was served on gold, and he was careful to insist that none of his Spaniards should share the honour done to the four English lords who bore the canopy over their heads.

The Spaniards muttered that they might as well be turned out as vagabonds; at the dance that followed, they took their revenge by not giving the ladies any of the Spanish leather gloves that they had brought as presents for them, and by memorizing rude comments on their looks and clothes to write home. The ladies for their part held a poor opinion of the Spaniards' dancing.

The Spaniards consoled themselves next day by going sightseeing in Winchester, and the new King Philip took the chance to escape with them. They were impressed by King Arthur's Round Table with the names of all his knights inscribed on it, but thought it a pity that Henry VIII had had it new painted with a huge Tudor rose glaring aggressively out of its middle. And then one of their English guides, a lamentably would-be conscientious old man, thought he did remember his grandfather saying he did, that there great table there had been made for the old King Edward, and when asked indignantly which King Edward, he thought it might have been one King Edward or it might have been t'other, but no, it wasn't one of the last three King Edwards, so he figured that it rightly was Edward III. But in any case, if not the original, it had been made in *memory* of King Arthur's Round

Table, for King Edward always thought a deal of that King, he did.

'So did Queen Mary's grandfather, presumably,' said Philip drily, when Bishop Gardiner had translated this piece of local colour which he evidently considered comic. He did not at all like Philip's reminder that Henry VII had christened his eldest son Prince Arthur, a name never before chosen by an English King; for both knew it had only been chosen in order to bolster up the Tudors' legendary Celtic ancestry.

Prince Philip's lowered eyelids showed that he knew the Tudors to be past masters at such tricks; Bishop Gardiner's heightened eyebrows showed that he'd never liked this Spanish match and never would, but they'd all got to make do with it now. He did his best. He showed the gardens. The green lawns, the luxuriant masses of roses tumbling over the old walls were a wonderful sight, but one was apt to get a shower-bath in picking them.

'If these are the groves of Amadis,' said one of the disillusioned Dons, 'then give me the barest stubble-field in Toledo.'

CHAPTER FOUR

Mary would wake herself up when she lay dozing in the early morning to make sure that it was indeed true. She was no longer a lonely old maid; she was married, and to a Prince whose nature was as noble as his looks.

'It was no dream; I lay broad waking.'

Who had written that? But no, she would not remember, for it had been the poet Sir Thomas Wyatt, who had loved Ann Bullen, and whose son had risen against her this spring to prevent her marriage and put Ann's daughter on the throne. He had been beheaded, and his father's verse should lie buried and forgotten. But you can give no orders to poetry; the simple one-syllabled line paced slowly into her head and stood there looking at her in wide-eyed wonder like her own flower the Marygold, opening to the sun.

No, it was no dream. She convinced herself of it by writing to her father-in-law that she was 'happier than I can say' in the daily discovery of her husband's 'many virtues and perfections.' The Emperor remarked drily that Philip must have changed a good deal; but then, he chuckled, lovers made poor judges. Soon, however, he received from others almost equally glowing accounts of Philip's affable behaviour. The

English nobles declared 'they had never yet had a King in England who so soon won the hearts of all men.' Panegyric poems composed for London's welcome to him praised his 'grace of speech so frank' and declared England's 'chiefest joy is to hear thee, Philip, speak.' Only a poet could think of such inappropriate praise for one who was taciturn enough in his own language, and apt to go dumb in any other. But it did look as though he were putting a severe strain on himself, and his father hoped it wouldn't make him break out the more violently later.

Mary's tender conscience had been worried by Philip's broken betrothal to the Princess of Portugal, but now even that little wound was healed, for the Princess had been so very understanding and kind and had sent her a most handsome present of dresses, and head-gear a foot or two high in the Portuguese style (had Philip contrived to send a hint to his former bride-to-be of the unbecoming English fashions?) and Mary could not stop trying them on and gloating over them.

At last, after years of scrimping and saving on her meagre dress allowance so as to afford the presents she loved giving to her friends and their children, Mary had as many fine clothes as she could wish to wear; and it was not after all too late, for here was a handsome young husband for whose sake it was her bounden duty to make herself look also as handsome and young as possible. She was already looking younger, the hollows in her face filling out and its colour brighter; even the Cockney crowds noticed it, suspicious as they were of the Spaniards (but there were only a few in the procession, Philip saw to that) when she brought him in triumph to London.

Why shouldn't she have a husband, poor woman, the same

as other folk? It was high time she got a fine young man, so they decided in the benevolent haze induced by the fountains running with red wine, and free banquets set out on trestle tables in front of the wealthier houses as soon as the procession had gone by. They danced in the street to music of their own making on lutes and rebecks, the butcher and baker and candlestick-maker and their wives and children all hopping and shouting and screaming with laughter as they joined hands and dragged each other round and round in a ring, and even the Oldest Inhabitant in Cheapside sitting on a stool and banging time with his stick.

No wonder that for the moment they could speak kindly of Philip and even say that you might take him for an Englishman as he was so fair; but then wasn't his father a Fleming like those big fair weavers from Flanders that had settled in England? This young fellow wasn't near their measure; but as pretty as a picture, a proper Prince in white and gold on his white horse.

And a good sportsman, so they said; had been hunting at Windsor where he'd been made a Knight of the Garter, and he had ridden in a tourney, though the Frenchmen did say (but they *would*!) that they had never seen worse lance-play than his. In any case he had given them all good sport with these shows and pageants and above all the cartloads of American gold, solid ingots from Peru, so heavy that it took near a hundred horses to draw them trundling along on their way to the treasure chests of the Tower.

The shrivelled human heads of Wyatt and his rebels stuck on spikes at the Tower and on the Bridge had all been taken down, also the corpses that ever since the spring had hung dangling on gallows at street corners; another sort of scaffolding had been built up for everyone's pleasure; a young man had danced on a rope attached to St. Paul's steeple and jumped the whole height of it down on to a feather bed. Orpheus sang to his 'counterfeit' wild beasts of prancing children in masks and furry skins (it was Orpheus who had to compare his music, unfavourably, with Philip's eloquence); the giant figures of Gog and Magog stood on guard over the City; and perhaps best of all, for the sly jokes it caused, were the painted figures of the Nine Worthies, and among them Henry VIII with an English Bible in his hand and 'Verbum Dei' on it – 'and God's body! if you could have heard how Bishop Gardiner swore when he spotted it only just in time before the procession, and got the Bible painted out, but by God's soul, the fingers got painted out with it, so there's Old Harry holding up his maimed stump like any old soldier beggar from the French wars asking you to give him a halfpenny. But you can still see the shadow of the Bible, and where's the worry, for no one's going to swing for *that,* I'd say.'

'Not swing! Burn. The Bible, Verbum Dei, the Word of God, that's heresy they say. And they'll make it English law as soon as the Cardinal, that Italianate Englishman Reginald Pole, comes over to hand us all back again to Rome and the Pope.'

'But he's English – a Plantagenet, one of the old stock.'

'Small odds that'll make to him, and he in foreign parts so long. It's as like as not he's forgotten his own mother tongue.'

The Oldest Inhabitant cackled shrilly; 'His own mother didn't forget the use of her tongue when she ran round and round the scaffold, as I saw her with my own eyes, *and* heard, she screeching like a pea-hen with stout butcher Giles after her, for the head executioner was away busy up North, chopping off the rebels' heads as thick as nettles, and young Giles was new to the work – a nasty job he made of it, the bungler, when he did catch her. It took him near a score of strokes to finish her off. Plantagenet blood, my arse or her head! It ran as red from it as any other.'

His granddaughter Mag told him not to be a nasty old man – if he must talk of red heads, then why not their Princess Elizabeth? She should have been riding in the procession, as she had done a year ago beside the Queen, and had clean outshone her sister, as though *she* were the Queen and Mary only her governess. No doubt that was the real reason they kept her shut up far away in the country, especially now the Queen had got herself a young husband.

But Grandfather Talbois, who couldn't keep away from executions, dared swear 'that jilt the Lady Elizabeth' had been the real cause of the rebellion this spring, and all these pesky bodies hanging till now at the street corners to bump your hat off if you weren't careful, 'they should hang 'em higher'; and his son, Will Talbois, the best candlemaker in Cheapside, agreed about that jilt with an admiring chuckle, 'she'll give 'em more trouble yet, mark my words, for all they've tried to mew up the eaglet, but they'll never clip that one's wings. *Mag*!' he shouted to his daughter, 'where are you strolling off to with that black foreign Moor?'

'It was only a poor young Spaniard, Father, who had lost his way and had no English to ask for it.'

'Then how could *you* tell him? I know, by signs and taking his hand and pointing to our house, I dare swear. Let Spaniards alone, I say.'

So said most Englishmen. Diego Valdez of Malaga, who

would have run any man through the body who dared call him a Moor, had learnt his way to pretty Mag Talbois' house in Cheapside; but for the most part, as the Spaniards wrote home pathetically, they found it safest to avoid the English, as the English did them, as though they were strange animals.

The English complained that there were four times as many Spaniards as Englishmen.

The Spaniards complained that they were charged twenty-four times as much as the proper price for everything.

The children in the gutters shouted, 'Spanish apes who steal our grapes,' and threw stones after them.

The Spanish Ambassador suggested to his young master that it would be a good way to relieve the tension if he passed on straightaway to the fighting in Flanders with his Spaniards and a large body of English as well, and thus unobtrusively, said Renard, as sly as his name, involve England in war against France. But Philip had too much to do first.

He had not yet decided whether the Lady Elizabeth were more dangerous dead or alive; he was not yet crowned King of England, he did not yet know if his wife were with child; he had not yet given permission to the Cardinal, Reginald Pole, to return to his own country.

Every man was thinking of that return, and of what it would mean to himself, when the form of religion would be changed by the law of the land, and anyone denying it would be subject to pain of death. No sensible Englishman dreamed of denying it; but a vast number were in terrible fear that their pleasant houses and lands and yearly rents might then be taken away and given back to the monks and nuns.

Even Mary was nervous of Reginald Pole's return, though she had for twenty years been longing for it.

He wrote to her – interminable letters, complained Philip, who had also received some – so long-winded ('so high-minded,' said Mary), so touchy ('so sensitive,' said Mary), so unpractical ('so eager to do God's will and that only,' said Mary).

'And do not *I* wish to do God's will?' asked Philip.

'Yes, dearest, yes.' But Mary, even now, and with another new silent hope springing in her heart, the chiefest, most miraculous hope of all, could see that in Philip's eyes God was a Hapsburg.

And in Reginald Pole's eyes she was no better. He had practically accused her of taking God for a Tudor. God had done her will, set her on the throne, rescued her from her enemies and their devilish conspiracies, given her the strongest country in the world for her support, and its magnificent Prince for her husband. But she had not yet done God's will in bringing this heathen country back to *His* loving care. With every week that she let go by, thousands of the souls in her charge were dying without the Last Sacraments, and so lost to all hope of heaven.

'He is right,' sobbed Mary to the pale impassive face of her young husband as he read the letter. 'We cannot "go easy, play for time," as even you have suggested, and even Bishop Gardiner of Winchester, even your dear father, yes, and even the Pope. But souls dying in sin cannot play for time.'

'Nor can those living in it,' said Philip with a strange smile. He had his own reason now for wishing the Papal Legate's arrival in England. It could be very useful to him.

Yes, he must write. But carefully. Reginald Pole must understand the conditions attaching to Christianity in these days, and especially in this country. So he wrote to him that he and the Queen passionately desired his return to England, that all the English longed for him to bring them Absolution from the Pope for their great crime in following their former rulers into rebellion against the Holy Father, and prayed to be allowed to return into the fold of his sheep – only Pole must remember that they had taken an enormous amount of spoils from the shepherds of it. Those spoils could not now be returned. The Pope's Absolution must therefore be coupled with a Papal decree confirming all the gentry who had annexed Church lands and property as perpetual owners of their gains. Without that decree, the aforesaid gentry would have nothing to say to the Absolution, to the Pope, nor to Pole.

He then returned to his wife, and told her he had written in most cordial welcome to her kinsman, entreating him to come and restore this wretched country to God. 'And if I were backward before in this matter,' he said, with so subtle a smile of his full lips above the pale gold fringe of beard that she did not at once perceive it, and he had to do it all over again, 'then you, of all people in the world, have reason to excuse it.'

'But why?' she asked bewildered, and he, looking down into her eyes (she was, fortunately, seated) saw, unbelievingly, that they must have looked very like that, though brighter, when she was eight or nine – 'why have I in particular, any reason?'

'My Queen,' he interrupted her softly, raising her hand to his lips (what a pity that hands grew old sooner than eyes, for he had always a partiality for beautiful hands), 'have you forgotten that Reginald Pole had been suggested as your husband, years before myself? And – but I do not ask you this, remember – how do I know that he himself has not suggested it? Or, if he had come before me, might not have done so?'

His clear eyes penetrated her, they made her shiver in a delicious sense of guilt that she had never before felt at mention of any man. Was it possible that this glorious young man could be jealous of her?

At that moment she could have worshipped him. And she told him her secret belief that she was with child.

If she were right, then one of the objects was achieved that stood between him and his departure from her; with sincere gratitude he expressed his satisfaction.

Mary wept, for joy, she said, but the resulting tears were as unbecoming as those of grief. He no longer found it intriguing that her eyes had looked like those of a little girl instead of a grown woman's; he found it irritating.

Did none of the English ever grow up? 'I'm nothing but a great boy – a little girl – at heart'; that seemed to be their perpetual covert boast. Mary's idea of duty was a child's, to be kind and conscientious. She had no understanding of the duty of a ruler. He was kind and conscientious himself; but he could think clearly.

He was doing so now while he gently stroked his wife's hair. 'Those living in sin cannot play for time,' she had said, and he had thought of the Lady Elizabeth, that unavowed heretic and hidden enemy, who had continued to play for time. But when the Papal Legate arrived in England, then Papistry would be made the law of the land, and death the punishment for breaking it. That would put an end to her anomalous position. It might even put an end to her altogether.

Yes, Philip had his own good reason for wishing Reginald Pole to come home.

CHAPTER FIVE

And late that autumn he came.

After twenty years of exile, most of them under sentence of death as a proscribed traitor in his own country, and with a price on his head for any private assassin who chose to murder him abroad, he returned home to hold greater official power than that of the Queen's Consort.

He came in the more than royal state of a Prince of the Church, such as had not been seen in England for a generation. In his Cardinal's robes and scarlet hat he stood on the Queen's own barge that had been sent to bear him up river from Greenwich; and before him stood the standard bearers holding up the insignia of his office, the huge cross and silver pillars and pole-axes that glimmered through the misty November sunlight, to announce the arrival of the Pope's Ambassador to all the waving, welcoming crowds along the river shores. The chief Bishops and Nobles of the land with their households in blue and red waited to meet him as he landed, and the London crowds ran to see the gay sight and shout and cheer as madly as though they had been saying mass in dangerous secrecy ever since he had gone into exile.

Philip was dining with the Queen in Whitehall Palace when the news was brought of the Cardinal's arrival. She turned red and then pale and clasped her hands to her side; and the King rose in haste from his unfinished dinner and walked out to do this Prince of the Church more honour than he would have paid to any Prince of this world, except his father. Bareheaded, in the faint but chilly mist from the river, he stood only a little apart from the crowds that thronged down to the water's edge, for Whitehall Stairs had been a right of way ever since the Palace had belonged to Cardinal Wolsey; King Henry had shamelessly commandeered it from the greatest of his subjects, but would not interfere with the rights of his meanest. So King Philip was half deafened by the cheers close round him of the fickle Cockneys who had dreaded the return of the Papal Legate, but now in their inconsistent fashion were hoarse with sudden joy to see a tired old Englishman come home.

He watched a very tall thin man wearily mounting Whitehall Stairs towards him. Reginald Pole's fair, greying head stooped a little, partly from weak health, partly from courtesy, since he so often had to speak with those of lesser height. He looked tired; 'who would have thought this fellow could give so much trouble!' went through Philip's mind at the approach of the languid elderly scholar who had sustained such obstinate conflict with Mary's terrible father, and with Philip's.

He led him up the stairs to where Mary awaited them, surrounded by her ladies; she curtseyed as Pole advanced and knelt to her, then kissed him as her cousin and stood, a moment longer than etiquette demanded, while she held his hand and looked up at the lean face that had aged so much since she had seen him. Yet it had grown the more familiar, for it was now so like the finely cut face of his mother, the Countess of Salisbury, her very dear Governess, who had been torn from her to the Tower and then to the headsman's block. Mary still treasured the portrait of her in all her finery of ermine hood and ruffled sleeves, but carrying in her exquisite fingers a sprig of wild honeysuckle from the hedgerows. And here again was her reflective calm in the deep-sunk eyes that looked down into hers, a touch of her ironic humour in the questioning curves of his long mouth above the forked grey beard.

The intent sympathy of his gaze brought a trembling question into her mind; it had been his mother's wish, and hers, that they should marry; had it been his too? Was it because of her that he delayed so long in taking priestly orders, had been made a Cardinal against his will, had refused to be made Pope?

She flushed like a girl at the thought, and prayed that neither he nor Philip guessed the reason. Hurriedly she turned and led him to a seat beside them under the royal canopy, making polite inquiries about his long and fatiguing journey.

He conversed with them in slow and sometimes slightly tentative English, but glad to be talking it again; 'I have dreamed of doing so, here in England, so often,' he told the Queen, 'that I seem to be talking in my sleep.' He told her of his progress up the river in the royal barge and how he seemed to be returning to his childhood as the banks of the Thames floated slowly past him, the grey-green fields dotted with sheep, the great trees he loved so well, the reedy wastelands of the Kentish marshes, streaked silver with water, the grounds of the old convent in the Hundred of Hoo where as a small boy he had visited the tall black-and-white nuns who had fluttered round him like a flock of clattering pigeons and led him away to pick red plums off an old grey wall.

He asked of the Carthusians' Monastery at Sheen to whose Grammar School he had gone when he was seven. But then he remembered what he had heard of its fate, and was glad that the Queen spoke instead of his later education at Oxford; Sir Thomas More himself had praised his virtue and scholarship, 'as your dear mother told me long afterwards.'

He smiled. 'I chiefly remember the furious mimic warfare between the Grecians and Trojans; we at Magdalen were all hot Grecians like our tutors, but there was one Oxford tutor who proclaimed all students of Greek to be devils and heretics.'

'How insular!' murmured Philip. 'In Spain we encourage the classics. But then we have many universities, whereas here, I believe, you have only two.' But he said it in rapid Spanish and neither of them understood.

'Her Grace's royal father,' Pole said to him in Latin, in the rather difficult attempt at a common language, 'gave us poor "heretic devils" most royal support when he wrote his commands to the University of Oxford to devote itself with energy and spirit to Greek studies.'

Pole's mother had been brutally butchered by Mary's father, and here they were casually mentioning both of them in polite conversation. Pole noticed that she blushed as they did so; there was no need; she had shown there was nothing in her of her father. Except in the button nose, the occasional steely look in the eyes, but that might be from short-sightedness.

He looked down at her tightly tucked-in little face, all bunched and crumpled up in smiles at the moment, but what would it be like when the lines ran the other way, in the deep furrows of a frown?

She was sixteen years younger than himself, a sweet and docile girl when last he had seen her, and the only woman whom he ever might have married, though the possibility had been more of others' planning than his own, and more from motives of policy than of his cool cousinly affection. He had never wanted to be involved with politics any more than with women; yet he who had tried so hard to keep himself disentangled from both, would he ever be free of them now?

Already she was urging him, begging him, she said, but in a voice that had shrilled to an imperious note, to become *at once* the Primate of the Church, the office that had been waiting for him ever since Archbishop Cranmer had been put in prison for his heresy.

'I too have waited,' said Pole gently.

'I know! I know! Oh! if *you* could but know the shame, the agony I have suffered these eighteen months, ever since I came to the throne, in triumph, they said, a conqueror – but what conquest was that, when I could not at once get the cruel Bill of Attainder against you reversed by Parliament? Obstinate, insensate brutes that they are, thinking only of their own stolen property, and so fearing your coming.'

'They were not the only ones to fear it,' said Pole, and turned his eyes on Philip. 'Your Highness and Your Highness's father the Emperor, and His Holiness the Pope have all combined to keep me dangling for months at Dillingen and Brussels, to send me as emissary to France on the pretext of trying to patch up peace with Spain, a ruse only to keep me from England until I would consent to sell God's Absolution to the English nobles, at their own price.'

'But you *have* consented?' Philip interposed, a shade too quickly.

'I have consented. Because I am to be allowed no other way of restoring the many thousands of innocent souls in this country to the Church of God. We sit here and talk at ease, while thousands are dying unabsolved by the rites of that Church, because it has not yet been made law. Your Highness had the power to save their immortal souls – and rejected it.' He added in slow and careful Spanish, 'You have rejected Christ.'

Philip's eyes turned to pale stones.

His anger was shot through with fear. Was this, could this be true of *him*? It could not be. Yet his father had said that one could not be a statesman and also a Christian, as Christ had understood it; his father feared to gain the whole world and lose his own soul; and so was going to renounce the world.

Suddenly Philip remembered that he had wished to do the same, and when he was only fourteen. He forgot that he had been helped to do so by dread of the difficulties he would meet in the world; he knew only that once in his boyhood there had been an autumn night of storm and despair when he too had wished to be a monk. He had had a vision in the tempest-torn darkness of a nun's face, a nun who was now winning a saintly reputation at Avila; but she had denied saintliness to him; she had told him to go back and become the ruler of the world. His father was that now, but he was going to give it up, in order to save his soul.

But Philip could not do so; he would have to carry on his father's work. He had not rejected Christ; but Christ had rejected him. For a moment he was aghast, for he was angry now with God. He had given up his earthly inclinations to do his duty by his father – yes, and God. Was he, for that, to lose his reward in heaven too?

It was blasphemy to think so. This tall fellow was a fanatic; he knew nothing of what it meant to be a statesman. And what had he ever done or could ever do for the Church?

'We are not living now in the days of the Apostles,' he began, but that would not do. He would never admit – and it would never be true – that he could not be a real Christian as well as a wise ruler.

He said quietly and clearly, 'Our latest Holy Order of the Soldiers of Christ has the motto that "the means justifies the end." Parliament refused to restore England to the Church, unless the Pope promised they should keep the private property they had robbed from the Church. The means are bad, but they lead to a good end, in England being once more a Christian country.'

And that 'end,' as Pole saw, would be the means to Philip's own ends. He would find a Roman Catholic England easier to rule. But of what use to say it, to say anything? He had accused the King just now with simple, almost inadvertent courage, and for a moment he thought he had shaken him, so rigid and silent had Philip sat. But no, he had again shown himself the astute politician, and Pole's attack had been of no more use than his futile errand of peace to the astute worldling Henri II of France and his gross, complacent, clever wife, Catherine de Medici. The Emperor Charles had sent him on that mission not as a diplomat, but as a stool pigeon. He had been baulked by all these potentates, until he himself was forced to reject Christ.

For that was what he must do in four days' time when, as Legate and Ambassador of the Pope, he would stand before the Queen's Parliament at Westminster to tell them the Pope had absolved them for their betrayal of the Church, and had confirmed their rights in all that they had robbed from it.

For all the pomp and glory of his return to his country, it was a sleeveless errand he had come on, to strike a base bargain with God.

He turned his head away to hide his bitterness, but as he did so he saw the Queen was crying. She at least had no part in this bargain; she had given back to the Church all the Crown's property from it; and had passionately desired to make her subjects do likewise. She hated compromise as he did, and had been called a bungler for it; as he had been proved one.

He bent towards her, speaking with great tenderness as he took his leave. He tired easily these days; he must go across the river to Lambeth Palace, now his home, and rest from his journey and gain repose in which to think out all that he must say so soon to the Parliament and people of England.

She could not let him go like this, and after the terrible words he had spoken to Philip. What if they were true? And if so, what could she do? Or say?

Surely the future, that she now held within her body, would make amends for the past? She opened her mouth to say goodbye, and found herself telling him, breathlessly, that at the news of his arrival she had felt for the first time the child leap in her womb.

CHAPTER SIX

'So now,' purred Philip, stretching his bare legs to the comfortable blaze of apple logs while Ruy Gomez warmed his night-shirt, 'we have that young Lady within both jaws of the nut-crackers.'

It was four days after the Cardinal's arrival; and he had that day accomplished the greatest work ever done by a Churchman in England since St. Augustine had converted it to Christianity. So all had agreed with awe, which had passed as the evening wore on into somewhat maudlin expressions of self-congratulatory joy over their saved souls. Reginald Pole had preached a very long and deeply sincere sermon, extempore, before the Parliament at Westminster, and all the Members had fallen on their knees and confessed themselves 'very sorry and repentant' for their past heresy; he had then pronounced absolution from the Pope, and the Members wept and sobbed for thankfulness that they had regained the Church, and retained the Church property.

To the two Spaniards now talking in the seclusion of the King's bedroom, it had afforded a scene of exquisite farce, highly gratifying to their sense of superior fine feeling. The English conception of 'honour' was clearly very different from the Spanish *pundonor*. 'Our common soldiers,' said Philip, 'gave up their pay, even their few personal possessions, to meet the demands of their allies the German mercenaries before the battle of Pavia. The English would call them fools.'

So would Ruy Gomez, an astute Portuguese man of business; but he quickly agreed, and gave poignant instances of how the Spaniards were being robbed by their London lodging-house keepers. The famous English hospitality had proved a hard bargain; they were a nation of shopkeepers. Philip, warming to his subject by the fire, declared that 'they may brawl and fight for their "honour", but they will not pay a halfpenny towards it, not even when their debtor is Christ himself.'

And he gave his rare sharp bark of laughter when his friend described seeing Sir William Cecil, who had been Secretary of State during the Protestant Edward VI's and Lady Jane's nine-day reign, ostentatiously fingering a rosary of extra large beads.

'The Queen thinks he is "really a very honest man." I had difficulty in restraining her from making him our Secretary too!'

'Then he should be careful, sir, not to pay so many visits to the public-house of the Bull at Woodstock. Our spies say there is continual secret correspondence between the Bull and the Lady Elizabeth up at the old Palace, and not all her guards can prevent it. So much for a country house as a prison!'

It was then that Philip reminded him that today's Act of Parliament had closed the other jaw of the nut-crackers on the young Lady. 'She's escaped beheading as a traitor, but may now be legally burnt as a Protestant.'

'The Lady does not protest very much,' murmured Ruy Gomez.

'True. She seems most anxious for guidance. Her letters to

her sister are full of the right sentiments. It looks as though she only needs a touch, a firm masculine touch, be it said, to propel her in the right direction.'

He dipped his bare toes in the basin of warm scented water on the floor beside him, then twiddled them over the fire, sending a shower of drops to hiss and splutter in the flames.

Ruy Gomez's small dark face peered curiously at his master's over the white shirt he was holding. Never had he seen something so like a leer at the corners of Philip's voluptuously curved lips. In any other man, it could only mean one thing; in Philip it might mean two. Was he hoping to amuse himself with Elizabeth's love, or her death?

'The Queen would be ill advised to make a martyr of her,' Ruy said. 'It is doubtful if the country would stand it.'

'That would make small odds to her. The Queen can be as much a martyr as a martyr-maker. She would probably enjoy being dethroned, perhaps murdered, for her Church.'

Ruy turned the shirt round and stared over it at the fire. 'There is another point to consider,' he said carefully. 'The doctors are now certain the Queen is with child; they cannot naturally be certain of the result, especially at her age and with her delicate health. She may very possibly die in childbed. Even if the baby lived, the undoubted heir to the throne, yet this turbulent country might easily boil up again in yet another revolution to upset the Succession and make Elizabeth the Queen. Then Your Highness would lose all hold on England, perhaps even your life.'

'The more reason then to make away with Elizabeth, if not publicly, then by private means.'

'I think not, sir.' Ruy was firmly making use of his ten years' seniority that had stood him in good stead since Philip was a baby. 'You would be in an even more dangerous position, with so small a force of Spaniards to guard you against the rebels, and with no one to use in bargaining with them.'

'You suggest I should secure the Princess as a hostage?'

'Or possibly, sir, as an ally.'

'Hmph. I can hardly put these arguments before my wife. However much she desires my safety, she might be unreasonable about my planning it in the event of her death.'

He held up his arms, and Ruy pulled the shirt down over them. As Philip's fair short-cropped head emerged, a trifle ruffled, he told Ruy casually how Renard had described their enemy as 'a spirit full of enchantment.'

Ruy guessed him to be more curious than casual. 'My spies bring me some queer stories about her,' he said, and told them while Philip, reluctant to leave the fire, brooded on this unknown creature who haunted the minds of the English. The more they avoided speaking of her, the more he was aware of her in their thoughts; he himself was apt to avoid speaking of her to his wife as it upset her; but often he had seen Mary's eyes harden and stare as if her sister were actually before her.

But to many that invisible presence was not a shadow but a quickening light; it brought a smile, a questioning shrug, as it now brought to Ruy Gomez while he slyly recounted his gossip.

The young Lady had a reputation for being 'marvellous meek,' yet she could rage like her father and had openly defied the Queen.

A Protestant nun in dress and behaviour, yet, when confined to her apartments in disgrace, she had given a fancy-dress dance for her friends, who had practically amounted to a rival Court, and had danced at it, dressed, but not over-much, as Diana.

Even in the Tower, when the axe, that had just struck the head off her little cousin Jane Grey, swung so imminently above her own, it was said that she had contrived to meet a paramour. Who was he? Probably Edward Courtenay, the young Earl of Devon; it was known that he had once planned to carry her off and marry her by force. And now, released from the Tower, he was writing heart-broken letters to her.

'And why released? *And* his paramour?' exclaimed Philip in a rare burst of impatience. 'After a rebellion to put them on the throne! My dear Aunt' (he still persisted in so calling his wife to Ruy Gomez; he seemed to think it amusing) 'carries mercy to extremes.' It irritated his tidy mind that Mary should have missed her perfect opportunity to cut off two such inconvenient heads at a blow.

But Ruy was right as usual. The Princess's death was no longer, at present, opportune. Therefore the best alternative was to cultivate this impudent and beguiling foe; it might also afford some contrast to the drab duties of matrimony.

He went to work cautiously with Mary and burrowed with mole-like patience to his purpose, through a seemingly endless damp tunnel, for that was what England smelt like, sodden earth and sour beer and boiled puddings and musty clothes and wet dogs, turning him sick with longing for the sharp smell of wine and of small herbs growing in stone paths in the hot sun, and spicy oranges dangling in a grove, and even of garlic. As for green 'resting the eyes,' his own felt tired out by so many heavy trees piling themselves up into the blurred shapeless landscape of never-ending woods. He would give them all for the single minute flash of a lizard across a wall, and the clear-cut cruel line of rocky hills, their tawny earth bare against the blinding sky.

They went to Hampton Court, and the green, now browned by winter, covered them, smothered them with a soggy blanket of moss, lawns, trees, and drifting clouds of dead leaves. The river flowed sleepily between softly waving rushes. Mary loved 'my father's favourite home,' so she was always calling it, and Philip refrained from mentioning that it had been Cardinal Wolsey's before Henry filched it; and that it was Wolsey's genius, not Henry's, that was impressed on the red-brick Palace that rose like a sunset cloud from the river-bed valley where one could never see above the tops of the trees.

Yet even this royal seclusion was considered a right of way by the casually intrusive English. King Henry's own Privy Garden seemed a bitter misnomer when the public were at liberty to hang over its hedges and little gate to watch Philip pacing up and down its paths. He insisted that at least the Palace should be kept immune; and the shocking report went round that 'the hall-door within the court was continually shut, so that no man might enter unless his errand were first known; which seems strange to us Englishmen that have not been used thereto.'

Suspicious, secretive, foreign, that was what it was. King Hal had never minded who strolled through his palace to get an eyeful of him.

Philip, holding a sprig of rosemary to his nose as they walked past the people in the gardens, complained to his wife that the Lion of England had respected these mice more than a pride of lions. In this country it should be a pride of mice.

But Mary liked the common people; she had sometimes

called at their cottages with one or two of her ladies and sat and talked with them about their work and families and often helped them secretly, without letting them know who she was.

It sounded a childish idea of royalty to Philip, who was trying to work himself up to a properly royal command and finding it unwontedly difficult.

'Your sister,' he began, saw her brows knit, and added hastily, 'the Little Bastard, as her father called her' –

'If he *were* her father,' muttered Mary.

Philip had no wish to hear her theories on the possible paternity of Elizabeth. Even if she were, as Mary declared, 'the image of Mark Smeaton,' the handsome young musician who had been executed for adultery with Ann Bullen, along with four others, including Ann's own brother, it had been made plain to him by Renard and Ruy Gomez that the bulk of England looked on Elizabeth as 'True Tudor' and 'Old Harry's Own,' – and all the greater menace for that.

'Whose-so-ever daughter she is,' he expounded laboriously as he launched himself on his carefully prepared speech, 'she is an ever-present factor to be reckoned with, and we must reckon with her. Since you have refused to put her to death, it would be wiser to come to terms with her.'

'*What* terms?' demanded Mary.

'Whatever terms may prove most expedient,' he replied smoothly. 'But it would be safer to have her as an apparent friend than a declared enemy. As a prisoner at Woodstock, she is proving dangerous. Sir Henry Bedingfeld is as trusty a jailer as any bulldog; he plants his troop of soldiers every night to keep watch on the hill above the house; he lets no one enter it without his permission. Not even the cofferer, Thomas Parry, who has to arrange all the housekeeping, is allowed to stay in the house. No, but he stays at the public-house in the village, at the sign of the Bull, and God knows who else with him. Half the disaffected elements of England appear to stay constantly at the Bull, and your bulldog Bedingfeld knows of it, writes, "if there be any practice of ill in all England, they are privy to it," yet he cannot keep them out of it – such is the licence granted to the English public-house! Your bulldog is no good at baiting the bull. Therefore, Madam, let *us* take the bull – or shall I say the cow? – by the horns.'

Mary was shaking all over, a symptom that he found inseparable in her from any mention of Elizabeth.

'It's true, it's true,' she gasped on an hysterically sounding sob. 'She is taking advantage of every inch I give her and stretching it to an ell. First Bedingfeld tells us that she asks for a volume of Cicero and the Psalms in Latin, then for a Bible – an English Bible, mark you, to flaunt her heretic inclinations in our face! – then for leave to write me one of her teasing letters, all innocence and false colours; then for leave to write to the Council, and makes poor old Bedingfeld her secretary to write complaints of his own treatment of her, "worse than a prisoner in the Tower," he has to write, and next day, "worse than the worst prisoner in Newgate." And then she's ill and won't have any but my own physicians, for she is "not minded to make any stranger privy to the state of her body," if you please! Are those the words of the worst-treated prisoner in Newgate? They are the words of – of "this great lady," so Bedingfeld himself, her very jailer, speaks of her! But *that* she is not! They are the words of an insolent traitor and pretender to the throne.'

Philip listened fascinated to his wife's outpouring of furious yet halting Spanish, like a lame dog run mad, he thought, and so strangely old-fashioned. She had quite forgotten her mother-tongue in all the long years of separation from it, but now that she was striving hard to take it up again, it had come back to her in all the out-of-date colloquialisms that her mother had used from the time when she in her turn had last spoken Spanish freely as a child. The result was that Mary's use of the language seemed two generations behind the times, and she herself as not merely his aunt but his great-aunt.

'Will the Lady Elizabeth speak Spanish?' he asked.

'I have no doubt she is busy acquiring it,' Mary replied on a biting note, 'and she can also speak French or Italian to you or Latin or, if you prefer it, Greek. She is very clever.' No wonder her tone was biting; she could have bitten her tongue out for it – after she had spoken. She loved Philip, she hated Elizabeth, yet could not resist using even her and her cleverness as a whip to flick at him, and his placid assumption that everyone should speak his language, and he none but his own.

But he was too certain of it himself to perceive any gibe at his stupidity.

'That is well,' he said; 'it will be well for many here to learn Spanish.'

Even Mary needed a reminder that her country was now a province of his. It amused him that even Mary flushed at it. And it pleased him to conceal from the majority that he could by now understand English pretty well, and even speak a few carefully prepared sentences quite correctly if necessary, though it would have to be a strong necessity to make him risk any possibly ridiculous mistake.

He had his way. Elizabeth was sent for to Hampton Court. But Mary would not have her in the Palace under the same roof as herself. She was lodged in the gatehouse on the river, a square red-brick block of masonry as strong as any fortress, and still under the close guard of Bedingfeld and a picked force of his men.

And still Mary put off seeing her; would not see her with Philip, dreading the effect of her own jealousy; did not feel well enough to see her alone; was afraid that her passive insolence, her false words, her subtle dangerous smile might infuriate her so much that it would provoke a miscarriage.

'You do not know what she is like,' she sobbed angrily to her husband. 'You have heard of her from the Court, no doubt, and they will have told you that she has done nothing down at Woodstock but sit and sew at her embroidery and study the classics – yes, and devout books so as to learn to be a Catholic – and that she knows nothing about all her unruly friends at the public-house down in the village. But I don't trust her an inch – and – and – I don't trust myself either when I am with her! One day I shall do something terrible to her – and then I shall be blamed for it, not her.'

Her head sank in shame. He looked at it, then laid a cool hand lightly on it. She clutched at his fingers before he could draw them away. 'Oh, do believe me. But when you see her you will not, for she charms all men to believe only what she wishes. And you, of all men, she will set out to deceive. But if you could see her as she is sometimes when alone with me—'

'Why not, if you wish it?' he conceded indulgently. 'I could be in the room, behind a curtain or a screen if you like, and hear all she says to you, without her knowing of any witness.'

'You will do that for me? Oh, but how good you are to me! You understand my fear of doing anything without you – and yet I know I ought to see her first alone,' she added hastily.

Philip agreed, but said that if she intended to come to terms with her sister, he must meet her openly some time.

'How do I know what I intend until I see her?' demanded Mary pettishly – at least she thought it was only the natural pettishness of a woman in her condition; but Philip thought she looked and sounded just as her father must have done in his quick rages. To tell the truth he was really afraid of her uncontrollable bursts of temper when her voice, most unexpectedly for such a little mousy-looking woman, would suddenly swell into the loud roar of an angry man's.

She was working herself now into a passion as she walked up and down, twisting her hands together, forcing herself to come to a decision, to be bold and resolute, to be like her father. 'I shall send for her tonight.'

'Without any warning? Then she will surely fear the worst.'

'Let her!' shouted Mary. 'It would be no more than her deserts.'

Certainly she was not to be trusted by herself in that state; it would be very awkward if in a rage she committed her sister to instant execution, or the Tower again, or even if in simpler fashion she threw a knife or something at her, or even, still more simply, scratched her face or tore her hair. One must remember what barbarians these English were. He braced himself, not unpleasantly, for the scene he was to watch that evening.

CHAPTER SEVEN

He took up his position behind the gilded leather screen in which, without mentioning it to his wife, he had thoughtfully cut a small slit. It was a pity the Queen's room was so dark; she said her eyes were too weak for a strong light, but he suspected that even with her sister, perhaps indeed especially with her, she preferred a flattering dusk.

It was after ten o'clock on a chilly night and gusts of wind, smelling of the river below, hurled themselves against the rattling windows. He thought almost with fellow-feeling of the girl now coming towards them in the flickering torchlight through the dark damp gardens, even as he had had to stumble his way at just this hour to his first meeting with the Queen. What a night-owl she was! He put his head round the screen and said on a note unusually imperative, almost exasperated, 'When you have said and heard all you want, give me a sign, say some word in Spanish, and I will come out and present myself.'

Mary was about to expostulate, but at that instant they heard the tread of men's feet on the stairs. Philip moved back behind the screen and Mary huddled herself down on a low seat at that end of the room. Sir Henry Bedingfeld entered the door at the other end, followed by some of the guard, and all stood there at attention.

A tall girl in a dark cloak walked quickly past them with her head held high, and down the long room towards the crouched bent figure of the Queen. Her appearance, after Philip's long waiting for it, was startlingly sudden, like a spirit called up by that hunched grey Witch of Endor on the stool, as she came so straight and swift towards her out of the black night.

She fell on her knees, but with her head still high, her face upturned, seeking, beseeching her sister's answering gaze. It was a transparently white face in the midst of the bright hair that had been dishevelled by the night-wind, and the eyes were wide and wary as a hunted animal's. She looked as though she knew her last hour had come – and so it well might, thought Philip, were he not there on guard.

Mary was speaking in English too fast for him to follow all she said, but the tone told him of the spate of accusing questions. Elizabeth's complicity in Wyatt's rebellion last spring – was she not guilty of it, would she not admit it, would she dare imperil her immortal soul by denying it?

But it was not fear for her soul, it was the sheer bodily fear of a trapped wild beast that darted from the eyes of the kneeling girl. Philip imagined them fixed and staring in death, the red head cut from the body, and the ruby-bright blood flowing from the white neck. Yes, she would make a good execution – and lucky to get it, it seemed, from the turn the Queen had now taken. For it was her sister's heresy that she was now urging her to confess, even more furiously than her accusations of treason; and Philip could see the straight slight body bound to the stake, the clouds of smoke, the long flames leaping up to consume that tossed cloud of flaming hair. He was glad he had thought of slitting a spy-hole in the screen.

What would the girl do now? One look at Mary's shut face, rigid as a mask, must show it to be deaf to pleading. Would she shriek and wail instead, shed floods of tears? He waited in hopeful curiosity. But Elizabeth spoke softly, faltered, fell silent, spoke again, in low scurries of speech, like the gusts of wind that flung themselves against the windows and then, like them, died of themselves. It was almost as though, finding herself unheeded, she sought another listener.

Suddenly, out of silence, there came a cry from her as passionate and tender as if she were pleading to a lover. What was it she had cried? Something that sounded curiously young and innocent, beseeching the Queen 'to have a good opinion of her.' What a way to entreat, when she must have been seeing the imminence of a fearful death as clearly as he had done!

She spoke again, but more continuously and composedly, and he noticed how ringing and musical her tones were now, throbbing like the strings of a lute, and sweet, full of the love of life rather than the fear of death. They seemed to be moving the Queen too, but in a different way, making her restless and uneasy; she tried to check her sister, then rose and walked hastily up and down, passed near to the end of the screen where she could glance behind it and catch his eyes in question. He nodded; she turned back to Elizabeth and spoke in an exhausted, exasperated voice, dragging the words heavily after each other like the trudging footsteps of tired men on the march. How old her voice was, old and tired, after that other! She was trying to make it kindly, but it only sounded despairing, too weary to go on disputing. 'You *may* be speaking truth,' came in grudging, gruff admission, 'God knows!' and then repeated the words in Spanish, '*Sabe Dios!*'

and caught her mottled hands together as if to wash them of the matter.

But it was a signal, and the girl knew it. She was crying out in terrified question, pointing at the screen. He had to answer it, to come out and meet her at last after all these months – or was it years? – that he had been waiting for this moment.

His usual reluctance towards any decided step became enormous, ominous; he could only overcome it by telling himself that it was because he might have made himself ridiculous by this childish device of hide and seek. He had to draw a deep breath, to fill himself with majesty and a sense of power more than human, as he stepped forward slowly from behind the screen, bowed low, and advanced towards the girl.

She gave one startled glance at him, then sank low, lower, down to the ground, her head bent till it all but touched her knee, remained thus while he had time to remember how a swan folds its wings and sinks upon the water; and then rose, as slowly and exquisitely, looking up at him until their eyes were on a level.

Odd that his first fanciful impressions were all of her in death, and by violence, beheaded, burnt, and now drowned, drawn up from the sea, for so pale she was that the candlelight flowing over her slowly rising face seemed blue and opalescent, and ripples of fear shimmered over it in waves of light rather than shadow. The long eyelids, sandy-fringed, lifted themselves at last, with no maidenly flutter, but wide open now. Looking straight into his were the eyes of no dying nor swooning victim, but the eyes of an equal. As a rival? an enemy? a lover?

They were utterly alien from the troubled eyes of her jailer, his wife, those starved eyes shadowed with pain and doubt, afraid of herself, of life, of him, praying for affection like those of a spaniel.

The eyes of this girl, he thought, would never pray to man or God; they were Pagan, perhaps even inhuman; clear as water, the eyes of a mermaid who could lure men to destruction under the cruel, softly curling waves of the translucent sea. He had seen death surrounding her high white brow, her lurid hair; but was it hers, or that of her enemies?

He could not stand looking at her, before his wife, in a moment that had caught them up beyond this present time, on throughout both their lives.

He had to move, to take her hand and bend his head over it, feeling how strong and sinuous were its fingers. He had to speak, and for once he heard his words before he knew what they would be. He bid her welcome to their Court, assured her she was no longer a prisoner, but their dear sister.

And then he had to kiss her, not on the cheek, but on her quivering red mouth.

Why had he thought of death to do with her? To kiss her was to kiss life itself, warm, tingling, and, he could have sworn, laughing. He longed to ask her why she laughed, but his wife was standing by.

CHAPTER EIGHT

Only an hour ago she had come this way under the swaying sighing trees, their shadows leaping forward across her path in the light of the torches carried by her silent guard. She had thought then she was walking, stumbling over sticks or grass tussocks in the dark, to her death, perhaps by fire. But in that hour her life had leaped and shaken itself into another pattern; the time and form of her death had fled away, become distant and unknown. She was not to die now after all, she was no longer to be a prisoner, closely guarded by Bedingfeld and his men; she was to go to Court again and be the Queen's, and her husband's, 'dear sister.'

She had to keep her feet from dancing on the wet grass; she turned at the door into the gatehouse and laughed in Bedingfeld's beard as she bade him good-night.

'You'll soon be free of me. Did ever a guardian have better reason to thank his stars? I've plagued you nearly to death.'

His breath caught in his throat at the sight of her face. 'I know well,' he said huskily, 'that it was in order to plague others.'

'Oh, in part! But in greater part to amuse myself. Prison teaches cruelty.'

He wanted to say that she could continue to tease and mock him without mercy, if only she would always look so at him, breathing the very spirit of young life and hope into him; but he could only clear his throat and bend stiffly to kiss her hand and curse to himself as he heard his knee-joint crack.

She lowered her head near his and whispered with the very devil of mischief dancing in her eyes, 'When I am Queen, I will not bring your rheumatism out in the middle of a wet night!'

'*When* I am Queen!' it was more reckless than heresy, with Mary drawing near her time, and prayers and processions in all the Churches to ensure her and Philip an heir. None of his men were near enough to catch the words, but that only made his enforced share in her criminal levity the more shocking – and just when he had longed for one crazy instant that she might go on teasing him for ever! Let her do it to her husband – if any man should be bold enough to marry her – and he hoped it would be one with a strong arm and no compunction in using the whip.

'Oh yes,' she said, exactly as though he had spoken aloud, 'but there may never be one, you know.' She swirled round on her toes, whistling a tune like a schoolboy, kissed her hand to him and vanished.

Philip was coming to see her. By himself. Mary might well not have been able to prevent it; and doubtless policy demanded it before she should be received at Court – but why had Mary sent a special message telling her to wear her best dress and jewels for the occasion? To do honour to her husband, ostensibly, but many wives in her case would have preferred him dishonoured. Perhaps she 'owed it to herself,' as dear Cat Ashley was always saying, not to appear as a mean jailer. Or, yes, that was the more like her, she was determined to fight her jealousy by being over-generous. In any case Elizabeth was delighted to obey her, and spent the morning trying on all her dresses and pronouncing them not fit to wear.

She tried first her ruby rings and then her emerald to see which made her fingers whiter, and could not bear to part with either. She had her hair dressed in a cloud of curls, and declared it made her one of the vulgar, and then smooth and pure as an angel's in an old Italian picture, and cried out that it made her a milksop, so went back to the curls – but would Philip be alarmed lest they meant she had designs on him? – or amused rather than alarmed? He had had plenty of experience where women were concerned; those pale eyes were very far from a fool's, they were likely to see through any feminine pretence at maiden modesty. Had he also *heard* through her that night? Had he detected when she had guessed his hidden presence, and used all her charms to plead to him, rather than to Mary?

No doubt, too, he knew all the standard tales about her shocking conduct, and dozens more that she herself had never known. Yes, it would be better to be quite natural, she told her mirror, as she rubbed a touch of rouge on her cheeks. In any case there was no time to change, for out of her window she could see a cortège come riding over the Palace bridge between all the stone griffins and dragons, towards the gatehouse.

Now she must go down and be careful not to laugh till he did, and congratulate him on his coming heir and Mary's healthy looks (she had never seen her look so ill) and lead him on to talk of Spain, for which he must be dismally homesick, and especially for his mistress, de Osorio, and all their children. It would not be his fault if Mary did not produce an heir and yet – Mary? – even now Elizabeth could not quite believe it.

She went down with her women and stood by the window with the light on her face, for he must be sick of shadows.

He was. He stood still for an instant by the door, suddenly realizing it. So long he had waited for the sun while weeks lengthened into months, and the weather worsened as an English summer became an English winter, until colder winds and sharper gales proclaimed an English spring. But now the real spring stood before him, bright and upstanding as a sword, with all its flowers spangling the embroidery of her white brocade, and jewels flashing red and green from her elegant fingers; it pleased him to see that they were shaking slightly. It was all rather bad taste by Spanish standards, but he would change all that – or perhaps he wouldn't.

He advanced between his grandees, bowed and looked down on the sunlit head bent low in curtsey, on her young face as he raised her, and then kissed her. England had some good customs.

The rest of the company drew back towards the open door of the anteroom. Elizabeth sat on the window-seat, leaving him the ceremonial chair; she could see him clearly now, as she could not do in the agitation of her first meeting with him.

She thought, 'He is handsome. He has a great deal of majesty, too much. If he were taller he would not need it. And his eyes are like a prawn's. They have grown cold in the study – no, they were born cold.' But his lips had not been cold, nor did they look so now. They were full and sensual. But they gave her a sense of fear. She wished he had not first seen her in that hour of her terror before Mary. He had probably enjoyed it.

They finished their polite enquiries and talked politics, which of course meant religion, and that he wished to sound her on her views. She agreed with him that men were always making some new religion, of earth too, she said, as well as of heaven.

'They preached "Communistic Law" here just lately – that no man should own any property and all should share alike, so they pulled down the palings in the great parks and slaughtered the deer, and said it was following Christ's own words.'

'They should never have been permitted to read them,' said Philip severely. 'Ideas are fertile.' A faint smile caught the corners of his lips as he added, 'They say "Erasmus laid the egg and Luther hatched it." And "Reform" is a bad egg.'

'Certainly it is explosive,' said Elizabeth.

'My father did one wrong thing, which he now has bitter reason to regret, and does. He had Luther in his power at the Diet of Worms, and he did not kill him. He let him go.'

She did not say 'But he had given Luther safe-conduct!' only, 'But then by your own showing he should have killed Erasmus too.'

'Assuredly. He was the father of heresy.'

'With others. The broody hen Luther flirted with a clutch of cocks.'

'Who accused each other. Even your advanced thinker Sir Thomas More called your translator of the Bible, Tyndale, the father of all heresies. Do you agree with him?'

'Oh yes,' she said lightly, 'because Tyndale made such mistakes in the translation. How right More was to complain of that word "charity" for "love". Words derived from Latin are all as cold as – charity.'

She felt his eyes upon her at mention of More, whom her father had beheaded because he would not acknowledge his marriage to her mother. Agreement with More would be slippery ground for her. She slid off it gracefully with a compliment on the new University Philip had just established at Mexico City, the first to be founded in the New World. What a triumph for the civilization, the initiative and enterprise of Spain, to be carrying her faith and learning into the dark and savage corners of the heathen world!

'I signed the order for its establishment,' he replied, 'on the same day that I signed the contract of marriage with the Queen of England.'

As another crusade against the heathen, his tone said clearly. But difficult to congratulate him on it, except personally. So she told him how he had won all English hearts by his affability and readiness 'to put up with our rough ways, for I have no doubt we must sometimes seem to you like savages.'

Quickly, to prevent a return to heresy, she repeated – and invented – some golden opinions of him she had heard, or hadn't heard, while she was at Woodstock. Even in the remote fastness of her country prison, she said wistfully, echoes had sometimes reached her from the outside world.

He was well aware of it, but made no reference to the public-house of the Bull, which had made such a convenient sounding-board for those echoes. He inquired with grave sympathy as to her pursuits in her retirement. She drew him a pretty picture of herself reading Greek and Latin and working at her embroidery-frame, and sprang up impulsively to show him a black-letter edition of the epistles of St. Paul with a cover stitched in a bold design of scarlet and gold thread.

'Who drew the pattern?' he asked. 'Yourself? You are an artist.' He flicked the pages and she had an anxious moment lest St. Paul came within the compass of heresy, since Christ had seemed dangerously near it just now. But he only murmured, 'I dislike this old-fashioned black-letter. Printing has improved greatly. What is this – your handwriting?'

'Yes, on the blank leaf. One should not write in books, but I was not allowed any paper. Please, Your Majesty, do not read it. It was only to beguile my loneliness by talking to myself.'

But in spite of her modest protestations, or because of them, he read:

'August. I walk many times into the pleasant fields of the Holy Scriptures, where I pluck up the goodly herbs of sentences by pruning, eat them by reading, chew them by musing, and lay them up at length in the high seat of memory by gathering them together, that so having tasted their sweetness I may the less perceive the bitterness of this miserable life.'

'"Pluck up the herbs – eat them – chew them by musing –"' he repeated thoughtfully. 'It sounds as though you were a cow.'

'*Oh!*' she flushed scarlet and her hands flew out to snatch the book from him, but thought better of it, and clasped each other instead, with a laugh now instead of an indignant cry, peal upon peal, at first musical as a carillon and then an uncontrollable fit of giggles which she had to choke with her handkerchief while the tears on her light eyelashes caught the sun and turned them to rainbows. 'How cruel,' she gasped, 'and true, for I remember now that I was watching the cows in Woodstock Park when I wrote it. They were moving so slowly through the grass, pulling up the long moon-daisies and munching them, chewing the cud, and I wished I were a cow, never to think of anything else but that, and then a milkmaid came with her three-legged stool and bucket on her arm, and milked them and sang so merrily while the milk poured ting-a-ling into the pail as though it were singing too.'

'What did she sing?'

'Oh, an old country song – "for bonny sweet Robin is all my joy—"'

'And you remember that – from last summer?'

'Prisoners have long memories, sir. I remember the evening going, the summer going, and the shadows of the trees dark and heavy as long-cloaked guards closing in on me. I remember how I said, to one of my own guards I suppose, that I wished I were that milkmaid, for her lot was better than mine and her life merrier.' The laughter had trembled into the note of the pathetic prisoner again.

'Was it raining?' asked Philip.

'It had been, I think, but the sun's last rays had come out and lay red along the cows' white furry backs, and yes, the grass was shining with raindrops. But why does Your Majesty ask?'

'I cannot remember any day last August when it was not raining.'

His tone said clearly that whatever he had to put up with in England from its diet and manners, its politics, its heresy, even its Queen, he would never forgive its weather. She knew better than to laugh about it. But she wished he would notice how strictly she had been kept a prisoner all these months that he had been disporting himself in England.

'Even the rain could not spoil your "tournament of reeds"?'

she asked. 'I cannot tell you how I longed to see your "cane game" as they called it here, surely the daintiest exercise of chivalry, the jousters riding at each other dressed in green and silver, white and gold, and armed with nothing more dangerous than long reeds – all to the music of silver trumpets and drums made of kettles. I pray you, gentle and courteous brother-in-law, to have that game played again for me to see.'

He looked down at her, suddenly suspicious, for he was noticing for the first time that his ceremonial chair was higher than the window-seat on which she sat (had that been of her planning?) and said, 'I do not think that tourney will ever be played again in England. Your countrymen do not care for it. The more cruel the sport, the more popular.'

She felt she would burst if she did not say the Spaniards were at least as cruel as the English. But she did not say it. She looked at him with sorrowful eyes and said, 'No cruelty of raw combat can equal the cruelty of keeping a young live thing cooped up in a cage, as I have been these two years.'

'And with no other consolations,' he said slowly, 'than those of learning and religion? Do you then assure me, my pretty, my very pretty sister, that you had no other consolations?'

Her cheeks had grown pale under the touch of rouge: 'What other could I have had?'

'I have heard of some, and in a stricter prison than an old country house. Did you never receive a visitor in the Tower?'

'No, Your Majesty.' It came with too strong a fervour.

'Nor pay visits – to another prisoner?'

'But what does Your—'

'No, enough of Majesty. I am your brother now, and believe me, more kind a brother than you know.'

'I can believe it well, since my sister—'

'Yes, what of her?'

'I do not think she is always kindly disposed towards me.'

'No. A few nights ago, when you were summoned to her, you thought, did you not, that you were going to your death?'

'Yes.'

'And so did I, or thought you might be. That was why I concealed myself behind the screen. Well, I have saved your life for this once at least. And now have you nothing to tell me of the Tower?'

'Sir, there were two children who played with me in the little garden, and brought me flowers to cheer my captivity. The eldest was a boy of five.'

'And you will tell me nothing more?'

'I have nothing to tell.'

'And never will have,' he thought, scanning those downcast eyelids that had shut her clear face into a mask. 'So, no consolations, though even your jailers would be glad to provide you with them?'

The mask flashed open into frank laughter. 'What! Poor old Bedingfeld! Would you accuse *him*?'

'I accuse no one, my sister, not even your beauty. But permit me to envy him.'

'Then talk with him, sir, and learn how much he finds his lot unenviable. He would be so thankful to be rid of the charge of this nuisance, this plague, this monster, that am I, that only his bounded loyalty and duty to the Queen has made him prevent my murder half a dozen times.'

'Is that true?' he asked quickly.

'Very true. My enemies have tried to set fire to the house at Woodstock, to shoot me as I walked in the maze, to put poison in my cup. All of which Bedingfeld has prevented, through no love of me, but determination that such methods should not dishonour the Queen.'

'You are very certain, my sister, of the motives of others. It must be from your infinite experience of life – you who have been so closely guarded these last few years of it – you who are more than half a dozen years younger than I.'

'What do you mean to say, sir – my brother?' ('The last thing he could ever be to me, or to any other!')

'What do I say? Why, nothing – as you have nothing to say of your brief sojourn in the Tower. But not too brief for love. For love is brief—'

'As breath! Love is brief, and life too. That is why I wish to breathe my life a little space before I die – to see your grave grandees, now gathered in a thunder cloud at the end of this room, so dark and quiet, to see them deck themselves in purple and black and yellow and silver, green and white and gold, and ride a tourney of the reeds before me. And – before I die...'

'What else, my sister?'

'To dance.'

'With whom, my sister?'

'With you, my brother.'

CHAPTER NINE

'Now I am alive again,' Elizabeth sang in her heart in time to the jigging notes of the lutes. 'I am still only twenty-one and I am at Court again, and dancing with Philip of Spain.'

The last three words were oddly exciting; not only because she was dancing with the greatest Prince in the world, nor because she felt that he admired her, and unwillingly, which made it so much the greater compliment. Why did she have this sense of immediate importance in dancing with him, in snatching a few words with him within the formal enclosure of their dance? In their interview he had said nothing that showed originality; but she had continually found herself wondering why he had said this or that, whether he had held back some meaning for himself behind the bare words. There seemed an infinity of reserve behind them.

Did he too find a hidden urgency in their meeting, an importance far beyond this present moment in the brightly lighted room enclosed like a jewel in the surrounding darkness? She laughed at herself. Philip of Spain had none of her reasons to hear this moment ring like a peal of bells within her; it was she, the disgraced prisoner, the Princess degraded from her rank, who had reason to thank her stars that she was alive, let alone free to dance with a handsome young man whose dancing was nearly as excellent as her own.

But for his chin, she thought, smiling sweetly at it as they parted at the end of the dance (it was a bad line, that underhung jaw; would Mary's baby inherit it?), but for that, he was as personable as any man here, except one. 'Oh Robin!' she whispered to a young man who stood among the encircling background of courtiers that had been watching their dance, 'how glad I am that you are so much taller than I!'

He was handing her dropped handkerchief, to her, a square of embroidery and lace, large enough to cover his fingers as they gripped hers. 'Is that the only difference between him and me – a matter of a few inches?'

'No, you fool! There is the difference of more than half the world and the whole mastery of England.'

'He'll never leave a footprint in England – unless you let him.'

'Let go my hand. He's watching.'

'Let him! Let all the world—'

'Let *go!*'

Her nails were sharply pointed. He let go, hurriedly, and she left him, a little too hurriedly. She should touch wood when she touched Robin; it was tempting Providence even to remind that frail lady (for she must be one, as she could never resist temptation) that her worst hour of danger in the Tower had come from none of her enemies, but from this young man who had so passionately desired her.

'Who is that tall fellow?' asked Philip in their next dance.

She did not know which tall fellow he meant. Was it the son of the Earl of Arundel?

'No. Though he, I believe, aspires to your hand, or his father does for him. Or is it rather, now, that his father aspires to it for himself?'

'The aspirants are three times too many. When I was in the Tower, the Earl of Arundel was urgent for my death.'

'Until he saw the light – of your eyes, and swore on his knees never to trouble you more.'

'A chivalrous old gentleman. But marriage to him would trouble me worse – well, almost worse, than death.'

'My sister, you are a virgin. It is quite correct that you should find some things worse than death. But I do not think that the tall young man standing by the door is one of them. And now will you tell me who he is?'

'Oh – *that*! Oh yes, I see whom you mean. But that is a nobody – l only thanked him for picking up my handkerchief.'

'Yes, I saw where you dropped it. And who is this nobody?'

'Only one of the sons of the late Duke of Northumberland, whom the Queen has lately had the clemency to release from the Tower. His father, Duke Dudley they called him over here, was beheaded for his rebellion when my little brother King Edward died, and he, the Duke, tried to put his daughter-in-law Jane Grey on the throne. A very wicked man,' said Elizabeth virtuously, 'he would have killed both my sister the Queen and myself.'

'I know about the Duke. What of his sons?'

'Let me see. There was Jack, Earl of Warwick – no, he died of the plague in the Tower. And Guildford – no, he was Jane's husband who died with her, the only one to be beheaded. And Harry, but he's too young. And Ambrose, or did he too die of the plague? If so, this must be Robert.'

'Robin Dudley. I think I have heard of him by that name. And is "Bonny sweet Robin"—'

'Not "all *my* joy," I assure Your Majesty! He was married years ago to Amy Robsart in a boy and girl love-match.'

'The kind of match that burns out quicker even than the match-tape held to a gun. And he was put in the Tower after the Queen's victory over his father. So he was there when you were, a year ago.'

'Yes, but—'

'But, what? Will you tell me again that it was only a boy of five who gave you flowers in the Tower? And nothing else?'

She looked into his eyes and felt cold. Suddenly she laughed. 'Whatever I say to you will be disbelieved. So of what use to say it? But what, after all, can you do to me? Nothing worse than death. But I have looked at death too often and too long to fear it now. Only – if I were dead, and if by any evil chance the Queen too might die, Your Majesty might have an awkward rearguard movement to reconnoitre before leaving England.'

He could not believe her boldness. She had put it all into open words, the fear of dangers that even Ruy Gomez had only dared to hint at, but that was guiding all his policy in releasing her from prison. *What* was he releasing? A genie out of a bottle, as in the old Moorish tales, rising in a cloud of fiery smoke against him? Even in this country, where men who had never seen her seemed to adore her, there were hints of a cloven hoof in her ancestry, and a prevalent belief that her mother had been a witch. He would have liked to cross himself against this daughter of the Devil. But instead he spoke soothingly.

'What nonsense is this? You must give a brother licence to tease you about your lovers, or else I shall believe that they are all indeed your lovers in good, or bad, earnest; yes, even the bald Arundel and the bushy-bearded old bear Bedingfeld.'

She was laughing happily, not at his badinage, as he

flattered himself, but because she was thinking, 'Now he is playing soft in his turn. It is always safer to attack.' 'Be bold, be bold,' as the nursery tale had it, but in answer to it came a chilling whisper, as from an open grave,

> 'Be bold, be bold, but not too bold,
> Lest that thy heart's blood should run cold.'

'And that,' she said, not knowing she spoke aloud, 'was the end of the story.'

'What do you say, Princess?'

'Nothing, sir. I was thinking of a fairytale,' – 'and of a dance in the firelight with a dead man,' she added to herself, but not aloud.

She was thinking of Tom Wyatt, who had come to warn her before he rose in rebellion to put her on the throne instead of Queen Mary; and was beheaded.

The tinkling music struck its final chord. She curtseyed to King Philip, turned, and saw Queen Mary looking at them.

'The body is a traitor. It is not my mind nor my will that is jealous. I urged my husband to dance, and with my sister. Once she was admitted to Court, I knew that I should have to do this, that I should have to sit on this dais and watch them dance together, since I cannot dance now, and perhaps I never shall again. But that is no reason to be jealous, since the reason I sit here is because I hold his child in my womb. I am blessed among women.'

Mary said this last to herself many times, and, at the same time, that she had no need thus to reassure herself.

But so many were seeking to reassure her. They had

brought a woman of fifty to see her who had just given birth for the first time, and to a hearty pair of twins, and reminded Mary that she herself was not yet quite forty. They had no need to reassure her, she told them. God had already worked a miracle for her in setting her on the throne above all her enemies. It was because He had meant her to be there, to do His work in England, and to bear a child that should carry it on.

The cradle, gorgeously decorated, lay in her room all ready for the day – it was any day now – that the bells should peal out the news that she had reached the triumphant pinnacle of her life, for which God had created her. Baby clothes and swaddling bands were piled high, some of the embroidery worked by herself, but not much, for the fine stitching made her eyes and head ache. Even toys were all ready, a rattle with silver bells, a coral mounted in gold to cut his first tooth on, a jack-in-the-box, and even, from donors with long views, painted hobby horses for him to ride. There was never any question but that the baby would be a boy. The future Sovereign of the World must be a man, and a strong one, to hold the world together. God, having done so much already for her, would not be niggardly in this final gift. If He gave her a child, it would surely be the one best fitted to carry on His work.

And why that 'if'? The child was certain, his birth would come any day now, the doctors said.

Any day. Day after day. And as each day died, then it would come the next. There was no need for her women to fuss and ask her questions so tactfully. There was nothing to do but wait patiently, as her husband was doing in such exemplary fashion, in spite of the supposed eagerness of youth. But then he was able to occupy himself, riding and hunting, and Mary did not dare ask how often Elizabeth was of the party.

More often than she saw; though more than once she saw them ride out through the gates of the Palace gardens into the Home Park at the head of their gaily coloured cortège while she stood behind the window curtains, hoping no one would catch a glimpse of her, and peered out from the dim panelled room to see them ride into the sunlight. Short-sighted as she was, she could see his flaxen head turn towards the deeper ruddy gold of Elizabeth's, and her mind twisted and turned inside itself to try and guess what the two were saying to each other.

But nothing could be more innocent than Elizabeth's opening to conversation – in Spanish, for she had been working night and day to perfect herself in it. She had flung back her head to look at the chestnut trees above them and laughed with pleasure at the strange sculpture of the spring, the leaves bursting from the tight sticky swaddling bands of their buds into shapes as fantastic as the outlandish plants that his sailors had brought back from the New World.

'Or as your signature,' he replied unexpectedly. 'Never have I seen a signature so fantastically designed. I said you could be an artist, but I do not know in what craft.'

'It is pleasant to think so, and I have thought it – that if I were turned out of this kingdom in my petticoat I could yet contrive to earn my livelihood.'

He gave an uneasy glance at her and she gave back a resolutely candid gaze that met and held his eyes. There was something both cool and reckless about her which disturbed all the ideals he had built up for his way of living and thinking; it was such a disturbance as the old often feel in the presence of the young; and that was ridiculous, for he was only half a dozen years older than she. But he was of an older world and way of thought, and in her he confronted a new one, outside his ken; she was of another race, barbaric, he told himself, and even of another sex than he had known; as tantalizing as any woman, yet bearing the challenge of a man.

'And how would you earn your living?' he asked rather lamely, for it was not what he had wished to say.

'I know nothing of that. Only that I would make a fair shift of it. Will Your Majesty try me at it for a wager? Turn me loose in Europe tomorrow and see what comes of it.'

'God forbid! I'd as soon turn loose a young lioness! Your hair and eyes are of the colour of danger. You are not a craftsman but a conquistador.'

'A freebooter? Like your Cortez and your Pizarro who conquered a strange continent?'

Her tone showed her delight in the odd compliment.

'Possibly.' He turned over the notion with grave deliberation. 'My great-grandmother of Castile, Isabella the Catholic, she was a Crusader, a Conqueror, as great as any man, greater than her husband Ferdinand of Aragon, whom she had to urge to join with her in driving the heathen Moors from Spain. They had oppressed our country for seven hundred years – until she conquered them. You too might conquer.'

She turned her head and asked him, 'Whom?' He felt as though he were looking into the sun.

'Myself,' he said, and he could look at her no longer.

They jerked their horses' heads straight again and rode on in silence. They flew their hawks to bring down their quarry; the long grey bodies of herons lay under their talons, and the hawks turned their proud heads up, away from them, never looking at their kill.

They dismounted and sat to rest on cloaks that their attendants spread on the grass and then handed round small silver cups of wine and knacks of stuffed cockscombs on biscuits, and Elizabeth snatched a scarlet radish from the dish and peeled it into a fair imitation of her own spreading riding-skirt over the white petticoat. 'I am the radish that is sown in the new moon,' she said.

'So is rosemary and lavender, but they are too dim for you.'

'No, I'm a gaudy vegetable. You, sir, should stick to the colewort.'

'Which is sown in the old moon, with the sign of the cross.' It angered him that she had not thought he would guess at her reference to the Queen. 'Did you think I would not understand gardeners' talk after nine months in England?'

'Lord no! You must be with child with it! Any day now you may bear a herb plot or a knot garden.'

He caught at her radish-coloured skirt, but she sprang up to pick a primrose or violet she saw, she ran down to the edge of the little stream to watch a water-rat swim across, and the water-beetles spin circles on a shallow pool. How fast she moved! Mary's movements were quick too, but with none of the lithe strength and grandeur of this young wild creature.

Yet both these half-sisters, so unlike each other and unlike him, made him uneasily conscious that they had no need to consider their dignity, as he did. *Why?* he demanded of himself, grinding the heel of his riding-boot into the springy green turf. The Tudors were Welsh upstarts, foreign to the English. The Spaniards had complained of his father as a foreigner, despite his Castilian mother; and he, Philip of

Spain, had determined they should never call *him* that.

But these Tudor sisters had never needed nor heeded such a determination. Their Welsh father and grandfather had bolstered up their ancestry with fairytales, had claimed descent from Arthur in order to make good their precarious claim on the throne. The daughters of their line were the more instinctively royal.

He watched Elizabeth as she came back along the bank and called to one of the falconers, spoke to him about her hawk, asked his advice, as Philip would never do of a servant, then handed the bird to him to see to, whistled in answer to a storm-cock until he whistled back again to her, and sank all in one movement on to the grass again beside Philip.

'My father says that English is the best language in which to call to hawks and other birds,' he told her.

'And in German to horses, I imagine.'

'You guess right, as always.'

'And what is Spanish best for?'

'For God, and the King.'

'Being the same?'

'It is convenient to think so.'

They laughed. Blown petals of wild cherry fell into their laps. She asked him about the plain of Cordova, which she had heard was a vast cloud of white almond-blossom every spring.

'There is a reason for that which might please you, if you would care for a love story.'

'What woman would not! Tell it me.'

'It happened four or five hundred years ago when the Moors ruled the land, if locusts can be said to rule. There was a female mule-driver called Romaiquia – yes, women still drive mules in the South. She was of the lowest birth, a brazen hussy, but a beauty and of great wit – she could cap verses impromptu better than anyone in Seville. That is a game you can still hear played in Seville, the drivers of mules and goats making up verses and calling them to each other as they pass down the narrow streets. It was so that she caught the ear of the Sultan, and then his eye; she became his Sultana, and he her slave. He would have made the world anew for her. One winter it was so cold that for the first time in memory there was snow on the Cordova plain. Romaiquia was so pleased with the sight that she demanded it should be provided for her every year. The Sultan could not command the heavens to fall, but he could command trees to rise. He had white almond-trees planted all over the plain, so that every year in early spring Romaiquia should see the Andalusian plain as white as snow.'

He had flushed at the unwonted length of his speech, and also because, as he had made it, they had both felt it come near to themselves. Of low birth and brazen, a beauty and great wit – she knew he had been thinking of her as he said the words.

'Now *there* was a female conquistador!' she exclaimed. 'I wish I had been a mule-driver to cap verses in the Seville streets.'

'And capture a Sultan?'

'Yes, if for me he would spread almond-blossom like snow in Andalusia. Your Moorish locusts had some pretty fancies. I should like to see their stucco work in Granada, making fine lace out of stone.'

'Dolls' gardens, my father calls them' he replied contemptuously. 'Perhaps you would also have liked the

Moorish Prince Motadid's flowerpots in Seville, that held the skulls of his enemies, with labels to show their names instead of flowers.' The hatred in his voice showed her that she must not mention Moors lightly, and small wonder.

She dared not let their conversation end on that note, though old Lady Clarencieux was watching them out of the corner of an eye acid with disapproval at this prolonged interruption to the hunt. Fortunately Ruy Gomez was entertaining her very well; Philip must find the Portugee an invaluable fellow. And Susan Clarencieux was unlikely to worry her adored Queen at this juncture with any disturbing gossip; Elizabeth had more to fear from that lively forthright young widow, Jane Dormer, but all *her* attention was being engaged by the Spaniard Feria. Most of the company indeed were pairing off like the birds that shrilled above them in the new warmth of this early April day, and what more natural than that her brother-in-law should still be sitting at her side?

She led him on to tell her more of Spain, and so of himself, a subject rare with him, yet he found himself doing it with such unusual ease that he thought she had been talking most.

'Your mind is a dragonfly or a green lizard darting in the sunlight,' he told her; 'you catch ideas as they do insects. But I,' – he hesitated, then took the plunge, 'I am slow. I am not clever. Nor was my father. He has told me that he was stupid as a boy and a young man. Yet he had to pit his brains against the cleverest rulers in Europe – François I of France, that treacherous fox, and Henry VIII of England—' He paused.

'Yes, please say it. You have no need to paraphrase your father's opinion of mine.'

'No, I have no need. For it was an enviable tribute – that King Henry possessed "that nonchalance which is the best secret of politics." Only a rich and rapidly working mind can possess that. My father, on the contrary, has had to work like ten men to make himself a great ruler. And I therefore must work ten times as hard as he.'

A really mediocre mind could surely never admit as much, or rather as little of itself. She was impressed by the dignity, and the determination, with which he recognized his limitations. And for all the frankness, almost simplicity, of this unusual mood, there was still some secret meaning, or perhaps secret power, retained behind the suave voice, which he did not choose to show.

The seed of what strange growth lay deep within him? A saint? A satyr? A great ruler? A fanatic? A frozen monster?

Any of these was possible; but also, at any rate at this present, a worshipping boy when he spoke of his father. Who might develop into a man capable of an equal give-and-take of passion and friendship with a woman? She wondered, weighing the unnatural formula of etiquette and piety which had bound his youth in rigid swaddling-bands long after he had ceased to be a child, and forced him to regard his body and soul as a public institution.

Against such upbringing, compared with which her precarious and often neglected childhood seemed sheer freedom, there was now this moment of springtime when he was falling in love with her.

And she, at this moment, might soon find herself in love with him. What might they not make of it? Might he not shake off his swaddling-bands, his ancient inheritance of a sense of guilt that he must atone, of belief in an angry God that must be appeased by sacrifice; and become a living hopeful force that would wield the future, with her help?

She could see him thinking this too, and believing it more than she. She knew more clearly than he what had already been made of him; how small a chance was left for him to become the partner who could help her in the work she might one day do. There still might be a chance. If not, would she ever again find such a partner? She thought not. She was alone, and must be so always, unless she met her equal; without any conscious pride she knew that to be unlikely.

Playfellows, not partners, were all that she could probably afford. She was playing with Philip now, and knew it, hoping that he did not. Her purpose would probably be always different from his. He certainly did not see that. But she for her part no longer saw his eyes as a prawn's.

A man came riding down the glade and after a quick glance round the company went up to Ruy Gomez and spoke to him. Ruy Gomez came towards Philip, who stiffened and froze as he approached. 'He knows it is from Mary,' thought Elizabeth. 'She has sent word that his presence is urgently required.'

And so she had. They all rode back to the Palace, and this time as they came through the grounds Philip kept his horse at a much further distance from Elizabeth's, and did not once turn his head towards her.

But to Mary, again watching from behind the curtain, the sight brought no comfort, and no appeasement of her rage.

CHAPTER TEN

'I might have died,' she stormed at her coldly wretched young husband. 'I felt so ill, in such pain just now, that all my women feared it. But *you* wish it!'

'Only your illness could make you think it.'

She clutched at his hand. 'Yes, yes,' she sobbed, 'it must be my illness. How could I say such dreadful things of you! You are kind. But you cannot know what it is to feel as desperately ill as I am doing, almost more in mind than body. Questions twist and turn within me, they are serpents gnawing at me.'

She had flung away from his hand, which had been as limp as his glove, and was walking up and down, up and down. Suddenly she threw over her shoulder, 'I know *she* wishes me dead.'

'Very likely,' observed Philip. Obviously Elizabeth would wish Mary's death, since she had everything to gain from it. Why could not Mary see and admit it? But she could see nothing clearly. The room seemed dim and small after the sunlight, and she like a dark bat flitting up and down in it, weaving her way blindly and her words with it, as if she did not know what way she or they would take.

'She may even work my death. It may well be possible. She is the daughter of a witch. Nan Bullen had the beginning of a sixth finger on one hand, a devil's teat for his imps to suck.

And her daughter' (she could not bear to speak Elizabeth's name) 'has a strange look in her eyes at times. I have seen the pupils go narrow and upright like those of a cat.' Her voice had died away into a mutter, ashamed to speak such haverings clearly before his coolly watchful gaze. Yet surely if a witch might overlook her or her child and cause their death, that witch must first be put to death. But there was only her own fancy to prove it.

'What *can* I do?' she cried, and he tried to answer sympathetically.

'Nothing; but wait for your hour and God's will.'

But she could not wait. Was there indeed nothing she could do? Nothing it seemed but to antagonize her husband, call him back from hunting on what he plainly regarded as a flimsy pretext, and then nag at him. She would give her life for him, but he would not believe that, and would not care if he did. She must not say it.

If only she could give her life for the child, if she could die in giving birth to him, then she would accept the sacrifice with resignation – no, with thankfulness!

She jerked herself to a standstill, staring open-eyed at the sudden dreadful knowledge. It would be no sacrifice; it would be a blessed relief. What heaven not to have to struggle on with life; to feel more and more tired and sick of her aching body; to see herself get older and older in Philip's eyes; to see them turn from her to Elizabeth; and, when he knew that she was watching, to see them turn away.

What a fool she was not to have known this before – or had she always known it, even before it had happened, before he had even met Elizabeth?

Being herself, she could not refrain from showing Philip

that she knew it. 'You watch her very carefully.'

'As I would the Devil,' he replied.

Her heart leaped. 'Then – you *don't* like her? You, too, don't trust her?'

'Not an inch.'

As she did not look convinced, he added, 'If you keep a panther in a cage, then suddenly release it, would you trust it?'

'I only released her because you wished it,' said Mary, and, Oh God, there she was crying again. Her sobs turned to hysterical little shrieks. In another minute her women would come running to her and he would be silently accused of endangering her life and their child's. He must stop her crying. He must say something quickly that would reassure her about Elizabeth, for that was plainly the trouble.

'You – and I—' he added hastily, for it would comfort her to link herself with him, 'need not trouble ourselves unduly with that young lady. In England admittedly she is an ever-present nuisance, a possible danger. Then let us get her out of England. We have already considered the plan to marry her to Emmanuel of Savoy and so link her to a Spanish dependency. And moreover give her a husband who, if he is half as forcible in the marriage bed as he is in the battlefield, should be fully capable of keeping a tight rein on her.'

He watched his effect. Mary was looking at him doubtfully. Did she think this too good to be true on his part? Uncomfortably he reviewed the conversation he had just had with Elizabeth in the woods, he did not know for how long; it may well have been longer than he had thought, and someone may already have told the Queen of it. But what he had just been saying to her surely gave good reason for it.

'I have not been merely amusing myself with the chase,' he said virtuously, and to his annoyance caught the echo of the self-exculpatory tone he had so often used as a boy to his rigid tutor. 'I have been putting forward this project to her, as indeed it has been put before, and with your approval – but this time, I think, with greater urgency and persuasion.'

'Indeed,' said Mary. She had quite stopped crying; in that at least he had had the effect he intended. But he was not so sure of this new steely stillness. He had better go before she had time to think of anything else. But she had already thought of it, and before he reached the door she said it.

'A Spanish dependency. And that would place her in most convenient dependency, and proximity, to you when you return to Spain.'

'This, Madam, is ridiculous. Her husband—'

'Is a soldier. So was Uriah the Hittite.'

For the first time he saw a resemblance in her to Elizabeth. What a pair!

But the resemblance was already crumpling up in her now puckered and sagging face. '*You* thought of that!' she cried, 'to have her near you, away from me.'

He had thought of it. But he had not thought she would do so. He would never have suspected her of being so suspicious. These virtuous women were always evil-minded.

For the first time she saw clearly the distaste in his eyes as they opened full and pale upon her. But distaste was not a thing she understood; and she read the look as one of cold hatred.

Her next words horrified him. 'The only safe place for her is where your father long ago wanted her to be – on the scaffold.'

'He does not now.'

'No. You have all changed, all of you. Your policy shifts and veers like a weather-cock, because it is only policy, because none of you care what is right or wrong. I spared her life when all my friends advised me against it, because I thought it right to do so. I do not think now that it is right. If I were to die now she would be a worse enemy to England than all the invading armies of France and Scotland. She would undo all my work for the Church and lead the country back into heresy. I will not risk it. If I should die of my unborn child, at least I shall first rid the country of this subtle canker.'

'Do so, and you will remove my one chance to defend myself here, alone, against your country. If you should die – which God forbid – then leave her to me as hostage – that is all the interest I should have in her.'

It was comfortable to believe it. She felt too sick to fight further.

Philip disliked having been led into a direct lie. Besides, it was unsafe. He decided to make it true at the first opportunity, and soon made the opportunity by walking with his sister-in-law in one of the pleached alleys that led down to the river in the gardens of Whitehall. It was out of sight of the Palace windows.

Elizabeth listened with respectful interest to his proposal of Emmanuel Philibert of Savoy as a husband for her; she had heard it before, she said, and agreed that he was a most worthy and honourable choice, young, good-looking, a good soldier, and so good at mathematics, of which she had always wanted to learn more; 'we could work out Euclid's propositions together,' said she, clasping her hands in girlish pleasure, 'and he could teach me algebra, but perhaps not that, for didn't the Moors invent it, or was it only the alphabet?'

'Is that all that he could teach you?'

'I doubt he'd have time to teach me anything – yes, *anything* – for I hear he sits up all night studying the arts of engineering and mechanical warfare.'

'Well. Would you rather choose a carpet knight?'

'I would not choose to sleep on the floor, but if I did, I should prefer a carpet to a steel plate. Marry him? I'd as soon marry a lobster! They say he lives and sleeps in his armour for as long as a month at a stretch.'

'You seem to know a great deal about him.'

'Naturally, sir. I made it my business, since he has often before been suggested as my bridegroom. But –' her light voice deepened, hesitated, it was a different woman speaking, 'I did not think that you would have done so.'

'Should I not have a brother's care for your welfare?'

'You did not speak of this when we talked so lately.' She sounded wistful, a little hurt. 'Did you have it then in your mind?'

'I had then, and have now, this in my mind – that I must have you near me. If not here in England, then in Spain. Let us speak freely—'

'Good God!' breathed Elizabeth.

'Well then, as freely as any man can draw breath in this heavy air.' He looked around and behind him, but no one showed through the thin lattice-work of the still all but leafless trees. 'The Queen *may* bear an heir to me, and live. What then? Why, then I am tied to her, and to this country, at intervals; but of shorter and shorter duration.'

'Why?'

'As she grows older, there will be the less and less chance of her bearing heirs to our two countries,' he explained patiently. 'And there will be the less reason for my presence here – the more for it in Spain, the centre of the world's government.'

She only nodded.

'In that case,' he doggedly pursued, 'what place would there be for you here, among a minority of suspect heretics? You would have small shrift from your sister, let me warn you. Nor does she choose to believe that you are her sister.'

'Who then, in God's name?'

'Scarcely his, Madonna mia. Yes, I can speak that much Italian. You'll find no Archangel Gabriel among the fathers she suggests for you. But a choice of five others.'

'With my mother's own brother, George Lord Rochford, among them!'

'I think she fancies rather the hireling musician, Mark Smeaton, as the favourite.'

'Tell me, Your Highness, is it your own opinion that my true name is Elizabeth Smeaton?'

'No. From what my father has told me of him, I should say that you bear all the markings of King Henry VIII.'

'I thank Your Highness. But in any case, if King Henry's elder and undoubted daughter Mary continues as England's Queen and your wife, and the mother of your heirs, it matters little to you who and what I am.'

'It matters little – *nothing* – in any case.'

They had reached the bank of the river below. It gleamed silver between the feathery gold of its waving rushes, it slid down below them past their elegantly shod feet, his in white buckskin, hers in green leather, it flowed on through London to the great Tower itself, its gentle ripples lapping against the steps of Traitors' Gate, where just a year ago she had been forced to land and enter that narrow prison from which so few came forth alive.

Well, she had done it – once. But a second time was too much to hope for.

'It matters a deal to me,' she said, 'if the Queen should consider double bastardy as equal to treason.'

'I fancy,' he replied judicially, 'that the truer and nearer your claim to the throne, the greater your danger. It is in your best interests that I advise your leaving England, and if not as the bride of Savoy (or, as you prefer it, of a lobster) then it might be as the guest of my Aunt Margaret, the Regent of the Spanish Netherlands, who has more than once invited you to the safe shelter of her Court.'

'I am greatly honoured by your aunt and indebted to her. But I could never bring myself to leave my country, however dangerous it be to me.'

'Why? Because your highest hopes are rooted in its soil?'

She did not answer. He changed his tack and said carelessly, 'I shall have to give close attention to the Netherlands in the near future.'

'So that, whether with your aunt or with my bridegroom, I can rest assured of Your Highness's continued brotherly care?'

'Assuredly.' He laid his hand on hers, which by a furious effort of restraint lay still under it, instead of flinging up to box his ears.

So this was the lover and possible equal partner she had imagined in the forest glade only two bright mornings ago! No equal, but a strutting little superior, farming out his secret slut with one pander or another! She could permit herself at least to flout away his hand in a show of pique that could not really offend, might even flatter him. 'And I thought you wanted me for myself!' she exclaimed, with an air of childishly brazen frankness.

'I want you for *my*self.'

'But only at second-hand, it seems.'

'How else, at present? Since that is only how I can make offer of myself. I am tied at first hand to the Queen of England, and must be while she lives and gives hope of an heir. But if she should not—'

He waited, but Elizabeth gave him no help.

'It is possible she may not survive childbirth,' he said. 'In her low state of health it is, I am told, even probable.'

Still she did not speak, and the reflected light from the running water below played up and down on the pale oval of her face, making a mockery of its stillness. So it would stay still for ever, while the emotions of others wove their pattern of life and death against it, but left it untouched, a mask hiding the woman beneath.

His words came up against her, each sentence groping, daring a little further, but fell back from her, leaving no mark.

His voice dropped very low. 'Then your hopes might match with mine.'

This time he drew an answer, though only in the form of a question. 'Does Your Highness know so well what mine are?'

'To be Queen of England.'

'And yours?'

'To make the match I spoke of just now.'

'Is this a wooing at first hand this time?'

'As near first hand as "ifs" and "ands" will allow it. We are neither of us free – yet.'

'Nor will you ever be,' she thought, and aloud, 'Spain is indeed a constant lover! Fifty years ago Katherine of Aragon married first my father's brother and then my father, so as to keep England in the family. And now you would marry first one sister and then the other, in the same good cause. But the precedent was unlucky. King Henry annulled his marriage because it was incestuous to marry with his brother's wife. Your deceased wife's sister would stand in no better case. And believe me, sir, I will not claim Mark Smeaton as a father in order to clear it!'

'I think,' he said slowly, 'that your true father is the Devil himself. You affect to know nothing of what I feel for you. But you must know it. I want you, whether at first or second hand, whether in Savoy, the Netherlands, or in England. But you will give me no shadow of a sign in answer.'

'Have pity! Such a shadow may well lead me into the shadow of death.'

'Then – is it only fear—?'

'"*Only.*" Your Highness can never have known what that is. You laid your hand on mine just now. If anyone passing at that moment saw it, would you bet high on my chance of outliving the Queen?'

'No. You are wise, and cautious.' They were the two qualities on which he had most prided himself, and now he hated them. 'Tell me this at least—' he paused.

'What, sir?'

'That if – that one day you might—' he began, then stopped outright. It was not for Philip of Spain to beg for love, when he was so uncertain of the answer. 'I will ask you nothing,' he said. 'But one day I may take.'

He bowed low and formally, turned on his heel and left her.

She watched him go back up the pleached alley. The neat criss-cross pattern of its branches cast a shadow like a gridiron on the slight figure as it walked away from her, with a little more dignity than became a rather small man, but that gave her no amusement, and some fear.

She wanted to call him back, but already it was too late, and then to run after him, but now it was too late for that too. It was always too late to retract, to try and retrieve what one had done. She had dared not encourage, but she need not have teased and tantalized him to such a point. And now he was moving away from her, up into the long tunnel of the trees that cast a shadow on him like a gridiron.

She shivered; she strolled on beside the river and wondered what would happen next.

It happened very soon; a tall young man, who waved his cap, then ran towards her, and her downcast heart flew up when she saw that it was Robin Dudley.

'The Queen has sent a page to look for you,' he told her breathlessly. 'Go to her quickly and be very careful. There's the devil to pay – it's because of John Knox – you know, the Presbyterian Scot, the preacher who gave trouble here even with the Protestants.'

'But he's not here now. Knox fled with Foxe and Cox and the rest of the box.'

'That's the trouble.' Robin was striding back in the direction of the Palace, she could scarcely keep up with him, his long legs went so fast without seeming to hurry. She found them curiously reassuring after the slow determined pace of the smaller man that she had just been watching.

'A tall man is safer,' she told herself.

'Knox sits snug and smug with his fellow Black-gowns at

Geneva,' Robin flung back over his shoulder, '*so* he can safely write a book to attack the Queen and add fuel to the fires at Smithfield. The Bishops have only lately begun to burn a few heretics there, but you'll see, the pace will quicken now.'

'At least slacken *your* pace. I'm out of breath.' (Even to Robin she would not admit that she had gasped for fear.) He slowed down, and she still more, planning desperately how she should answer Mary.

'He's going the best way to foul his own nest,' she called after him. 'His fellow Protestants here must hate him anyway for his quickness to save his own skin.'

'He's still saving it, or thinks so. The dirty coward's published it anonymously, but it's known to be his book.'

'What *is* the book?'

'It's called *The First Blast of the Trumpet against the Monstrous Regiment of Women*.'

CHAPTER ELEVEN

Mary had deliberately allowed John Knox to escape from England together with hundreds of other Protestant preachers at the beginning of her reign. She had believed then that she could lead back her country to the Church of Rome in peace and mercy, and had publicly resolved to use no harshness nor punishment for the error into which it had been led by its former rulers.

Her plan had not worked.

Since then, a priest's nose had been hacked off in Kent, a church full of worshippers set on fire in Suffolk, and in London's own Cathedral of St. Paul's a priest had been all but murdered on the altar steps, and the Host splashed with his blood. Words matched the deeds. Mr. Foxe was including the would-be murderer in his projected Book of Martyrs. Bishop Bale had written to Bishop Bonner, 'What is your idolatrous mass and lousy Latin service, you sosbelly swill-bowl, but the dregs of the devil?' And Mr. Knox had written a book that denied Mary any right even to the mercy she had shown him.

So this was how he returned thanks! This was what came of being merciful. She had tried to be, and her enemies would not let her. They had hardened their hearts against her and rewarded her mercy with hate. God could not have meant her to be merciful. This must be His way of telling her that He had sent her to bring not peace but a sword.

She sat crouched in her bedroom over the book, peering into it with her short-sighted eyes, and stabs of pain running up from them through her head as if the thick black strokes of the printed words were actual knives thrusting into her.

'That horrible monster, Jezebel of England,' they called her – 'a wicked woman, traitoress and bastard who has no right to the Crown.' She turned the page and read his prayer that 'God shall kindle all hearts with deadly hatred against her.'

She raised her eyes and saw Elizabeth standing before her; and in her the answer to John Knox's prayer.

That bright still figure was surely kindled with deadly hatred against her.

'This preacher – John Knox – what do you know of him? Speak honestly, if you can. No hesitation. I want no false abuse.'

Elizabeth answered rapidly, breathlessly, 'Then, Madam, I will say only what his own party said of him when they had made him Court preacher here – "he is neither grateful nor pleasable." The very first of his Court sermons was a long scream against what he called "the hideous idolatry" of kneeling at Communion. Afterwards he preached against his patrons under a thin disguise of names from the Bible; he protested that, even under their violently Protestant rule, no one but himself was Protestant enough. His own Archbishop Cranmer could not abide him; he said he was "a trouble-maker who could never let well alone." This is the character given him by his own allies.'

But Mary was peering at the book as though she had not heard. '"Heresies breed disorders,"' she muttered. 'Sir Thomas More said so long ago.'

Elizabeth tried desperately to distract her attention.

'Madam, there can be no surer proof of it than in this man's disordered mind.'

Mary thrust the book at her. 'Read it,' she commanded, 'read it to me. Do not turn the page. Read it wherever you are.'

Elizabeth read aloud, '"Woman having been accursed of God is to be for ever in complete bondage to man, and daily to humble and subject herself to him."'

'And do *you* agree with that?'

'No, Madam. Nor with any sentence I can see. This is not literature, it is "blotterature".'

'So you can quote too. More and Colet, we are in fine company!' Her laugh was dreadful. She snatched the book again from Elizabeth, bent her head almost on to the page and read out, '"It is more than a monster in nature that women should reign over men." – Ah, that touches you to the quick, too, you who look to be the next woman ruler! It's for *that* that you wait and watch. You stand there looking at me – there's another name for such watching – the overlooking of a witch.'

'Witch – watch,' the words yammered against Elizabeth's brain, thrown clean off its guard by this astounding new accusation. She had plunged into a nightmare, she dared not move nor speak, dared not look at Mary since that was 'overlooking,' dared not look away since that showed a guilty conscience.

She heard a voice loud as a man's, loud as their father's in a rage, telling her that it was of no use for her to wait and watch for signs of the Queen's ill health, to hope for her death and that of her child – 'no use, I tell you,' said Mary's strange voice, 'for you are a bastard twice over, you can never inherit the throne. What if I leave no heir? What even then? It makes no odds to you. For then the true heir to England is, without any question, Mary Queen of Scots.'

Even this was a respite. Elizabeth was not after all being ordered to her death. But she was now as much afraid, though more coldly. This last threat was blurted out in Mary's rage as it swayed uncertainly to this point and that; but it was none the less plain that it was her considered intention. She would hold to it. She would, if possible, carry it out in her Will. Philip would not like it; but that might be an added inducement, especially after one of their quarrels.

Mary cried out, 'Why don't you speak? What are you thinking?'

'That the little Queen of Scots casts a long shadow.'

'Which turns you cold, hey?'

'And will others. When she is Queen of France as well as Scotland – and –' Elizabeth baulked, but said it – 'and England, then Spain will no longer lead the world.'

'Always politics. It is all you think of, yes, *all* of you.' Yes, even Philip, she thought, and hurried on, 'At least that child would keep England's religion safe. She is a true daughter of the Church.'

'She was brought up in it, Madam, as I was not.'

'How should you be, by a mother known as "a spleeny Lutheran"!'

She was hitting feebly now, aimlessly. She would regret such a taunt instantly and be the more amenable. Elizabeth felt safer.

'But I am learning now,' she said meekly.

'You are taking a long time over it. And how do I know you are sincere, since it is for your safety? Life is sweet to you.'

The last words fell on so dropped and sad a note that a sharp pity caught Elizabeth unawares.

'Ah, Madam, and how should it not be sweet, now you have restored me to your favour, at least in part? But you,' she glanced at the cradle in the corner, 'with your great hopes, you must—'

'Find life sweet? Girl, what a fool you are, or would be if you believed yourself. But you are well used to unbelief. And how should I believe your faith in God? *I* forswore Him once, because I too was young and found life sweet, and feared to disobey my father – as you fear to disobey me. I acknowledged him to be the Supreme Head of the Church of England; I did "utterly refuse the Bishop of Rome's pretended authority within this realm"; – the words will stand for ever – I see them before me now in the flickering candlelight – a hot June night, Thursday it was, Thor's Day the heathen called it, and his thunder was rolling in the sky, but no thunderbolt fell to strike me dead. They made me sign each clause, forswearing God and my dead mother. She was hounded to death, but they could not make her forswear herself. It was I who did that to her, I who loved her more than anyone in the world. I acknowledged that her marriage with my father "was by God's law and man's law incestuous." And God has not yet punished me, not *yet*!'

With a blind gesture she groped out towards the cradle.

She had utterly forgotten Elizabeth who stood aghast before a misery so near to madness. Reason could never answer it; though she longed to tell her almost angrily that at least she had not hurt her mother by her perjury, since she had then been dead.

Remorse had been useful while it had helped Mary to be

merciful. But now it had begun to work the other way, what horrors might it not lead to in England? And anyway it was nineteen years ago, and how could one live, let alone rule, if one kept company with ghosts?

But the sagging, hollow face of the forlorn woman, whose womanhood seemed given her only for torment, stabbed her with a painful and unwilling emotion. She flung herself on her knees, and caught at the thin hands that were twisting and tormenting each other.

'God *has* punished you, Madam. Our father treated you vilely. You were a girl of twenty. He had kept you for years in prison. He could break the strongest spirit, but you stood up against all others. You told Edward to take your head but you would keep the mass.'

A little cold serpent of common sense whispered smiling to her that there had been no danger of the boy Edward taking his elder sister's head, it would have been most embarrassing to him – but that would not occur to Mary. The hands between hers had gone numb and dead. In anxiety that was only in small part for Mary, she chafed them, crying, 'It is over and past. You have fought a great fight and won the country to you. You have restored the Church –'

'But not the Church properties!' cried Mary on a cracking peal of laughter, and pulled away her hands.

Well at least she had heard and answered, so was not mad, yet. Elizabeth spoke more coolly, 'You have restored *your* share of them, Madam. What more can you do?'

'What more? You dare ask me that, who are the hope and figure-head of all these rebel Lutherans!' She was trembling, baffled and bewildered by Elizabeth's unexpected sympathy. She did not want to believe in it, and indeed Elizabeth herself was now amazed at it. Why had she been hurt even for an instant by hurt to Mary, who was crying, 'Oh yes, you can protest your innocence, you don't agree with their opinions, you know nothing of their plots, you can fold your hands and purse your lips and pretend that butter won't melt in your mouth, you can deceive all the world, even yourself – but your sin will find you out. God is not mocked. Guilt can only be expiated by sacrifice.'

So the storm's worked round again, was Elizabeth's thought, and as if in answer to it a rumbling, grumbling, thundering sound came bumbling from far off, from the streets behind Whitehall Palace, nearer and nearer, boring its way into this airless room. But it was not thunder. It was a curious animal sound, of many voices, not of an organized march of men, but a sort of muttering growl, now swinging into the rough rhythm of a tune. Involuntarily she turned towards the windows, then turned back.

'No. Go to them. Open them,' said Mary. 'Listen to what the crowd says. That is your forte, I think.'

'They are not speaking, Madam. They are singing.'

'What are they singing?'

'I can barely hear the tune, certainly no words.'

'But you know what they are.'

'No, Madam. London is always finding new street songs. I know very few.'

'Then I will tell you one. Do you know this?

> '"*Mary Mary quite contrary,*
> *How does your garden grow?*
> *Silver bells and cockleshells*
> *And pretty maids all in a row.*"'

'I have heard it and surely it is very harmless. The bells for church services through the day and night, the holy palmers with cockle shells in their hats, the nuns with their pretty faces all in a row, are "quite contrary" to the last reign, and all the better for that, so do many feel.'

She had shut the window and was talking fast to help shut out the sound of that other song. Not for her life did she dare admit that she knew the savage irony of its attack on Mary and Philip.

> *'Spare neither man, woman or child,*
> *Hang and head them, burn them with fire,*
> *What if Christ were both meek and mild,*
> *Satan our lord will give us hire,*
> *Now all shaven crowns to the standard!*
> *Make room! Pull down for the Spaniard!'*

There were louder, angrier shouts outside, shouts, the clash of weapons, a long shrill cry, then a gradual deadening of the noise as the Palace guards dispersed the crowds.

But the swinging rhythm of their song still seemed to echo on in the shut room between the two frightened women.

'Those are your friends,' said Mary.

'God save me from my friends!'

'Go!' Mary shrieked, and Elizabeth fled.

Mary sank her head upon her knees and folded her long-sleeved arms around them, shutting herself in with her dark wings, feeling her knees press against her heavy womb; but could feel no stir within it. 'I am with child with grief, and the midwife is hate.' Her foes, whom she had spared, hated her. Her husband, whom she worshipped, did he hate her? Did

God Himself hate her? Because she had failed Him long ago – or because she was failing Him now, in her weakness towards His enemies?

Her foot thrust out and kicked against the book that was poisoned with a heretic's 'deadly hatred.' Surely he had rent his mother's body asunder when escaping from her hated womb. Would God punish herself in such a way by giving her a son who would also hate her? Could she do nothing to prevent it?

The answer came to her from her answer to that bland and baleful face of her young sister. 'God is not mocked. Guilt can only be expiated by sacrifice.' England must learn that lesson. She harboured many obstinate heretics, but only a very few, and only just lately, had been punished. She must act quickly or her child would be born in sin, the deadly sin of her neglect of the souls of her country. In sudden terror she got up with difficulty and clambered across the room, heavy with child, heavy with guilt, towards the cradle that stood waiting, glittering, empty.

She read again the rhyme carved on its side.

> 'The child which Thou to Mary
> Oh Lord of might hast send,
> To England's joy, in health,
> Preserve, keep and defend.'

Oh, Lord, give her might to defend him!

Not mercy any longer, but might.

Others must help her. She must consult a man. Not her husband; he was kind and considerate, and she had been mad to wonder if he hated her. But if she asked him now about

English affairs he would only tell her that he could do nothing until she had made the Council give him the Crown matrimonial and an English expeditionary force in Flanders. She had asked, but the Council had refused.

'If it were my father he would have commanded them,' she thought, and then still more bitterly, 'If it were Elizabeth she would manage them.'

But even if she could give Philip all that he asked, would he help her? His own private chaplain, the learned Spanish friar Alfonso de Castro, had just lately preached a sermon declaring that persecution was not a religious duty. Philip must have allowed, even encouraged him to do so, and why? The answer struck on her heart like a blow; because persecution 'was not always expedient.' That was Machiavelli's word; it never should be hers.

Only one man she knew despised expediency. In her mind's eye there stood again the tall scarlet figure of Cardinal Pole dominating the Members of Parliament last November like a messenger from heaven, his arm outstretched over the abjectly weeping, kneeling forms as he pronounced their absolution.

He had rebuked this guilty nation; and herself. His words to her still burned her mind; 'I do not know if your councillors who urge you to set your kingdom's affairs in order first, and *then* restore religion, believe the words of the Gospel.' He had written that to her, and she could not refute it. He was strong and she was weak. She had once renounced God and her mother. He would never have done that. He alone could help her expiate it.

She would confront Elizabeth with Cardinal Pole.

INTERLUDE: THE PRIEST

CHAPTER TWELVE

Reginald Pole had not always wanted to come home. Italy had indeed been his true home ever since he had gone there to study after leaving Oxford. His scholarship was so excellent that when he was still only twenty-four one of his professors in Greek sent him his book to correct and edit at will; the 'immodest modesty' of which his friends accused him, preferred this to any task of his own.

He had not wanted public life, nor any share in the ruling of his country, nor of the Church. He had refused the Archbishopric of York from Henry VIII; he had done his best to refuse to be Cardinal; he had as good as refused to be Pope. He hated politics and the modern cynicism about them. He had been given a copy of Machiavelli's *Prince* by Henry's minister, Thomas Cromwell, who always carried it about with him as his Bible, and thought it would teach the young dilettante some practical sense of the necessity of force and fraud in statecraft.

It did, but not as Thomas had intended, for Reginald declared the author to be an enemy of mankind and that his book was one to poison Christendom for centuries to come.

Nor did he feel any better about the management of affairs by the Church. At Rome he was horrified at 'the abomination of the Cardinals and Bishops, the detestable vices of the city';

he fled from the capital of Christendom to Venice, where on Ascension Day he watched with joy the purely pagan ceremony of the Doge in crimson and cloth of gold flinging his ring into the water to 'espouse the everlasting sea'; then back to his villa at Padua and his friends and their delightful way of life, as near as possible to that of the patricians of ancient Rome.

His friend Cardinal Bembo preached sermons on Platonic love and avowed himself an Epicurean philosopher. His friend Longolius had abjured his French name, Longueil, vowed never to read any book for five years but those of Cicero, and was solemnly created a Roman citizen as of old; when he died in Reginald's house he bequeathed him his classical library.

The influence of his friends lay like sunlight all over Reginald's early manhood.

'Friendship, dear boy,' Bembo had said, twirling the little moustache that followed the disdainful curve of his lip, 'that is the field of your genius, your nation's genius. You are cold to women. Stay cold. You would make neither them happy nor yourself. You love argument, conversation, though never did any man converse in so few words – but that is the cause of conversation in others. You love the rush and swing of Greek verse, the slow measured cadences of Latin prose, things that no woman has ever truly loved. I, too, love these things, but I love others, which women also love. I love to gather my strawberries myself, to spread them in these flat blue dishes of coarse pottery that the Tuscans have made for centuries, and leave them lying within my darkened rooms during the heat of the day so that their cool scent shall awaken appetite before even the first incredulous rapture of their heady savour. And I love to fill my house with roses, freshly plucked each day. You also love these things, Rinaldo mio, as long as you do not have to do anything about them.

'But, like all Englishmen, you are passive about them. Others must provide your delicate pleasures. That, my young friend, is an unfortunate attitude to take up with regard to women. Therefore I advise you to continue to have nothing to do with them.'

Reginald did not wish to have anything to do with them, and he had not. He did not then remember that his mother was also a woman.

His exquisite life in his villa, with gardens laid out to the plan of the aesthetic Lucullus, was provided by the princely generosity of his relative King Henry VIII of England, who allowed him a hundred a year and with no other obligation than that of entertaining the English Ambassador to Venice and all his retinue, a mere nothing to Reginald, who was accustomed to have his house full of guests at all times. Too full, his house steward Bernardino complained, for they treated the house as though it were their own, and did not leave Bernardino nearly enough time off to copy and edit Greek manuscripts.

But then Reginald in his turn paid long visits, chiefly to Cardinal Bembo and his voluptuous mistress Morosina and their three children who were like Raphael's dark-eyed bambini. He sat among gleaming statues of naked goddesses dug out of the dark earth, and portraits of poets and their loves, Dante and his Beatrice, Petrarch and his Laura, of Boccaccio, of Roman maidens by Mantegna, of Bembo himself by Raphael; he explored Bembo's library, his collection of ancient classic manuscripts, Greek coins and vases, and cameos carved into rings for women to wear before the Virgin Mary was born. Bembo's profile was also a cameo, the high domed forehead, the finely chiselled nose and eye-sockets forbidding one to notice the too small chin under its tiny point of beard. He was the perfect example of the modern Italian Churchmen who had survived the Renascence of pagan culture by identifying themselves with it. As a youth he had been passionately in love with Lucrezia Borgia (he always said those stories about the Borgia family were grossly exaggerated); now as a Cardinal and secretary to the Pope, he advised the young deacons in his charge not to read St. Paul lest the saint should spoil their style; he put Plato above Christ; but even with Plato one should be careful to preserve the golden mean, and treasure philosophy not as an aim of life, but as an added elegance to help the refinement of 'delight and play' which was its true purpose.

Reginald listened to him, looked at his Morosina with delight but not desire, played with their children, admired his antiques, followed his advice and wrote a Life of their learned friend Longolius in faultless Latin prose, using no word that had not been used by Cicero, a tribute so appropriate that surely God would permit Longolius to appreciate it even in an all-Christian, non-pagan heaven.

But life could not go on being all roses and strawberries and other men's mistresses. After seven years, the correct term of years in fairyland, he had to go back to England at his King's command. Henry had grown twice as large and loud and terrible. Reginald felt the shadow of fear that lay on all his own family; and the hush that fell on the crowd of courtiers whenever the King's glittering bulk strode into the room and his darting capricious glance put every man in terror lest he be the one whom its lightning would strike next.

The magnificent royal cousin, 'to whose generosity and care I owe my knowledge of letters,' as Reginald gladly acknowledged, now showed that he expected payment. He was busy collecting a bodyguard of learned and ecclesiastic opinions to support him in saying that his marriage of twenty years' standing to his late brother's wife, Katherine of Aragon, was incestuous; that the former Pope had no right to give him a Dispensation for it; that in fact he had been living in sin with her all these years, and their daughter the Princess Mary was a bastard; and therefore, finally, he was free to marry Ann Bullen.

Reginald, finding himself one day unexpectedly created Dean of Exeter, as an obvious step to conscription in this bodyguard, packed his books, musical instruments and fustian mattresses, and left for Paris. But Henry sent after him to consult the University there about the divorce, *i.e.* to persuade them to Henry's view of it. He did so with satisfactory results, and returned home to retire to the Carthusian monastery of his schooldays, not as a monk, but for board and lodging and peace to study.

But Henry dug him out again, threatened to make him Archbishop of York, commanded him to state publicly his own private opinion of the divorce. Reginald must either abjure his mother's friend, Queen Katherine, and his own sense of right, and help to ruin his pathetic little friend, the Princess Mary; or else endanger all his own family as well as himself. His elder brother, Lord Montague, implored him to find a compromise; he desperately sought one, thought he had found it, and went to tell the King.

Henry came on him suddenly at the end of a gallery; huge, overbearing, he stood there like a monstrous apparition of brute power. Reginald was appalled; the jolly kindly kinsman he had adored was now a tyrant who demanded toll even of one's private thoughts. He forgot every one of his perfectly prepared sentences; he tried to speak, gasped, and heard himself begging the King not to ruin his own soul.

Henry's hand flew to the dagger in his belt and jerked it up to strike, then flung it clattering on the floor, turned on his heel and swung out of the gallery. 'There was so much simplicity in his manner,' Henry said later, 'that it cheated my indignation. I could not think he meant me ill.'

He was right. Reginald, left alone, was weeping broken-heartedly, not for the singular failure of his first effort at diplomacy, but for the wrecked nobility of the man he loved.

There was a partial reconciliation; Henry even accepted Reginald's reasons, chiefly economic and therefore sound, against the divorce, which he wisely put in writing this time instead of attempting speech. Henry then added, as brightly as a child claiming a prize for *not* learning his lesson, that if Reginald 'would now only show his approval of my cause, nobody should be dearer to my heart.'

But he let him escape abroad again, and even continued his allowance, and Reginald went back to Italy, this time for more than twenty years. He thought he was going home again. But it was not the same. The game of playing at being Greeks and Romans now seemed childish; Bembo's luscious verses would not last, nor his Epicurean philosophy; it might be original to argue against the immortality of the soul, as the philosopher Pomponazzi had done, but Reginald thought he would back Plato and even the Church against Pomponazzi.

'Even' the Church? He realized how little he had considered its teaching in comparison with classical learning. He began to study theology and divinity, and challenged all philosophy that did not lead to these as its consummation. Prayer came more and more to take the place of contemplation, the New Testament that of Cicero, and even Homer was beaten on his own ground by Isaiah.

He had always hated the active life of affairs; he had grown dissatisfied with the contemplative life of classic scholarship; at last he had come to know that what he wanted was to lead a life dedicated to reform within the Church. The world would never know peace as long as the policies of Church and State were based on selfishness and tyranny. His King had now made himself his own Pope, plundered the monasteries, turned out the monks and nuns, married the Courtesan, as Ann Bullen was called on the Continent, and beheaded the wisest and saintliest scholars in his kingdom, Bishop Fisher and Sir Thomas More, for the crime only of keeping silence.

Then Reginald also was forced to meet that charge. The King demanded his approval of his actions. Reginald asked for time, and took it, more than a year, to answer, not in a letter, but a book, a long book, a very rude book, and sent the manuscript to the King. He told Henry to his face that he had once admired and venerated him more than any other man, but that now he had become a robber and murderer and enemy to Christianity; one who 'never loved the people; – robbed the clergy; – destroyed the best men of your kingdom, not like a human being but like a wild beast.'

His final shot was a suggested epitaph for Henry's tombstone: 'He has spent enormous sums to make all universities declare him incestuous.'

The only hope, he said, of bringing Henry to his senses was to give him a severe shock. It did. Henry swore to make Pole 'eat his own heart.' He proclaimed him a traitor and offered huge rewards for his assassination in Italy. But he found Christendom gathering itself together against him. England rumbled with revolution, a bloodless one, that should bring the King to an understanding of God's law; it was to be called the Pilgrimage of Grace. Europe rumbled too, especially Rome and the Papacy. Reginald was summoned there and started for Rome. On his way he received such urgent letters from his mother and elder brother, Lord Montague, begging him not to go to Rome, that he all but turned back.

But his friend and fellow-traveller, the ferocious old Cardinal Caraffa, prevented him. Reginald had an enormous admiration for him, he was so full of vigour and ardour, though it was a pity he was also always so full of mangiaguerra or 'champ-the-war,' the nickname given to the thick black fiery wine of Naples; it should also have been Caraffa's nickname. Like Henry of England, Caraffa frequently held quite other opinions after dinner from those that he had had before; it was another point of resemblance in the two men most different from himself, whom Reginald had yet most nearly worshipped. He still worshipped Caraffa's fiery zeal for the Church, and it was the old man's violent persuasions that changed his mind again and led him on to Rome and the ruin of his family.

For there, to his consternation, he found that he was to be made a Cardinal. He saw the danger to his relatives, he tried to refuse, but the Pope sent along, not only his Chamberlain to tell him he was nominated, but his barber to shave his tonsure. Mildly protesting, he was led 'like a lamb to the shearer.'

Then, inevitably, he was appointed Papal Legate for

England, to bring the King back into the fold of the Church under threat of excommunication and of moral support to the Pilgrimage of Grace. But the 'Very Catholic King of Spain' noted that the moral support lacked financial support, so gave none. Both he and the 'Most Christian King of France' continued to support their anti-Papal brother of England. So Henry, undisturbed, squashed the bloodless revolution in an ocean of blood, and turned like a tiger on Pole's family. Pole's mother, the Countess of Salisbury, was the daughter of the Duke of Clarence, whom his brother, Richard III, was believed to have drowned in the Tower in a butt of Malmsey wine; her children had a claim to the throne closer than that of Henry; he had been waiting for an opportunity to destroy this branch of the White Rose Plantagenets. Reginald's younger brother Geoffrey, an odd uncertain weakling, was threatened with torture in the Tower and confessed to whatsoever his judges wanted. His mother had embroidered a coat of arms with marigolds, the emblem for the Princess Mary, and pansies, the emblem for Reginald Pole. This was considered a clear indication of a plot to marry them, as both their mothers had always wished, and put them on the throne. So the old Countess was beheaded or, rather, butchered by a bungling executioner, and also her eldest son Montague; and his son, a child, was put in the Tower and never seen again, just as two other little princes had been put in the Tower by their uncle King Richard nearly sixty years before, and never seen again except once or twice in the winter twilight as two small shivering ghosts.

Only Geoffrey, having turned King's evidence, escaped; if it can be called escape to live on, shrinking from all men, starting at shadows, hating to live, and trying in a futile frenzy to smother himself with a cushion, but failing even to die.

'Pole must now eat his own heart and be as heartless as he is graceless,' wrote Bishop Hugh Latimer in exultant congratulation to his King, whom he called the 'instrument of God' in wiping out the noblest family in England.

There was some reason to call Pole heartless. His blood ran thinly in an effete body; no human emotion was urgent in him, neither love of family nor of country, and certainly not of women. But now he was forced to remember that his mother was also a woman, and to realize that her fate had lain at his door.

A villain like Thomas Cromwell, or even Machiavelli, would have managed to avoid it. But he dared not twist the knife of remorse within him. He had to make of it something that should not turn his brain.

So he wrote in a letter that he had been 'the son of one of the best and most honoured ladies in England; but now God has wished to honour me still more, by making me the son of a martyr.' His friends commended his pious serenity; it was also his courtesy that hid his unceasing ache from them.

He showed no rage against Henry. He did not even take the revenge of publishing his attack on him; he had never intended to do so; and Henry's crime against him could not make him change his mind. He had spoken out his blame of the King in it, and so made amends for his cowardly hesitation in not doing so before. That was the importance of the book to him; he had declared his true mind in it, and the consequences were beyond his control; but they left their mark in deep lines on his haggard face. He wrote of them, 'the hatred with which the King pursued me acted on me as the ploughman's furrows on the earth,' and so, he hoped, 'the seeds of faith, hope and charity might take deeper root.'

He seemed almost to welcome the tragedy that made him know he had a heart as well as a soul to offer God.

He still kept his genius for friendship; was still broadminded. He took two young men into his household who were strongly suspected of heresy. Even more surprisingly, he made great friends with an odd, ugly, violent artist whose nose had been broken in a fight with a rival sculptor, and whose loud abuse of other artists struck Reginald as not only un-Christian but ungentlemanly. But then his painting in the Sistine chapel had earned Michelangelo the right to be an 'original.'

And he made close friends, for the first time in his life, with a woman, ten years older than himself, a famous poet under the name of Vittoria Colonna, also a friend of Michelangelo, who gave her drawings of his and they wrote sonnets to each other. 'You, gracious lady, might create me new,' he told her; Reginald called her 'our dearest mother in Christ,' and she called him her 'son and Master.' They formed a group of which she was the 'mother,' and the 'father' was the pious, learned Contarini who had dared tell Pope Clement VII that 'nothing is stronger than truth, virtue goodness, and a right intention.' It was not as witty as the sayings of Cardinal Bembo. But Vittoria, like Reginald, had outgrown her friendship for Bembo: for years she had imitated his smooth verses and it had brought her a great reputation; no literary party was complete without her, and one met everybody at her house, uncouth artists, uneasy poets, and now that interesting austere new English Cardinal who was such an aristocrat that his family had been executed for being too near the throne.

But Vittoria was outgrowing also her taste for parties, and the arid brilliance of the society which she outshone. Like Reginald Pole she felt the need of religion, and he of her motherly consolation. Their new coterie was called the 'Spirituals' by those who liked them; those who did not, like old Cardinal Caraffa, called them 'crypto-Protestants.' Prayer-meetings and theological discussion gave a purifying influence to their companionship; only a new disturbing spirit of criticism made Pole wonder if it were not all rather too pleasant to be much use.

The 'Spirituals' stayed at each others' houses, walked and talked in shady groves, sat by playing fountains for their alfresco meals; almost it seemed that the sunlight of his early days in Italy had returned. But the light was colder, the friends were older. They walked more briefly, talked more lengthily, thought more slowly, and both friends and foes were much more apt to die.

King Henry died, and the gentle 'father' Contarini, and then Reginald's 'new mother'; yes, Vittoria Colonna, noblest of Roman matrons, lay dead; everyone seemed to be dying except Cardinal Caraffa, older than anybody, who swore he would never die.

He was now openly an enemy. He had forced the Pope to establish the Inquisition in Rome, bought a building with his own money to house its dreaded officers, and gave secret information to them of Pole's circle of scholars and 'Spirituals,' both of which were 'plain heretics' to Caraffa. Michelangelo's nudes were an abomination and should be decently covered – or destroyed. Erasmus had been the arch-traitor and all his works should be put on the Index; though Pole reminded him that Erasmus's aim, like Caraffa's, had been the revival of religion within the Church.

Caraffa replied by hounding some of Pole's household to fly for their lives, and calling Pole himself 'worse than a heretic – a heathen cannibal, devouring his own kind.'

Pole's cannibal crime was that he had stated publicly that 'we, the shepherds, are responsible for all the evils now burdening the flock of Christ.'

Caraffa urged reform too, but it must be reform of others, not himself.

Then death struck his worst blow, at the old Pope Paul III, whom Reginald did not like. But his death left the Papal Chair vacant, and everybody said that the English Cardinal was the right man to fill it. All his friends implored him to take up the highest office, rescue it from political tricks and devices, and carry out the work of Church reform as only a man so high-minded and disinterested could do.

The prospect of being the first English Pope for four centuries, and the youngest for nearly as many, the easy winner of a prize that the magnificent Cardinal Wolsey had struggled for in vain, was too showy and vulgarly ambitious to affect him. His trouble was that so few others were disinterested. The Emperor Charles V was backing him with every Spanish Cardinal he could muster, but only so as to thwart French power by defeating the candidate favoured by France. Most urgent of all his supporters were the money-lenders and bankers; they told him the betting was so high in his favour that fortunes would be lost throughout Italy if he backed out of the running.

Was this the race that he must run for Christ?

He did not back out; well, not exactly. But he shrank from the ugly and immoral muddle he had got to clear up if he were once seated on the throne of Peter. The appalling stew of the Conclave of Cardinals shut up in the Vatican to decide his election, so crowded that the stench of the lavatories seemed certain to breed the plague; most of them guzzling and drinking when they were supposed to be fasting; admitting Ambassadors over the roofs and through the windows when they were supposed to be hermetically secluded, and slipping out betting notes to the bookmakers of Rome; and then the reports that what Pole had most to fear was not the rival votes for the French King's candidate, but the alarm of the Papal Court that if he became Pope they would all have to lead a new life; these things revolted him into calling the whole proceeding 'that comedy, not to say tragedy.'

What part could he act in it, even if he were 'called upon to be the ass who should bring Christ back into Jerusalem'? He told himself he would not refuse to answer that call; but every nerve in his body prayed against it. And when the crisis came, those nerves acted more mulishly than Christ's ass.

The Spanish Cardinals tried to push a rush election at night before a reinforcement of opposing French Cardinals arrived. Pole, faced with a sudden and slightly irregular action, took fright, and refused obstinately to enter the Papacy 'under cover of darkness.' But by daylight the other French Cardinals arrived, and the chance had been missed. Pole had lost his opportunity to work the counter-Reformation from within the Church. A safe, easy, worldly man was chosen instead, to compromise between the Spanish and French parties; and Pole tried to excuse his relief by thinking God had not really wanted anyone so ineffective as himself to be Pope.

Inaction yawned again for him in all its grey temptation of 'accidie,' that dull sloth and disbelief in life which is the worst and loneliest of the Seven Deadly Sins. He had escaped the Papacy, but only to find no place for himself anywhere, no true work that he could do for God. Was a monastery the only answer? Debating with himself and in long letters, dipping first with one foot and then with the other, he tried to take the plunge. If he took vows, he would no longer be in doubt as to what God wanted him to do; it could only be what his Abbot ordered him to do. And he would be more free than anywhere of the pitiful puzzle of human relationships. Even among the Spirituals there had been jealousy, criticism, pride in conscious piety; and he had felt impatience at such a refined little heaven of choice souls. Such annoyances in a monastery would at least be free from femininity; and under the discipline of Orders. To be told what to do; there at last lay rest for his uneasy spirit, in the final surrender of his will.

But was it God's will? He had drawn back his foot for perhaps the fiftieth time, and just in time, when he heard that Mary Tudor was now Queen of England; then, within three weeks of her accession, that the Pope had appointed him Papal Legate to his own country. Pole's first reaction was to ask if the Pope could not appoint someone better. But that was only habit. He quickly overcame it. He had at last received a clear call to action; it was, he knew, the last chance God would give him. In a spirit almost of exultation he resolved to take it.

Now at last his path lay clear ahead of him. It led back home, to his own country. His roots lay in that soil, like those of the great oaks that he had climbed as a schoolboy in the playground of the Carthusians' monastery, now dispersed, destroyed.

Many beloved things had been uprooted in that soil. His duty now was to plant them again.

The new Queen wrote urging him to it; she shared his sense of divine purpose in bringing both of them to power in their own country. They might indeed share even more. Their friends had long wished for their marriage; he had shunned the thought of it in his dislike of ambition; but now even his 'immodest modesty' had to admit that he was respected throughout Europe and that none would make that charge against him. He resolved 'not to retire from the busy scenes of life,' nor 'make more account of myself than of the public.' He might well serve the public best by marrying his cousin and Queen, and so keep England balanced between France, Spain and the Papacy. Still more might he serve God best by it. He had not even yet taken the priests' vows of chastity; was it because God had reserved him for the more onerous duty of the vow matrimonial?

Elderly and timid, he shrank from it, but Mary too was middle aged, modest and virginal. They would understand each other, and could work together. He remembered her as a delicate, pretty little creature, simple hearted and kind, a loyal and admiring friend to himself, and deeply attached to his mother, whose dearest wish had been that they should marry. In carrying this out he hoped to make himself believe that he would expiate the doom he had brought upon his mother.

But when at last he met Mary again she was the wife of Philip of Spain.

Pole had done his best to prevent it. He knew Englishmen well enough, even after twenty years abroad, to tell the Pope that a Spaniard as King-Consort would be 'universally odious' to them.

The Pope had replied that 'one could not swim against the stream' – not when the stream was directed by the Emperor.

For sixteen months Pole had struggled to swim against it, before at last the Royal Barge rowed him up the Thames – to take up a position of truncated power, a work deprived of half its value. He had to restore England to the Church without England making any restitution to the Church. His own enforced compromise embittered him as no enemy had done. Bitterness brings weakness. He was the less a man.

The first English winter he had suffered for so many years, at a time when he was far older and colder in blood and the less able to resist it, put him at his lowest ebb physically as well as spiritually. Coughing and sneezing his aching way through the riverside mist and rain at Lambeth, he came face to face with the task most alien to him. The Queen demanded his co-operation in the rooting out of heresy by 'blood and fire.'

He urged her to continue in the mercy she had shown when she came to the throne. Was her name of 'Merciful Mary' to be changed to 'Bloody Mary'?

She answered, 'What does it matter how men call me? I gave my mercy for crimes against myself, not against God.'

He said, 'Are we in our frailty to act as God's judges? My first promise to Parliament when I arrived was that "I am come not to destroy, but to build; to reconcile, not condemn."

She answered, 'And what have you built? Whom have you reconciled? The rich keep silent, but hold fast to their thefts from the Church. The poor blaspheme aloud.'

Her eyes were fierce, her voice rasped against his ears. This had been the warm kindly little creature whose work he had hoped to share. As he looked at her the blank fog of his 'accidie' darkened into the night of despair. He could never help her, nor his country, nor his Church, any more than he had been able to help himself, or his family, or his mother. He had had the courage to say openly to Caraffa, the most violent instigator of the Inquisition in Rome, 'I do not like the methods of the Inquisition, even though I agree with its aims.' He did not tell her that, but he said it again now. How hollow it sounded, how feeble, negative! In any case she was not listening, and he found himself wondering what would have happened if she had married Caraffa.

They were the people who got things done. She had all the force of a strongly sexed nature that had been starved of sex, and still was, though she did not know it; and that force was now set on doing what was right for the Church. He was doubtful of her methods, but his doubts led nowhere. Even his defiance of her terrible father had brought about nothing but the hideous death of his own mother.

'She is dead, she is dead, let it go, do not think of it, for you can do nothing.'

But Mary, who loved her, was alive. Mary, who had greeted his homecoming 'as though she were his mother.' Mary, who was the only woman he had ever thought of marrying, who was only not in love with himself because she was so much in love with her husband, who did indeed treat him as a second husband, as furiously, eagerly dependent on his opinion as she was on Philip's will. And Mary was appealing to him, entreating him to help her against her enemies, above all against the enemy who was the avowed or secret hope of every heretic and rebel in the country.

'Who is that?' he asked as his heart turned to lead; he had no need to hear the answer hammered against it, 'Elizabeth, Elizabeth, always Elizabeth.'

So families must turn and rend each other, a sister seek a sister's blood, and all in the name of God. What then had the Devil left to do?

This he thought and could not say, while Mary's harsh voice hurried breathlessly on, deaf to all but itself.

True, Elizabeth now went to mass, but how true was she in that? Elizabeth was slippery as an eel in argument, obstinate as a mule to persuasion. 'I have tried to speak to her, but can make no headway. She is not the sort of woman who can trust other women.'

'Madam, remember only a year ago you put her in the Tower, under constant expectation of death.'

'I released her. It makes no odds. She cannot feel gratitude. I gave her presents when she was a child. I never liked nor trusted her, but I was sorry for her then. I should not be now, whatever happens to her.'

'*What* should happen?' he asked heavily.

But Mary would not admit that she hoped to find justification for her sister's death. She would only urge rather incoherently that Pole must see Elizabeth alone, must make friends with her as he was so well able to do with such different people, that he must discover the secret workings of her supple mind and inflexible heart; and then, and then – well he must decide whether, in leaving her alive, Mary was not undermining all her own work and his for the Church in England.

He said coldly that he was not a spy. But the burst of hysteria that followed showed him that he was exposing Elizabeth to worse danger by his refusal to take part in the matter.

He said he would see what he could do, and left her,

wearied and in disgust at this homecoming to friends that had grown so alien. He had looked on death as the great divider in friendship; now he knew that life could be worse. It was better when friends died; then their memory could stay sweet in one's mind; but friendships that festered, what could be done with them? You could not discard them, put them on the rubbish heap; you had to breathe fresh life into them; and that was the last thing he could do.

'I am not for life but death,' he told himself in despair, his hand on the window-latch, his tired eyes watching the scurry of torn blossom in the cold wind outside, a puppy leaping and barking up at a little boy running against the wind. That child would have to live, grow up, to face worse than a spring gale – but, thank God, not himself! He would not have much more to face, he told himself droningly, longing to lie down by a warm fire – and then at that moment he had to face it.

He was summoned to a Council meeting assembled on the instant, in a fury of haste and alarm. They were ducking their heads like hens, pecking at a torn paper which at last, with difficulty, he learned had been found nailed on a gate of the Palace. Scrawled over it in a botched handwriting was the question: 'Will you be such fools, oh noble Englishmen, as to believe that our Queen is pregnant? And of what should she be, but of a monkey or a dog?'

A chill nausea crept up through his bones. Men could be more vile than devils. He thought of the poor distraught creature he had left; who was, in the last resort, only a lonely, frightened woman, longing desperately for her child; and was made the target for such filthy attacks.

BOOK II: THE PRINCESS

CHAPTER THIRTEEN

Pole did not trust Elizabeth, and needed none of Mary's warnings that he would find her sly, discreet, demure; it was exactly what he had thought her at his meetings with her in public. He was almost inclined to agree with Mary's opinion that she was not even King Henry's bastard; a still, frozen creature, wary as a young cat, begotten of the moon rather than by that huge sun of a man.

She had quoted Aristophanes at him and he felt she was showing off, and told her he had left Oxford without taking his degree. She murmured that with his position it was no doubt unnecessary, and he replied, 'It was uninteresting.'

'Like all achievement – to such Eminence.'

The mocking little compliment annoyed him more than he cared to admit to himself. It would be of no use for him to talk further with her; no one could be worse at it; even his most intimate friends had always told him he had fewer words in speech than any man alive.

'But that,' Mary told him with surprising astuteness, 'is why others say so much to you.'

People did indeed talk to him with extraordinary freedom, it was a part of his 'genius for friendship' they said, and it was often, though they did not guess it, because he knew what was in their minds.

But Elizabeth, he was certain, would never show him hers.

Yet when at last by sheer chance he saw her in private, on the last day of April, she showed it in a way that took him by surprise, even by storm, for she was in a blazing rage.

So he knew the moment he entered the long gallery at Hampton Court and saw a tall slight figure sweeping away ahead of him, then swing round and pull up short. He had entered a cage, and interrupted the headlong pacings to and fro of a young tigress; her tawny hair and eyes flamed before him, her lips compressed in a tight line shutting out the things she had been saying, even shouting to herself in the paroxysm of her rage. But she had not shut them quite in time.

'Fool! Fool!' he had heard her cry before she turned, and thought he had caught the words 'blundering dolt' and 'to presume to rule!'

No wonder she stood still, aghast; but not for more than a second; her skirts came ruffling back towards him like the spread wings of a swan, then swished to the ground in a curtsey that denied its gesture of obeisance and was more of a challenge, defying him to take note against her of whatever he had heard. She rose, and her blackly dilated pupils looked him full in the face, a girl of twenty-one facing a man of fifty-five, knowing that she must fight for her life, and that her only defence now could be attack.

'Listen, my lord Cardinal, if you have listened already and heard that which I spoke only to my own ears – but I will say it again for you, for you to do with what you will. I am angry, not because Protestants are punished, but because the wrong ones are chosen for punishment.'

'It is not for you to choose. Therefore you find it easy.'

'Is it so difficult? Have you not enough real traitors to God and the Queen – the men who made themselves rich by robbing the Church and now make the best of both worlds? Smug in their security, they practise religion as a mere State function.'

She checked on these words, for it was just what the Queen accused herself of doing, and she saw that he guessed her thought.

'That is not a chargeable offence,' he said drily.

'So they use their ill-gotten wealth to buy their immunity from the law, and offer up to it instead such humble victims as are too poor to buy themselves off.' She hurried on,

'Who are these devilish heretics, these mighty traitors to God that are being burnt? Such small fry as the Devil himself might throw back from the fires of hell! A Welsh fisherman who couldn't even read the Bible which he cherished because he had been ordered to do so in my brother's reign. Four washerwomen from Essex who had never known there were seven sacraments to believe in, had only heard of one, and "what it was they could not tell". One was a young girl who had been brought up to think "the mass was an idol". My brother's ministers of State made it law to think that. But *they* do not smell of the pan! Not a single noble has been brought to trial, nor any man of wealth and power. They get off scot-free while they put up the butcher and baker and candlestick-maker, and their wives and widows, yes, even their children, to draw the fires of Smithfield.'

She took breath at last on a gasp. He was watching her closely, and his eyes seemed to have sunk to the back of his skull. He was appalled by what she had told him. He should have known of it. But how should he know of it? The administration of justice in the ecclesiastic courts was not his province.

Then it struck him, how had she come to know of it? He asked her, and she shrugged. 'I? Oh, I have low tastes; I gossip with my servants.'

'You are a friend of the butcher and baker and candlestick-maker.'

'As my father was.'

'Yes, he had the common touch.' But the appreciation in his voice did not beat down her defensive attitude. He tried further.

'Why should you not admit your championship of the common people?' he asked, and saw her thought that he must be a fool not to see how dangerous it would be for her to be acclaimed the Friend of the Poor. 'Yet,' he said, 'your sister has shared that with you from King Henry. Even since she has become Queen she still loves to visit the poor in their cottages. She would be horrified if she knew of such injustice as you describe. Have you told her?'

'I have not dared. To you it is different. And you caught me unawares,' she added with a smile, but felt it glance off him ineffectively. Well, he was old. 'You must teach me how to view heresy,' she said.

'You see it clear enough. It is a plague which if allowed to breed will infect the whole State. No country has ever yet been able to allow a second religion within its borders. When it does, it will do so because its true worship is for a third religion, that of the State.'

'The herd cannot see that.'

'Every effort must be made to instruct them.'

'It is,' she replied in sudden weariness. 'Think of Bishop

Bonner! He will argue subtly with angry ignoramuses for weeks on end.'

'To save their souls and convert their hearts.'

'That is what they fear worse than the stake – to be turned from their belief. So they answer with vulgar abuse, to hurry on their death. Your Eminence knows well that the mental agony of doubt, fear and, above all, hope can be worse than the rack. But our fellow-countrymen are mules for obstinacy. Let the donkeys alone to graze in peace and quiet and they'll not have a thought beyond what to put in their bellies. But put words in their mouths and tell them to speak this and thus, and they'll dig their heels in and bray the contrary, louder than Balaam's ass. They'll rush on martyrdom, they'll long for a chance to "witness to the truth" and abuse a Bishop. They'll show everybody they can go one better than St. Peter.'

The flippancy of her change of front was bewildering. 'You are now mocking what you had championed.'

'Championed – I – those self-conceited fools!' She was doubling on him like a hare. Why? Somehow he did not feel it was only to ward off suspicion.

'Your sympathy is with the common people, not with their opinions,' he considered.

'I hate opinions. They split the world in pieces. They nearly split a pulpit when three or four brawlers clambered into it together to preach against each other! Some sects deny the divinity of Christ; some His manhood; some reject baptism; others churches; others turn the altar table to the west, or north, like apes who cannot tell which way to turn their tails. They call all ceremonies play-acting, all laws tyranny, and nobody ought to own any property, unless it's oneself, or to obey anybody, unless it's oneself. That's what happened in my little brother's reign, under the bigots who thought ideals should govern politics. This country was a football kicked to and fro by their precious opinions. Edward sided with the German Protestant States against Spain, because Spain was "reactionary"' and Germany "advanced". Advanced towards what? God knows! Though in due time He may show.'

Was this attack a feint to safeguard herself? 'What is your policy? Not, I think, the present alliance with Spain?'

'My policy is that policy should be kept free from emotion, from ideas that are valued as "new" and "old" only by those who do not study history. This poor silly football of England has now been kicked over to the other side, allied with Spain and therefore against France. But you, sir, know, as King Henry did, that England's safety and power stands in the middle of the see-saw, to keep the balance steady in Europe and never let it dip too far over on either side.'

Yes, he had known that. It had been the chief reason that he had considered marriage with the Queen, to keep England free of foreign entanglements. He wondered if this girl had guessed it, and did not like her any the better. 'I am not a politician, as you, Madam, so plainly are.'

It gave him an unwontedly malicious pleasure to see her eyes flash open in sudden perception of his view of her as a smart modern young woman, symptom of this modern England he had never known.

'A smart red-headed young gent.' That was the odious description of the upstart groom who had married Jane Grey's mother last year within a month of her daughter's and husband's executions. A feminine counterpart to young Mr. Adrian Stokes – God's death, was that how he saw her? – and how truly? 'You be a sharp young thing, but don't be so sharp as you'll cut yourself,' echoed back in her mind in old Dr. Turner's North Country burr. No, don't cut yourself. She had only an instant to stop Pole's distaste for her turning into a guarded enmity, and how could she, on the instant? Flattery, however subtle, would be seen through and scorned. Only sincerity, however savage, might serve.

It astonished her to find as she spoke how sincere she was.

'Is policy only a term for such as Machiavelli? Should it not be used as a bulwark for the Church against those who would destroy her authority? It is not the cynics, the atheists, the time-servers and State-servers who have the power to do that. Thomas Cromwell destroyed the monasteries, his followers stole from them, but they created nothing.

'It is Bonner and the other Catholic Bishops, it is *you*, it is –' (she gulped, but his eyes were looking deep into hers, seeing all she did not say, so she had better say it) – 'yes, and it is the Queen herself, who is giving Protestantism a soul. It will no longer be a commercial bargain, a vested interest in which half England has taken shares. Nor will it be the half-baked, ill-digested crank-belief of a disreputable rabble. No, the case is altered. The roughs who mishandled the priests, the church-robbers, the iconoclasts who broke all beauty that was held sacred, the atheists who denied God, the anarchists who defied law, they will all be herded under one banner now. The banner of a holy army. You have given haloes to the followers of those who sold their God for thirty pieces of silver.'

'If the haloes are false, they are of no more effect than the rings of gilded cardboard in a Christmas play.'

'They are to others. Think of their audience! Suffering purifies. You have turned this mob into a band of saints. Protestants will be remembered because of the humble folk who chose to suffer for their cause, who glory in the chance to be uplifted out of their drab, ignoble lives and feel themselves at one with the saints of God. Already their own teachers are having to hold them back from the ecstasies of martyrdom. That fisherman called the shirt for his execution his "wedding garment". The little Vicar of Hadleigh danced on his way to the stake, saying, "Now I know I am almost at home – even at my Father's house".'

'Such heroism is of God, but not the belief that inspired it.'

'How should *they* know that?'

'By the teaching of God, through the Church and the tradition of His Apostles.'

'But they deny that, and now the Church has sanctified their denial by their sacrifice.'

Her sincerity had overcome her after all. The tears had stood bright in her eyes and now they ran down her cheeks unheeded. 'Where will it all end?' she cried. 'How can there ever again be one Church in England? Why should there not be as many sects as there are souls, each holding his own opinion to be infallible, and heading to unutterable confusion? Authority is now condemned. Any rebel against it will think himself sanctified, and welcome any lying slander of it. They'll find any stigma good enough to beat a dogma with!'

Her tears broke into hysterical laughter. She flung away from him and leaned against the window, hiding her face against the curtain, stuffing it into her mouth. What had she been saying? She did not know, and dared not speak again. In another moment it would all come out, all that she must never say to anyone – that she was an outcast, that she could never belong to the Church if it remained split in England, as these fools were ensuring that it should be. Her whole position, her chance of the throne, depended on her belonging to the Protestants – and now there would be no hope for her to bring them back gently and gradually into the body of the Church, so as to resume the old worship by degrees, almost without noticing it, and make an English Catholic Church, not Roman. This her father had wanted to do, and others before him. Now it would never be done, and she would always be outside, associated with a rabble of crazy cranks.

'I might as well give up Christianity and worship the Devil,' she thought, and wondered for a horrible instant if she had said it aloud. There was an uncanny silence in this man that made one say things one had never dreamed of speaking. The silence was still going on, it seemed to penetrate even through the back of her head to the thoughts within it. She had to speak in order to break it. She turned back to him.

'I have been too bold.' She was shivering. 'At least tell me what you are thinking,' she said, and her hand flashed out and brushed his, as light and cool as a butterfly's wing, yet he felt as though a flame had touched him. He was still silent. 'Do not be angry with me,' she pleaded. 'You have given me a rare and dangerous pleasure – no, not dangerous' (how she hoped that was true!), 'since I spoke in confidence to a great gentleman. Which is more than can be said of my great father!' she ended on a spurt of astonished laughter. What power was there in this sad, tired old man to draw her hidden thoughts from her? He could not like her. She was raw, crude, vulgar in his fastidious eyes; yet she had never seen disdain in them, for her or anyone. He honoured all men. But what did he think of her?

What he thought was that for all her frankness he knew

little more than before of her religion. But on one point he was at last assured; she was not begotten of the moon. He saw life burning in her as it had done in the enormous sun that had sired her, 'the greatest enemy I had in the world, that King whom I loved above all other men.' He did not know if this his daughter was his enemy. But to watch her, hear her vibrant voice, still more to feel that fleeting touch on his dull hand, was to catch something of King Henry's fire, his sense that one life on earth was not enough, that he needed as many lives as he did wives to compass the overweening arrogance of his desires.

But he must answer her. He said slowly, 'I am not sure you love the Church truly. But very sure you hate her enemies. Perhaps because you identify them with the enemies of the State.'

'Isn't that what they are bound to become – finally?'

'Yes. But that is not the reason one should hate them. One should not hate them at all.'

'No. Only love and pity – and burn.'

'There is love and pity in the judges who wrestle for weeks on end, in the face of their prisoners' furious abuse, to try and save their souls. And not only theirs. The worst danger in false doctrine is in its inverted pride. It cannot rest until it has led others also into damnation. The Church has had to fight through centuries against those who were willing to risk death and torture for the liberty to pervert thought. The worship of the State, Heathenism, Satanism, Witchcraft have all had their devotees.'

Had he indeed seen the passage of her thought just now? She spoke hurriedly. 'They say the Pope has just died.'

'It is true.'

'And your Eminence?'

'They have asked me to go to Rome. I shall not go.'

'Why not, in God's name?'

'Because it is not in God's name. If I do not go, Marcello will certainly be chosen this time, the very man that the Papacy now needs.'

She was not listening to him, but to something else; the flame in her seemed to shrivel and die, her eyes stared dull and blank at him for an instant before they hid under the dropped eyelids. His slower ears caught the sound of hurrying footsteps coming nearer, louder.

A sturdy dark-faced boy came at a run into the gallery; it was Elizabeth's new page, young Humphrey Gilbert, but he ignored her and bowed, panting, to the Cardinal. 'My lord, the Queen's labour has begun – they say already ended happily, with a boy.'

A hand shot out and boxed his ear, almost toppling him over as he rose. 'And what of the boy's aunt, you jackanapes? Do you not greet her too? "Why not?", I think, is the motto of your house!'

He gaped at the merry tone following so instantly on a hard blow, and raised his head to meet her brilliant smile.

'Come, no apologies. Joy can confuse us all, especially that of welcoming a new young master.'

CHAPTER FOURTEEN

It was still the last day of April, but it began to look like being the first, so Elizabeth muttered darkly to her faithful Cat Ashley by the evening, for might it not turn out to have been All Fools' Day after all? The bells had rung, the choirs had sung; Te Deums were already being chanted as far away as Norwich Cathedral, thanksgiving processions had borne their flickering candles through the churches, the shops had shut, the prentices run to light bonfires in the street and put out trestles for public feasting; a new envoy from Poland arriving in the middle of the excitement had publicly congratulated King Philip on his son and heir; and the parish priest of St. Anne-within-Aldersgate had described from the pulpit how fair and beautiful a child was their new Prince, 'as the like has not been seen.'

That was the trouble; nobody seemed to have seen him; messages began to come from Hampton Court contradicting the first report and saying there was as yet no delivery.

And still people went on contradicting the contradiction and dancing in the streets and feasting, for it was a pity to spoil an occasion for holiday; and still Elizabeth walked up and down in the privacy of her room and swore and tore her handkerchief and would not eat her meals, but kept on eating sweets, and felt that time itself had ceased to breathe, that the world had ceased to move, that for all eternity she would hang here in a vacuum between two reigns, not knowing if Mary would die and she be Queen, or a Prince be born to sit on the throne.

Very seldom on it. He would be, not Tudor first, but Hapsburg. A son of Spain, a grandson of Germany and the Roman Empire, three-quarters of his blood Spanish, and only a quarter of him to carry on the ancient British blood that had flowed in the veins of all this island before the Romans and then the Danes and Saxons had driven it away, higher and higher into the Welsh mountains. Never before had Elizabeth, now contemplating her alien, unknown nephew, been so proud of being mere English and half of that Welsh. Proud but panic-stricken.

The future was so near, yet out of reach. So often she had asked herself, would this be the end or the beginning of Elizabeth?

'If only I could see Dr. Dee!' she cried aloud. '*He* could cast my horoscope.'

'They say he's back again,' said Cat Ashley, 'and wants the Queen to buy a library, but she says she doesn't care for strange books.'

'*Back?* Why did no one tell me?'

'My lady, my darling, it wouldn't be safe—'

'Tell me where he is. Never shake your head. I know you know.'

Cat Ashley whispered, 'In Mortlake, by the river. But are you going to—'

'Bed? Where else? It's late.'

Tick, tock, went her mother's clock. It stood on a bracket looking down on her bed, and a rushlight in a silver pan shone on its fantastically inlaid face. The signs of the zodiac surrounded it, the heavy pendulum swung below, the minutes marched on towards the hours. It was still the last day of April. The stars shone bright outside her uncurtained window. The Palace watchman went his rounds and called,

> 'Twelve o' the clock, look well to your lock,
> Your fire and your light, and so good-night.'

It was no longer the 30th of April 1555. It was the 1st of May. The clock struck one, then two. Her mother had lain alone in the dark and listened to it striking those same small hours on the 1st of May nineteen years ago, until she could bear them no longer and had risen and wandered about the garden. In the white light of dawn King Henry's ministers came to arrest her and found her standing under an apple-tree in bloom, and led her away to her death.

'Stop the clock!' shrieked Elizabeth.

Cat Ashley came running to the side of her bed, but Elizabeth was already out of it. 'Cat, Cat, we must go a'-maying. No, never mind the clock. I was riding the night mare. I'll ride my new gelding instead, and you'll come with me. Too early you slugabed? Go to the ant, thou slug! Why, it's May Day, and all the boys and girls of London town are out in the woods of Westminster by now!

> '"Is't not fine to dance and sing
> When the bells of death do ring?"'

She was whirling round the room in her white shift, her red hair flying loose. Involuntarily Cat Ashley crossed herself. 'What mischancy words!'

'Then we'll have the next ones—

> *"Is't not fine to swim in wine*
> *And turn upon the toe?"*

She was turning like a spinning top, picking up a garment here and there and pulling it on her as she twirled, finally snatching up a dull, rather shabby old cloak of Cat's and flinging it round herself.

At last Cat was ready, their two most trusted grooms had saddled the horses, and they rode out.

In Hampton village the birthday bonfires were guttering down, and so were the stars, paling fast before they were snuffed out. The river, first to catch the still hidden light, gleamed like the grey steel of a sword behind the huddled shapes of the dark cottages. They rode towards the darker, shapeless mass of the woods, and the trees began to stretch their groping fingers against the lightening sky.

The woods were already awake. People were rustling among the trees, whispering, giggling, in excitement and awe; unconscious worshippers in a heathen rite whose meaning had long been forbidden and forgotten. They knew only that they must be in the woods this night, to greet the dawn and 'bring in May.' The birds, who had cheeped a sleepy questioning note or two, suddenly shrilled into full chorus, and with it there rose here and there young human voices scarcely distinguishable from the birds, so closely they imitated their notes. A band of dim figures trooped past the horses, branches of white hawthorn glimmering like sheaves of moonlight in their arms; one was piping on a flute and the others trilled and gurgled an almost wordless song to it in mimicry of the nightingale –

> '*Dug, dug,*
> *Jug, jug,*
> *Good year and good luck!*
> *With chuck, chuck, chuck, chuck!*'

From deep in the wood another human-bird chorus answered back,

> '*Then derry come down, derry come derry, come derry!*
> *Come derry, come down, hey ho!*'

The light woke suddenly, astonished, on a cluster of young rabbits in a glade, sitting up and washing their faces with their front paws wet with dew. They leaped up and down opposite each other, then sat suddenly still, upright, their ears cocked at the thud of horses' hooves, and disappeared in a scurry of white scuts into the silver-green grass.

As the light, now pale gold, struck the tree-tops, a chain of young men and girls came crashing out of the undergrowth hand in hand and swung into a many-coloured ring, their flushed faces split open with their shouts. Their bird-song had turned to words;

> '*Round-a, round-a, keep your ring,*
> *To the sun we dance and sing,*
> *Ho ho! Ho ho!*'

Those final yells made the horses rear; the ring whirled faster and faster till it broke, and some fell headlong with shrieks of laughter, then leaped up and chased each other back among the trees.

'Disgraceful,' panted Mrs. Ashley, trying to soothe her horse, 'they might be heathen savages.'

'They *are*, on this day!' Elizabeth laughed. 'Papists and Protestants are not the only worshippers left in England.'

Mrs. Ashley wished she would not speak so. 'It's not safe to be out here,' she stammered; but she felt Elizabeth herself was not safe on May Day.

A young man rode down the long ride through the trees with a hawk on his gloved wrist and silver bells on its jesses; he wore a shabby old green velvet hunting-coat and fine white leather riding-boots; his horse was old but a thoroughbred, his saddle was patched but it fitted, his spurs were bright, and at his heels pranced a couple of good hounds. He drew rein at sight of Elizabeth, and from sheer surprise forgot to sweep off his hat and bow.

The light shone full on him, cutting him off from his still shadowed horse.

'The sun is lifting you from the saddle,' she cried to him.

'And who has lifted you from yours, my Princess?' he asked in amazed laughter. 'Not a maid in a hundred who has gone to the woods this past night will come out again a maid.'

'I'll swear I've done nothing but what could be done on horseback.'

'I'll have to believe you – unless you'll give me the chance to disprove it.'

'Too late, Robin Dudley! The sun is up. But I'll see your hawk fly at a heron before I go back.'

'Why back? Come on with me and break our fast at Chelsea. It's the prettiest village along the river bank and you can get curds and cream at the farmhouse. I know Mrs. Ashley there, yawning her head off, is a very Cat for cream.'

'Hush! Don't wake her or she'll say it's as much as her place is worth, won't you, my Cat? Never mind if she nods. My grooms are a very vigilant pair of guards, even against my bold Cock Robin.'

'The hen is bolder. What the Devil took you into the woods at dawn on the first of May?'

'The Devil. And the fear of what he's doing at Hampton Court.'

'Nothing happened last night.'

'Then the chances are it's happening now. Ah me,

> '"*The chances most unhappy*
> *That me betide in May!*"'

'That's not a maying song.'

'No, it's a mourning song. One of her lovers wrote it of my mother. The devil took her in the garden on the first of May.'

He had never heard her speak of her mother, and it frightened him. 'Why think of the past?' he said as they jogged on together.

'I do not. I think of the future, and a Spanish Prince on the English throne. We'll be dragged into war with France.'

'Well, that's nothing new. England always used to be at war with France, it was the only way to get our fellows abroad across the sea.'

'There are other ways now. And other seas.'

'Oh, you mean the New World. But the Spaniards have got that.'

'Not all of it. And they may not keep all they've got.'

He leaned forward in his saddle to scan her face, rosy in the new-risen light. She looked like any milkmaid sallying forth on a May morning adventure, yet she never stopped thinking, planning – or rather straining forward to see into the plans of others. For that matter he could do it too, he was not to be outdone by any clever girl some months younger than himself.

'An expeditionary force might be a good thing,' he said; 'it would take people's minds off religion, which is an unhealthy thing to have your mind on. Philip might give me a company of horse to lead in Flanders. He asked me lately if I wanted employment, and I told him, "Urgently, since all our family is bankrupt!" Not a bad fellow if you know how to handle him.'

'And do you?'

'Not as well as you, Princess. You must give me lessons.'

Their laughter rang out through the shining air where all the birds were shouting with joy. The sun was gilding the edges of the leaves with a rim of wet light, dewdrops were sparkling everywhere, they breathed in the damp delicious smell of new grass and budding may, they were the only pair in the world to be young on a spring morning. She snatched at a branch above her head and brought away a cluster of white blossom. 'The buds are as tight and trim as a page's buttons,' she said. 'There's no embroidery half so fine on the cradle of the new young Prince. But there's no new young Prince in the cradle – yet. There may never be a new young Prince.'

'For Christ's sake, what are you saying?'

'Treason, isn't it? But only your hawk is near enough to hear.'

'There's myself. You can trust me to the death. But you should not. No, not your own shadow.'

'My shadow isn't here yet. The upper air is filled with light like a cup, there's no room for our shadows. But ssh, look, they are there behind us after all, stretching away like ribbons.' She flicked her branch over her horse's ears. 'I fill my rooms with blackthorn and may, though people call them unlucky.'

'Not for you. For they are sacred to Queen Hecate.'

'Do you call me that, Robin Goodfellow? Well, he too is of the Devil.'

'I always said we were a pair.'

But she fell silent. They were riding along the river bank, drawing near to Chelsea village, and she could see the square tower of Sir Thomas More's Church rising above the trees; and soon she would see the red garden walls of Chelsea Manor House, where she had lived as a child, and the postern gate opening on to the reedy marshes through which Tom Seymour had come one early spring day when the wind was high; and that, she now thought, was the last day that she had been a child.

The village street had blossomed white and green with branches stuck before the doors, the village green rang with happy shouts, as the great painted maypole swayed into place, hung with ribbons and wreaths of primroses and wild daffodils. A bagpipe shrilled on a piercing note, a flute answered it like a bird, boys and girls joined hands and capered round the pole.

Never did any banquet taste as good as the curds and cream in earthenware bowls, the sticky buns hot from the oven. But as they turned and rode back out of the village, a horrible thick cloud of depression came down on her as heavily as a curtain. Her high-cut nostrils quivered as she realized why, for into them had begun to steal the smell of burning flesh. She turned her horse's head and struck across the fields. Robin spurred after her. 'Where are you going?'

'Anywhere in the world that will take me away from *that*. And this is to please God! Or her husband!'

'No. His chaplain thumped the pulpit and called the burnings "repugnant to Christianity".'

'So you were there, my Protestant Dudley!'

'When in Rome, or keeping in with Rome, do as the Romans do. Or as my Protestant Princess does.'

'Michaeli's as shrewd as most Venetians. He says England would turn Jew or Mahomedan if ordered by their sovereign. Well, there's one poor devil behind us who didn't. A pest on this wind, it's carrying the stench after us. If Mary herself had ever smelt it – by God I'll get some cunning chemist to manufacture it and give it her as a present!'

'For the christening?'

She swore volubly and pulled up her horse to wait for Cat Ashley, who had been following in a flurry at such haste.

'Robin, will you come with me on an adventure?'

'To the end of the world.'

'It might be that for us. There's some danger. I am going to Mortlake to see Dr. Dee.'

'Then let no one know of it.'

'Cat must know, and keep guard in my rooms.'

She beckoned Mrs. Ashley close beside her and spoke low and urgently. She must go back to Hampton Court with the grooms, and into Elizabeth's apartments, and conceal her absence until she returned and would slip unnoticed into her apartments with her private key, which she had long ago had copied, of the side gate from the tennis courts. No one had observed them ride out so early, and she could pretend that the Princess had a megrim and was keeping her bed. In the meantime Elizabeth would take Lord Robert as her escort to visit a learned Doctor.

Cat was too much troubled by this last to worry over the proprieties.

'O Jesu!' she sighed, 'I knew there was mischief afoot when you took my old sad-coloured cloak that you'd not be seen dead in if you were in your right mind – but sure, to go a-maying was mischief enough. Pray heaven you keep the hood well over your face. To rush off like this without any plan or preparation, on the spur of the moment—'

'The best spur of all. Come, Robin, use yours.'

She had swung her horse's head round again and cantered off.

CHAPTER FIFTEEN

Here he was riding all alone with Elizabeth, the chance of a lifetime, thought Robin, and no chance to use it, even to show his skill in flying his hawk; and far less to make love to her. She seemed scarcely to know that he was there, so intent was she on riding as fast as they could to Mortlake. Besides, it had begun to rain in sharp cold gusts, and who could make love, or even conversation, at this rate, and with wet slaps continually stinging one's face? The villagers huddling off, with cloths and sacking pulled over their heads, had deserted their maypoles, whose gaudy colours were now all dripping in the rain; a melancholy bear had been left tied to his stake, and when Robin thought it would be a good joke to set him free to frighten his intended baiters, Elizabeth did not even answer, but rode on, on, along the sulky sluggish grey river, until at last they came to a small stone house, so near the river it was like a pebble washed up by the tide.

It did not look like a magician's house.

And Dr. Dee was not in the least like a magician. He was young, not yet thirty, tall and fair, with a face as clear and rosy as if he spent his days out hunting instead of poring over forbidden arts. Robin instantly suspected him of drinking the blood of freshly killed children to keep his youthful complexion, like the sorcerer Gilles de Rais.

He wore a loose white artist's coat slit up the back, with hanging sleeves, but somehow looked elegant even in that, and no whit put out at being surprised by a Princess in his workaday garb.

If indeed he were surprised, for he showed no sign of it. He greeted them as a charming host, asked after Elizabeth's tutor, his old friend Roger Ascham, and smiled over some scandalous story of their college days together at Cambridge. Elizabeth wickedly reminded him of another scandal, when he had produced a Greek play with startling scenic effects, and he airily admitted that he had been sent down after it; one of the characters had flown up to the ceiling on the back of a huge scarab, and it had shocked some of the old dons, who suspected him of sorcery.

'They had some ground – or should I say ceiling – for their suspicion!' murmured Elizabeth, with difficulty restraining an hysteric giggle.

She looked uneasily round her at the room, a fortress of secret learning, armed and barricaded by enormous books. There were nearly four thousand of them, he said, and many of them very rare. But books would soon cease to be rare; the Printing Press was not merely another new invention, such as was continually startling this learned and inquisitive age; it was a revolution. The Papacy had recognized it as that from the beginning; fifty years ago they had tried to control the Press – but in vain. No Caesar could again destroy the learning of the ancient world; the library of Egypt had been contained in a house, and burnt to ashes; 'but the library of the future,' declared Dr. Dee, raising his white-sleeved arm like the wing of an avenging angel, 'will have no limits but the world.'

All the same he agreed with Elizabeth that it would be a pity if the Queen would not buy his books to found a National Library; England needed it, and he needed the cash.

Robin asked eagerly of the Philosopher's Stone – did Dee think it was hidden in Cathay or in the undiscovered city of El Dorado? Did it hold the secret of life and death? Could it really transmute base metal into gold?

Dee answered him with a touch of impatience, 'Yes, yes, gold is money now. But money could be anything, however flimsy, even paper. Money is nothing, except that particular substance that men have agreed shall be important to them.'

'And to you, if the Queen buys your library,' said Elizabeth.

But it was evidently too important to laugh at.

'Metals *can* be transmuted, made interchangeable,' he declared, 'and the power released therefrom may remake or perhaps destroy the world. That may well be the secret of life and death that is hidden as yet from mankind.'

'And long may it be so!' cried Elizabeth. 'When would such fools as men are, have the wisdom to use such knowledge?'

This man might look like an archangel, but so did Lucifer, who chose to reign in hell rather than serve in heaven.

Robin gazed awestruck at his crucibles and astrolabes and new scientific instruments; he was eager to hear of the lectures at the Sorbonne that Dee had given when only twenty-three, on Euclid, the first ever given on him in an European university.

'Were you afraid that no one might come?'

'No, my lord. The Parisians, like the Athenians, are always eager to hear new things. Even the herd can guess that higher mathematics hold the highest secrets. But I did not expect the

Sorbonne to be so overcrowded that the rabble of students who couldn't get in fought each other to climb up outside the windows to listen from there.'

'Still higher mathematics,' observed Elizabeth.

Robin whooped in self-justification, 'And your precious Roger Ascham, Madam, said I'd never learn to be a politician because I gave up Cicero to study "Euclid's pricks and lines". That's how he snorted at 'em. But I say they hold magic.'

'That may be,' said Dee, smiling. 'For what charm is wielded by an isosceles triangle so potent as to risk a broken neck on the Sorbonne roof? And does mankind, yes, even the rats from the Paris gutters, so crave certainty as to find a benediction sweeter than the Church in the curt syllables of Q.E.D.?'

There was more scorn than sweetness in his smile, and not only for his ragamuffin admirers, but for the great Duke of Mantua and the Emperor himself, who had come to visit him at Louvain in order to learn from him and his inventions. He let them know this, not with complacency, but a fiery snatch at his triumph, as he offered to show his laboratory and his designs there for an instrument that men had been trying to make ever since Roger Bacon had propounded it three hundred years ago – a glass at the end of a tube which would enable one to see distant objects, even the very stars, as though they were quite near.

'Still more useful to see an advancing enemy on land or sea,' said Robin, all agog to go into the laboratory but already too busy talking about navigation, and why had the Spaniards mastered its art above all other nations?

But Dee had a plan for a Petty Royal Navy to be kept always on guard round the coast of England.

'And will you propose that too to the Queen?' asked Elizabeth.

'Not to this Queen, Madam.'

She caught her breath. She could fend him off no longer. She sent Robin packing off into the laboratory to look at the designs for the magic glass; then sat quiet an instant before she spoke.

'I also risk my neck for certainty. Do you guess why I have come?'

'Do you fear to tell me, Madam?'

'No. I wish you to cast my horoscope.'

'And yours only?'

'No. King Philip's – and the Queen's.'

'That is indeed to risk your neck.'

'And yours. Or it may bring you great fortune.'

He did not speak. He did not move. As he stood there before her he seemed to tower above her, an arrogant archangel, and his eyes plunged down into hers as from a great height. They were the strongest eyes she had seen; they dragged her up out of this dim book-lined room, out of all their urgent scurry of talk that had raced over time and space; they dragged her out of time and space; into a silent infinity.

None of her hopes nor terrors counted here, not even of death. That was not the final extinction. She knew it now.

A veil was closing round her, but through it she could still see his eyes. And now, from a great way off, she heard his voice.

'The future is not ahead of us. It is around us and with us now. Our death is in our life, and our life in death.'

His eyes loosed their hold. She could now see before her the leaded panes of glass in the window, down which the raindrops were running thick and grey. She could see nothing else through the blurred glass. There was no one else in the room.

She sat there alone, staring at the rain, her head light and empty as a blown-up bladder banged by a Fool at a fair; at any moment it might float away from her. Perhaps it was because she had eaten nothing since sunrise, and the light was fading as though it were already afternoon, so she told herself, struggling to get back to today, this morning, this afternoon, to prevent this small stone house on the river drifting off the edge of the world.

Something stood outside the grey window; 'It is a sunbeam,' she told herself, and then remembered that it was raining; 'It is a rainbow,' she told herself; and then saw that it was looking at her. It was the form of a child that shone clear for an instant outside, then glided through the closed window into the room, where it appeared as a coloured shadow, the bright hair rolled up in front and hanging down behind over a long dress that gleamed now red, now green. She was walking upon the bookshelves, where there could surely be no room for her, yet as she moved, prancing, playing up and down, the books seemed to move too, displacing themselves to make room for her. Elizabeth knew she could not be seeing this, yet she was seeing it.

This many-coloured little creature, whose childhood flickered as her own had done in the flame of danger, was herself; a being not afraid to walk through the world alone, a world whose purpose it was to overcome her – and here she was, nearly twenty-two years old, and not yet overcome.

'Shall I then live after all?' she asked, and heard the answer, 'You will live, as long as the name of England lives.'

She knew that whether her body lived on in splendid vigour, or was burnt tomorrow to the dismal smell of ashes that yet clung to her nostrils, she herself would travel on throughout eternity.

The grey air round her slowly darkened; she could see nothing more; she thought that night had fallen, that she was dead; but a strong pair of hands was chafing hers, a hot urgent voice was calling in her ears, calling her back to this discomfortable and anxious life; eager kisses were pressing her cheeks and lips; desire of life, of the body, was dragging her unwilling spirit from eternity into this frightening world again.

'My love, my beauty, come back to me, come back, come back!' cried Robin Dudley's young and furious voice.

She had to come back; she did not want to, she was so tired, but 'I am here,' she thought she cried aloud, and heard it as a whisper. Her eyelids opened an instant on his face, she had forgotten how handsome he was. 'I was dead asleep,' she said, and he answered, sobbing, 'Too dead, dead asleep. I thought you were dead. You shall never die – while I am here.'

'How long will that be?'

'Ever – for ever.'

> *"So you and I*
> *Will never die?"*

'What a posy for a ring!' she murmured.

'To bind the two of us together for ever. Here it is.'

He was thrusting the ring off his finger on to hers, and then because it hung so loose, on to her thumb.

'So now I'm an alderman with a thumb-ring,' she said,

sleepily, 'and that's well, since my mother had an alderman in the family, a Lord Mayor of London. "Turn again, Whittington, Lord Mayor of London!" Shall I ever get the chance to turn again?'

'You'll turn and turn and turn again, the slipperiest serpent and daughter of Eve that ever coupled under the Tree of Life! But now you'll not turn again. I hold you in my arms now and for ever, my spirit of enchantment!'

Once before he had held her to him like this, a year ago in the Tower. She had eluded him then, she should not now.

The rain lashed against the little windows, the river lapped and roared in the wind like the sea, they were all alone in the dim book-lined room, there was nothing now to keep her from him, only a long pale face beneath his, swooning under his kisses, growing paler and paler. God's breath! was she fainting indeed, perhaps dying? He sprang back with a curse from her cold face. 'For Christ's sake, what ails you?'

'Oh, Robin,' she wailed, 'I am so hungry!'

It never seemed to be the right time for seduction, Robin reflected as they rode back to Hampton Court after a savoury knack of brawn and bread and a draught of ale, taken standing in a hurry, for the sooner she was back, the safer for her. But his disappointment did not weigh too heavily on him, for he was full of this fresh attempt that Richard Challoner was going to make to discover a North-East passage through Russia to Cathay. Robin had been studying Dee's maps, for Dee was geographer to the expedition and held the opinion that it would soon be accomplished, and should take only about thirty-six days, perhaps less. The Tsar of all the Russias, Ivan the Terrible, had belied his name and most courteously invited the English explorers to his Court to arrange a trade agreement with the West, and would send a magnificent present of furs to the Queen of these intrepid adventurers. He had also invited Dr. Dee to Moscow to be his Court Astrologer at a fee of a thousand roubles, 'and that shows you what Dee is,' said Robin with glowing cheeks (he had quite forgotten his suspicions of the probably unholy cause of Dee's fine colour). 'The money would be the least part of it – for even their Ambassadors wear clothes set all over with precious stones – yes, even their nightcaps are sewn with great pearls. They drink a fiery staff out of jewelled goblets and eat the little black eggs of sturgeon.'

'It sounds horrible.'

'No, it is delicious. Challoner gave some to a friend who sent it back, saying they had enough black soap of their own, but it wasn't soap, it's a stuff called caviare. I tell you, I have half a mind to go North myself. England is played out. Her only hope is to colonize. We no longer go to the wars in France. We have let Spain get in ahead of us in the far West – but why call it the New World as though it were the only one? Dee is sure there are others, that there is a vast Southern Continent far down in the globe below Cathay, the Terra Australis he calls it. No man has yet discovered it. How if I should be the one?'

'What, first North and then South?'

'I would sail all round the world if I could. Some man *will*, one day, and why not I?'

'"Why not?" "Why not?" That is the motto of my new page, Humphrey Gilbert, who wants to sail to all winds.'

'Yes, and I'll sail West too, despite the Spaniard, and find El Dorado. Think of that fabled city built of gold and jewels lying hidden in the black heart of the impregnable forest! A sailor told me that the jewels come alive at night and flit through the trees like the burning eyes of witches. But John Hawkins says those are insects that carry fire in their wings. And he said that the most dangerous fire he had met was the light of the African moon. He always made his sailors shut their cabin windows against it. 'Juan de Aquines' he calls himself now since Philip knighted him at Plymouth, but he says it with a wink, and spits out of the corner of his mouth. I tell you, John Hawkins and I will see to it that the Spaniard doesn't have his own way all over the world. Why should England not win a new continent, and you be Queen of it? And Hawkins goes to Dee for his maps too.'

Elizabeth huddled Cat Ashley's shabby cloak about her; she felt cold and old, a hundred years older than Robin, who was less than a year older than she, but was now like a boy, as all men were when they talked of the adventures they wanted. Once, before she was quite fifteen, a man of thirty-five had wanted to lead his fleet to oust the Spaniards from the Western World, and there carve out an Empire for himself – and for her. He had ridden with the Magyars, feasted with the mountain robbers of Hungary, talked with the Sultan, Soliman the Magnificent, cracked jokes with François I of France and Henry of England.

But he carved no empire for himself, nor her.

For her, the Lord High Admiral, Tom Seymour, had laid down his splendid head upon the block.

'Are you listening?' asked Robin. 'I tell you, it's feasible.'

'Eggs in moonshine!' said Elizabeth tartly. 'That is what I say to young Gilbert when he talks as you are doing now. But *he* is only sixteen.'

'Yet you like to talk with him.' Robin's tone was sulky.

'He's a clever lad, though like you he thinks the classics old-fashioned, and studied navigation at Oxford instead. But how could you have had all this talk with Dee? And—' she turned her head quickly on a sudden suspicion, 'how was it you were not ravenous – as I was?'

'Why, I had a knack or two in the laboratory after we had left you alone...'

'For a few minutes only—' she broke off at his stare.

'How long then *was* it?'

'Look at the sky,' he said. 'Now it's stopped raining, can you not see it's growing dark?'

Bewildered, she looked about her. A few wild blossoms in the hedges waved like pale flames through the wet gloom. Where had she been during these hours that had hidden themselves in the compass of a few minutes?

The day had passed without her knowing anything of what it might have brought.

She reined in her horse abruptly, stopped an old farmer trudging towards them through the mud, and asked if any further news had yet been heard of the birth of the Queen's baby at Hampton Court.

He told her at great length all that she knew already of the bell-ringings and thanksgiving processions, while she checked her fidgeting horse in an agony of impatience.

'But for all this great labour,' he ended at last in his broad slurring voice, 'for our yoong maister so long looked for, in the end there's been neither yoong maister nor yoong maistress that any man to this hour can hear on. Eh!' he added reprovingly, while pocketing the coin she gave him, 'there's no call to laugh at honest folk neither.'

And he splashed aside into a puddle, where he stood

glaring at them and muttering about a cackling gaggle of geese, while the two rude young people, riding on, rolled in their saddles and shouted and hooted with delight.

'"No yoong maister." Oh Rob, think of the priest describing him in the pulpit!'

'"Nor yoong maistress neither" – oh Bess, think of the Polish envoy congratulating Philip!'

'Think of Philip *still* not a father!'

'*Still* not crowned King of England!'

'*Still* not getting England into war with France! All "Eggs in moonshine", all of 'em, Robin, and addled!'

'A fine pair you think you are, Maister Cock-up-Spotty and your smart yoong drab,' growled the farmer, well out of earshot, as he trudged away and looked back again and again over his shoulder. 'Splashing me with your horses' hooves and giggle-gaggling about your betters. The Queen's a lady, and that's more than you'll ever be.'

And even Elizabeth might have agreed if she had heard him.

It was quite dark by the time the Palace loomed across the river, the lighted windows glimmering on the rough dark water. She parted from Robin at some distance from the gates, leaving her horse with him, and would not heed his protest that it was dangerous for a female to go on alone through the dark.

'A deal more dangerous for me to be caught with you,' she told him, and he had to admit it; dared not linger for more than a snatched kiss and a whisper; but had to stand and watch her slip away – to become captive or Queen, criminal or conqueror? She slid away swiftly, a shadow lost almost at once in the black dark.

She went down the long alley of the tennis courts, her hood pulled well over her face, then with her secret key through the small square enclosed garden under the windows of the rooms where her little brother King Edward had stayed while at Hampton Court; but there was no one there now, and all the windows were dark. Then into the servants' quarters, the narrow passage of Fish Court, and under the great arch that led to the kitchens, and so, keeping close against the wall, towards the door of the staircase to her own apartments.

There was a torch flickering in a bracket further down the passage, but all was silent and empty. She had only to glide through this arch, open the door noiselessly, she was all but there—

A figure stepped out from the dark archway just in front of her. She had either to turn and run, which was hopeless, or to go on. Desperately she sank her head further under her hood, hunched her shoulders into a low stoop, and set herself to shuffle past. A hand fell like a stone upon her wrist, another thrust back her hood. She was looking into the grey, deep-shadowed face of the Prince of Spain.

CHAPTER SIXTEEN

So this was what Dee had foretold. All the future Dee had shown her had been the spirit of her past self. To see the wraith of herself. What a fool she had been not to recognize in it the sign of her own immediate death. That was what he had meant by all his fine, vague talk of death in life, and life in death; that was why he had said nothing really of the future. What a fool she had been not to see it till now, 'What a fool!' she said aloud, and then instinctively repeated it in Spanish, and was answered so; and was asked,

'In what folly? Or treachery?'

'No treachery.'

But to cast the horoscopes of King and Queen was treason. To cast her own, in her case would be treason. She waited an instant, practising in her mind the tone she would use when she could speak. At last she forced it to her lips, and it did not sound forced, but like that of a reckless wanton.

'And what folly? What other could there be when a woman slips home in the dark hid in a cloak? What else was Your Highness waiting for here, so near the kitchen quarters, but to catch some errant scullery-maid?'

'I was waiting for you.'

'As I said! So you knew of my absence?'

'I knew. I wished to see you. Your governess protested

you were sick in bed. It is a game you have played too often. I walked past her into the room, and you were not there.'

'Is this Spanish etiquette? You shock me, sir.'

'You mock me, Madam. All England is mocking me now. If it had but one neck I could cut it off with a blow. I cannot. But I can yours.'

His hands flew up and fastened in a murderous grip round her throat, then as suddenly dropped to his side.

'I do not believe,' he said, in a quiet, almost casual voice, 'that the Queen has ever been with child. I think she has a tumour.'

Elizabeth, feeling her throat tenderly, gave a gasp that was more of a croak.

'Well?' he said. 'You may speak your thought.'

'Not easily. It hurts.' She swallowed, then began again. 'But the Queen is convinced—'

'Of course she is convinced. Of course everyone has been convincing her. And now they say she was mistaken in the time; she may have to wait another two weeks; perhaps another two months. Do the women here carry their young for eleven months?'

Was it possible she might after all escape death yet again? Philip did not seem to be concerned with the reason for her absence, disgraceful as she had hinted it to be.

'Why did Your Highness wish to see me? I should not know near as much about the Queen as any of her women.'

'I did not seek you as a midwife.'

'Well then—?'

'It seems you have been absent a long time – since early this morning perhaps. Have you then heard nothing of the battle?'

'The *battle*! But where?'

'Here. In the very precincts of the Palace. Five hundred of my Spaniards attacked by near twice as many English. Not another brawl, but a pitched fight.'

'How many killed?'

'Of your English, I suppose? Ask of your own people – who shouted at mine that I am impotent to get an heir.'

'Sir, you did not seek me as a mediator any more than as a midwife. Why then?'

'To tell you that I must leave England. I will not stay here to be insulted, my people murdered, while I am enslaved by the fraudulent pregnancy of a brainsick wife. I am nothing here. I am *called* King only as my wife's consort. To be crowned King, that is denied me. I am no King. I am here merely as a borrowed stallion – to a barren mare.'

'O God,' she thought, 'if Mary could hear him she would run mad.' And if Philip had heard her and Robin on the road, their cruel laughter at his humiliation – but she dared not even think of that, lest he should hear her thoughts.

But he was intent on his own. He was deliberately pulling them together out of the fury of his almost unconscious attack on her, dragging them into sane and reasonable words.

'My father demanded my sacrifice on the altar of this heathen island, and I did his will, for as long as he required it. But now he demands my presence. He only awaits my return so that he can retire into the monastery of Yuste and make his soul before he dies. If he should die before then, I shall have his soul for ever on my conscience.'

'What the Devil!' she longed to shriek, and 'What a family!' The cruel laughter was welling up again within her; she choked it back and said gravely, 'Your Highness's conscience is too tender, and the burdens laid on it too heavy. There is not only the fear for your father's soul – but for your wife's reason.'

'You wish me then to stay? For whose sake? Never tell me it is for your sister's.'

She looked at him for a moment in silence; then said, 'No.'

He gave a short bark of laughter. 'You are wise as usual, my sister. It is very necessary for your sake that I should stay. I have saved you from death at the hands of the Queen more than once. If I stay, I can still save you. But if she dies, as is likely, I would be in danger of death from your English rabble.'

She spoke very softly. 'It would then be my turn to save you, my brother.'

'I wonder if you would,' he mused doubtfully, but without any sign of resentment.

She dared not try to assure him; put a foot wrong now, and the thin ice on which she was skating would crack and plunge her to ruin.

'But the question will not arise,' he said, 'for I shall go.'

Her hand fluttered out in the darkness and brushed past his.

'And leave me to die? Will not my death be also a burden on your conscience?'

'Your life endangers it far more.'

His tone, sombre and relentless, made her fear his love more than his hate. She tried to shrug it off. 'If that is a compliment, I have little liking for it.'

'It was not to pay you compliments that I forced my way into your room.'

'And why did you, then?'

'To tell you, for your own sake, that you must leave England when I do.'

'And go where?'

'To Spain.'

'As your—' she stopped, aware that he was enjoying her stupefaction.

'My daughter,' he finished for her; and she knew that he was smiling. She was glad she could not see the smile.

'My father,' he continued, 'wishes me to marry you to my son, Don Carlos.'

'That – little boy!'

'He will grow. And when ripe for matrimony he will be no younger than you, than I am younger than my wife. And your experience will be more apt than her virtue to ease the situation.'

Blind with rage, she tried to push past him, but he took her by the shoulders, forced her head back against the wall and struck kisses like blows upon her face. She turned her head this way and that, trying to escape them, she cried out, but strangled the cry, knowing that if she were seen in Philip's arms, there would be no escaping death from Mary.

He gave that sharp toneless bark of laughter. 'Are you now showing me your virtue, you who have just blazoned out to me that you have been playing the harlot?'

She cried wildly, 'No, it's not true,' and struggled free. 'But you believed it! Do you want a harlot for your son's wife?'

'Yes. Or any other's, so it bring you near me.'

And he laid his hands on her again, but she shoved them frantically aside. 'Let go. You had better. I am going to be sick,' and was.

It worked. He left her.

*　*　*

If she had not thought of that – for she *had* thought of it, she had felt sick with disgust and fury, pain and exhaustion, but she could have restrained it, one can restrain anything – if she had not thought of it, she would now be his harlot. Nothing else would have served to prevent it, not even a dead faint.

But he alone stood between her and her sister's hate. It might mean her death if she had driven him away in disgust for good – as she might well have done. How oddly fastidious, she thought, as she lay in bed under the cold wet cloths that Cat Ashley was applying to her bruised mouth, how finically fastidious in a man who wanted to marry his son to the woman he meant to make his mistress! A man who, she suspected, rather relished the spectacle of executions by fire or axe.

But no, not odd, for to him the unforgivable thing was to make him, or what pertained to him, ridiculous. He would never forgive his wife, nor the English people who had milled in the streets today to shout taunts at him and at her.

And how should she be forgiven, how retrieve her position as the object of his fastidious desire? For the first time she saw clearly now what that was – that he did not mind if she were a wanton, he preferred it; did not mind whom she married – the Prince of Savoy, Robin Dudley, even his own schoolboy son, as long as it would enable him to enjoy her in secret, and as a sin. It was that which he wanted of her, not matrimony.

As a wife, she was neither respectable nor safe. She might deceive him, or dominate him.

But towards her as a mistress he could permit himself the luxury of her forbidden dangers.

'I should be one of the "poesies" of Titian that he keeps concealed behind a curtain,' she thought, remembering the swift, bare-breasted Diana pursuing the stag, which he had once shown her so shyly, or, she now saw, slyly; and she began to shake with silent laughter.

'No laughing matter, you'll not be fit to be seen for days!' grumbled Cat Ashley as she took off the cloths and applied cooling unguents, 'My lamb, my pretty, you were mad to go alone with him.'

'Good God, woman, do you think young Robin Dudley made his mark here? What a fool you are!' She laughed a little shakily, to think how Robin had indeed kissed her so few hours before.

But she did not trouble to account for her bruises. She lay in the dim rosy light from behind the velvet curtains; she sank deep down into her goosefeather bed, while the edges of sleep came curling and rippling up around her. With the sudden force of a swimmer, all but spent, striking out in a last determined stroke for life, she shook herself awake, to realize that there was but one way to retrieve what she had thrown away with Philip.

She must show him that for her part she did not care how ridiculous or repulsive she may have made herself to an over-conscious young man who had been paralysed by his upbringing into a horror of natural bodily functions. He had been taught to be unnatural; the cold savagery of his passion for her had revealed that clearly enough. But she would let it have nothing to do with her. She would be true to herself. She would continue to show him all her natural audacity, her carelessness of reputation, yes, and of refinement. 'If *he* is refined,' she said to herself, 'then thank God for the coarseness of the mere English.'

With that she lay back again and let herself wander into the borderland of sleep, that enchanted country where the edges of one's world, of one's very self, become remote and unexplored. Was this still herself, with all the cares and busynesses that had clung to her like coils of tangling rope through the day? Or was she sliding away, gradually freeing herself, a boat slipping its moorings, gliding she knew not where, becoming she knew not who, losing herself – and what could be lovelier than to be lost? If such bliss lay in sleep, then why fear death? She fell deep asleep.

But then she dreamed, and the ropes coiled round her again.

She was telling Robin about Philip – 'He kissed me here, and here, to hurt, where you had kissed me so short a time ago,' and Robin swore to kill him in a tourney; it would be easy, for Robin was the best man with a lance in England since Tom Seymour had borne down all his opponents; he would strike through the opening of Philip's visor at his eye, and the point would drive through to his brain and he would fall dead.

'So die all the enemies of the Queen!' cried Robin in a loud swaggering voice, and that was the first time she knew that she was Queen of England, Elizabeth of England, how new it sounded, and yet she had always known it. She left her throne above the tiltyard and walked over the muddy ground to tell Robin he was her own true knight, and found him sitting there beside Philip, who was not dead at all, but also sitting up, comfortably discussing with Robin how he would help him to marry Elizabeth, and then Philip would invite them both to stay with him.

CHAPTER SEVENTEEN

In that month of May the cuckoos went mad with joy in the belated spring. It had rushed into flower on top of the chilled and sodden world, borne on the wings of innumerable birds that had waited till this moment to burst into vociferous chorus. But loud and shrill as they sang, the cuckoos shouted them all down. They piped from every tree, and some from where no tree was. They called from the street corners, they hooted behind the houses, they whistled up in wild mockery from the crowds that ran to throw stones and jeer wherever they saw a Spaniard. And the bird's cry ran on into new words for an old country song.

> '"*Cuckoo!*" *her singeth as her flies,*
> *Her bringeth good tidings, and all of 'em lies!*'

A ship sailed home from Antwerp up the river, and the sailors told how the great bell of Antwerp had pealed rejoicing at news of the birth of England's Prince, and all the English crews in the harbour had been given a hundred crowns to drink his health. 'May the Prince have a few more false births!' they guffawed, as they clinked their cups on the long bench in the Angel. It used to be the Angel of Our Lady, but they changed it in the last reign, and the inn-keeper wasn't going to spend good money on yet another sign, so just added 'Our Lady' in small letters at the bottom.

The Queen was still lying-in at Hampton Court; the doctors had admitted a mistake in the date, and that her child might not be born for a few weeks yet; but down in London taverns there were whispers that if a Prince were produced, it would be no son of Philip and Mary, but hatched from a cuckoo's egg laid in the royal nest.

An honest woman of Aldersgate, one Mrs. Malt, had been asked by certain lords in disguise (but she *knew* they were lords), if she would give up her new-born son to them, but she would not, not for all the gold in the Tower.

'Another mare's nest in Aldersgate!' cackled Grandfather Talbois on his stool at the door of their house in Cheapside, where he sat all day now it was warmer, to see the crowds go by. 'Did she get her boy by St. Anne's parson? Told 'em all just what the Queen's baby looked like, didn't he? But I'll have no mare lay a cuckoo's egg in *this* house, let our Mag mark that. Them Spaniards do be terrible oncoming with the maidens.'

> '*When Spanish apes*
> *Steal all our grapes*
> *What will Mag do for wine?*'

chanted her little brother Tom, and made a rude sign at her. She hated to be called Mag, her real name was Mary, but they none of them called her that any longer, for they didn't hold with the Virgin Mary now; nor with the Queen. Her mother often didn't hold with Mrs. Malt either (nor for that matter with most other women), but at this moment she chose to hold fast by her; she said that Granddad had no need to doubt Mrs. Malt's word, there were others in Horn Alley who would vouch for the lords' visit to her, and what's more they'd brought a fine lady with them to serve as rocker for the baby. These foreigners would go to all lengths to get their ends; the new Order of Spanish priests had a motto for it. 'The end justifies the means,' and the end of it all might have been that they'd have had young Timothy Malt from Horn Alley for their next King, and how would they all like that?

'Well enough,' objected her husband; for all he was the most prosperous candlemaker in Cheapside, the finest street in London, he'd sooner have a Cockney brat come to the throne than a lad who was three parts Spanish, who'd make them all pay Peter's Pence again to the Pope, another pesky foreigner.

His wife bade him speak low, for the prentices were going in and out, and already the streets were crowded with barrow-mongers crying their wares, and they the worst spies and tell-tale-tits in the town, and why was young Tom still dangling about, his ears growing long with listening, when it was nearly eight o'clock and he late for school and sure to get a beating?

The boy snatched up his satchel and grabbed an orange out of it which he flung at his sister. 'Fine Seville oranges!' he called, imitating the street cry, 'Our Mag will be a Spanish lady, as civil as an orange!' He ran hooting up the street to escape the blow she aimed at him, and she ran after, not to try and catch him but to run away from her odious family – and oh, would she really one day run away for good and all, with Diego Valdez of Malaga?

She couldn't run fast through the hustling crowds; a

spiteful little wind blew her flaxen hair into her eyes that were already smarting with tears, she stubbed her toe on a stone, she splashed her gown with filth, and this was Cheapside, 'the beauty of London'!

The fine buildings in Goldsmith's Row looked down on a filthy dunghill in the highway; the Lord Mayor would get it cleared for the next royal procession when Queen Mary came back to town with her baby, to prove all the unkind Protestants false; never for one moment did Mary Talbois doubt it. But they would find other nasty things to say, just as the dunghill would start growing again at once. The stench of it blew out on the breeze and curled up into her nostrils. She had seen and smelt London all her life, but only now that she loved Diego did she know how dirty London was; and how coarse and stupid her old grandfather, who had come up to it to make his fortune, but had never stopped being a countryman; and how harsh and crude and purse-proud were her parents.

Diego was a poor squire, but he held himself as much a noble as the King, and nobler, for the King was part Flemish. But Diego's family had lived in Malaga when the Phoenicians were there, long before the Romans came, and then the Moors; they had helped drive out the Moors, except those who were converted and were called Moriscos; the de Valdez lived in a white house with a walnut door in one of the former Moorish streets that twisted up the hillside like a white ribbon, and as clean, for Diego had to say that for the Moriscos, the town shone like a pearl above the sapphire sea.

She had never seen the sea.

His house had a little courtyard in the middle with carved arches to keep out the sun, for the sun was so hot that it made this English sun like the moon. There she would sit with a black mantilla over her flaxen head, and see flowers hang in purple bells and scarlet stars against the dazzle of the sky, and smell the figs ripening and the thyme and aromatic herbs blowing down from the mountain, and eat oranges plucked fresh from the tree, which tasted like none you could get here.

She bent her head to the orange still in her hands, so eager to sniff it and forget the dunghill as she ran towards the fields of Holborn that she rubbed her nose pink against it. She blessed her horrid little brother now for throwing it at her; it was a talisman to show that her dream would come true, it glowed like a ball of fire in the sunlight, she tossed it up in the air and caught it, running after it with dancing steps and singing,

> 'Oh Mary, Mary Talbois,
> The candlemaker's daughter!
> But I shall be Mary of Malaga,
> Far, far away in Malaga,
> I shall be far from Da and Ma
> When I go to dance in Malaga,
> With Diego Valdez of Malaga.'

She searched in a thick clump of thorn trees until she found a blackbird's nest, deep hidden, from which the birds had flown. Then from the pocket, hung with coloured tassels, that dangled at her belt, she pulled out a twist of paper, looked at the few words she had scrawled on it, kissed it and tucked it down into the nest.

'No cuckoo laid *that* egg!' she laughed, and took to her heels and ran back into the London streets.

A new crowd was forming somewhere, boys were scampering and calling to each other, she saw the glint of halberds moving slowly along amidst a welter of people; there were now no shrill excited calls, but an angry mutter of questions, exclamations, rolled to and fro:

– 'another prisoner' –

– 'is it another heretic?'

– 'another bonfire soon then!'

Now she could see the cart and a tall man standing up in it with his arms bound. A boy with a basket of turnips threw one at him; the prisoner turned and looked at him, and with a howl the boy dropped his basket and backed out of the crowd and ran away.

'Who is it? Why are people afraid of a heretic?' she asked, and got a shrug for answer and a whispered 'Heretic! If that were all!'

'It's the Lady Elizabeth again,' she heard. 'That's her servant Carey behind the tall fellow.'

But no one would tell her who the tall fellow was. She had to wait till she got home and found her grandfather cackling over 'that jilt again, she's always making trouble! Mark my words she'll be known for always as Bad Bess.' And then Mag heard that the prisoner, who had frightened the boy in the crowd only by looking at him, was a famous sorcerer newly come from abroad, and that the Princess's servant Carey had been arrested with him, no one knew why. But that the young Lady had been mixed up in some devil's work was plain as a pikestaff, plotting the Queen's death by magic as likely as not – 'but when will they get Bad Bess herself in the cart. That's what I'm asking – and she too, I shouldn't wonder!'

* * *

Elizabeth heard of Dee's arrest, and Carey's, who was to have brought her the horoscopes, as arranged with Dee; she did not know if they had been found on him, nor what the charge was against the two men.

Not for some days was she summoned to the presence of the Prince of Spain; not the Queen's. Did Mary not yet know of the matter, and was there in this some ray of hope for her the first after all these quaking days and nights?

She was taken privately to him where he sat alone in the little room that had been Cardinal Wolsey's sanctum at Hampton Court; the oak panels had already darkened with fire-smoke since she had sat here as a child with her father and played with his chessmen; but the gilding was still bright on the carved Tudor roses in the ceiling. Cardinal Wolsey had sat there with her father; he must have guessed his doom long before it took place. How long must she wait before she knew hers?

She could learn nothing from Philip's manner in receiving her; it would have the same chill politeness whatever he had decided to do with her. He had risen and bowed while she curtseyed, handed her to a chair and then seated himself again, all the movements timed with the deliberate grace of the preliminaries to a dance, or a duel. Her hands were icy, but she would not hold them to keep them from shaking, she would not let them shake; her lips were taut and her breath came fast, but she would not speak first; he looked at her, but she would not look away.

Was it herself sitting here, or was it Wolsey, waiting to hear her father say that this palace of Hampton Court was too fine for a servant of the Crown and should be for the King? Wolsey had given it all over to him, lock, stock and barrel, yes, all those barrels in the cellars, and made him a present of the ninety-nine years' lease at fifty pounds a year, and all the furnishings that had put King Henry's in the shade; but that had not saved him from King Henry.

She was mad to be thinking of this instead of what to say. Why did Philip not speak? She still did not look away from him; it was he who turned his eyes from her, towards the window. Was it himself sitting there, slight and pale, or was it a great gross man in scarlet and gold who looked out of the window at the workmen pulling down the initials H. and A., that had been carved over the courtyard gate for Henry and her mother, Ann Bullen? Ann had sat here too with Henry, had played at chess with him and watched the firelight flickering on the panels, and purred, sleek as an elegant black cat, with pleasure that it was now their home and no longer that overweening Cardinal Wolsey's. Ann had been Henry's 'own darling,' his 'entirely beloved sweetheart.' But Henry had ordered her death.

Soon she would run mad and scream at Philip to do likewise and get it done with.

At last she heard his stern, measured voice and had to force her wits to take in the brief words.

'You have been consulting an astrologer.'

Unexpectedly came her answer, pat, before she knew what it would be.

'Your Highness, it is one whom your own father has consulted.'

'But not in the same circumstances. Nor, I think, as an astrologer.'

'How then?'

(He had spoken as a judge. But he had not said, 'a sorcerer'; there was no hint yet of magic; nor of attempted murder.)

Philip shrugged. 'As a remarkable savant in geography and other sciences. Your Dr. Dee is a man of many parts. Too many. He must know, and you, that to cast the nativities of reigning Princes is treason.'

He had passed judgment. Still she spoke boldly.

'No treason was intended. I ordered them, but only to learn of the future.'

'What did you hope to learn? That the Queen would die shortly, and you reign in her stead?'

'I wanted to know what was going to happen next. The probabilities were – and are – that I should die rather than the Queen. It is not treason to wish to know if I should see this next summer. Which now seems unlikely.'

'The horoscopes did not say so.'

'So – you have seen them?'

Was he smiling? Her heart leaped, though she did not trust his smile, 'I'd keep it from the milk anyway,' she told herself with the almost hysterical gaiety that always flared up in her in desperation. And with it there surged back her resolve when she last met him, and fought his lust as now she fought his enmity. She would retrieve her position with him, and in her own way. He should never see how frightened she was.

'Come, tell me,' she said, in as casual and confidential a manner as if he had paid that visit to the little stone house by the river together with her, 'what has he foretold for you and me?'

'For "*you*" and "*me*"? Do you then put us together?'

She lost hope. There had been none for her in that half-smile, only the scorn that now snapped off his words like splinters of ice. But she came back to the attack, and drew her bow at a rash venture.

'Did not he?' she asked, still almost casually.

He stared at her. Involuntarily she put up a hand to hide the bruise that still showed near her mouth, then snatched it away, furious that she felt herself blushing.

His answer came at last. 'He foresaw that our lives would be linked.'

'How?'

He did not answer.

Had Dee said they would be deadly enemies? If so, her position was deadly, for Philip's belief in astrology and sooth-saying was stronger than her own. But surely Dee would have been cautious on paper, and not given Philip cause to fear her as a future enemy. Yet wise men could be singular fools. She braved it out, still on a quiet note. 'If he said that you would be against me, it is unfair that you should have the advantage of knowing it, while I go unwarned.'

'You seem singularly unwarned of the danger in which you have already placed yourself. You have committed a treasonable act against the State, and your associates in it are already in prison.'

'My servant Carey knew nothing of it. He is only the messenger who was to bring me some documents, he did not know what. And Dee obeyed my command, probably without knowing it was criminal, as indeed I did not – only that it was imprudent. There are so many crimes against the State now, it is difficult to keep pace with them.'

'You are overplaying your innocence.'

'But not that of my fellow-culprits. Indeed, Your Highness—'

'You have no need to defend them.'

'Are they already – dead?'

'No. They will shortly be free. Dee's defence had more power than yours. On the day that the informer, Ferys, brought the charge against him, one of Ferys' children fell dead, and the other was struck blind. No judge dares convict Dee after that, not any jailer keep him in prison. He will be allowed to go into exile abroad.'

Elizabeth had risen from her chair, and stood stunned. 'If he had the power – and will – to do this horrible thing—' she stopped, and then, 'He did not seem evil. Can he really be a devilish sorcerer?'

'An effective one, it seems. And when is sorcery not devilish? Have you practised it?'

He looked away from her, then added, 'It is said that you have a familiar spirit.'

She flared into furious denial.

But even as she spoke she thought of a child with long hair who had slid through the closed window in Dee's house and played among the great books on the shelves. Could he have sent that sprite to haunt her, invisible to herself, but not to some other? The terrible fancy broke down her courage.

'It is not true,' she cried; 'I am not a witch. If he has cast spells, I have used none. I went to him only for the horoscopes.'

But her protest sounded in her own ears like that of all who were accused of witchcraft. One could never disprove it. Her mother could not.

The Inquisition had first been instituted to deal with witchcraft; and the Spanish Inquisition was more ruthless than that of Rome. Philip had been her chief hope of protection against Mary. But what protection could she hope from him now? He still would not turn towards her; was he afraid to do so?

With a quick desperate movement she leaned over his chair and caught at his cold hand. 'Why do you not look at me? Do you fear that I will cast a spell on you?'

He looked. He put out his other hand and touched the bruise near her mouth.

'You have already done so.'

CHAPTER EIGHTEEN

The spell kept him in England against his will, against his judgment, against his father's urgent requests for his presence, and his own bitter feelings about the country that had refused him everything he had hoped for; had insulted him in the public streets with taunts at his impotency (he who had fathered more than a dozen children to the best of his knowledge), yes, and even across the Channel, those accursed narrow seas that hemmed this island into a little arrogant, ignorant world of its own. Yet still this witch held him dangling here, to endure the Cockney's disgusting gibes and Mary's damp devotion and his own awful pretence that he too believed in her hopes of an heir.

Once she accepted the fact that she was too old and ill to bear a child, she might run mad in good earnest, Ruy Gomez told him – and why might she not? he asked, shrugging his already rather high shoulders in contempt for her, and all women. How they loved to torment themselves! All save one.

Yet he agreed with Ruy he must stay a little while longer for the sake of the Queen; but knew it was for the sake of that one. The Queen pleaded with him to remain another month, another week or two perhaps, and he would see her hope come true. He hardly heard her. But he listened when

Elizabeth pleaded with him to stay, for her life's sake, that was true enough, yet she never mentioned so small a matter; and it was not her words that he heeded, he did not trust them, but the low, ringing, laughing tone she sometimes used that was like the thrumming of a guitar.

Her voice was an orchestra; he had the suspicion that she practised its various instruments before she played on them to him. But to whatever tune she played he had to dance, so he told himself, bitterly and in enmity, while in solitude; and then while he was with her he could only listen to her in pleasure and in confidence.

How amusing she could make even the Cockney insolence. 'You should have heard them even against my father, the Great Harry, when he could not get himself a male heir to England. The Tudors are a poor lot, they say, as poor in heirs as they're rich in ancestors, as *they* say.

> '"*King Arthur was a noble king,*
> *His breeches cost him half a crown,*
> *But ne'er an heir from them did ring,*
> *With that he called the tailor 'lown'!*"

'So now you know. We *may* be descended from Arthur, but even he can't guarantee our descendants. Who cares if the great bell at Antwerp did ring on a false report? You'll make it ring true on a dozen other births when you go, so soon, alas, to Flanders – but no, you'll keep those muffled! Who cares if the English sailors are rude? They are always rude. Our Lord High Admiral Howard called your glorious Armada a fleet of cockle shells last summer, and look how much bigger your new galleons are already – but our sailors would never see that. Sailors don't care. They say what pleases them – and they have little else to please them. It is the same with the crowds in the street, what else have they got? Scandal, sniggering laughter, we need not grudge them to the low; they have no other compensation against the great.'

'Not even here?' At last his anger fought through the charm of her comradeship, more potent than her coquetry. 'Here, in this country, where every heretic and robber still hopes for Communistic Law that shall make every man a law unto himself?'

'And, therefore, have no law – until all men be glad and wise. Jack Cade himself, a century ago, showed how far off all men still were from making their own law. So did Robert Kett only a few years since. If my poor little brother's Reforming – *de*forming – Ministers had not hanged him from his own "Oak of Reformation", he would have hanged himself, in despair at the lawlessness of his followers. He had hoped to lead them into the Promised Land and all they saw of it was to break down the palings of the deer parks!'

He looked at her in amazement.

'You pity all men,' he said.

'God forbid! It is necessary sometimes to be pitiless.'

'Then what is it that makes you seem almost to love all men, even the rascal herd?'

'Why, what is it that makes all men kin? I hope to feel that in all – even those I might have to hang.'

'You speak as a ruler – and born to it.'

'I am more likely born to be hanged. It is for that reason I never learned to swim,' she added on one of her sudden wild digressions that left him following her lamely, as with a dictionary. 'And for that very reason,' she hastened on, 'I have a fellow-feeling with the crowd, even when they jeer at me as "that jilt". It's some small compensation for all their squalid chores—'

'Chores?' he repeated, bewildered.

'Oh, that is an old-fashioned word meaning household tasks such as scouring the greasy wooden trenchers after a hot meal, and can you guess what that would be like? No, Your High Daintiness cannot, but I, you see, am a natural kitchen wench at heart. And I can see that, to such drab lives, scandal, especially royal, can be not only compensation but even a rough affection, a sense that the great ones are even as they under their silken robes, that we are all the same under our skin.'

'I have not observed any such affection,' remarked Philip.

No, he was a foreigner. She had gone too far, thinking of herself while speaking of them both. She had sought common ground with him (it would be easier with an English sailor), but she must not go too far. She must restrain her mockery even of her family and herself (God's life, would she ever be able to laugh freely with anyone? – Well, perhaps with Robin – in secret), even though it had been to salve the wounds of Philip's self-love.

At all costs she must keep him here in England until Mary was more safe to deal with. She must not laugh nor go on talking, she must forget her almost unbearable relief that for the moment anyway she was safe with him. The moment was going on, going past her ('tick, tock, said her mother's clock'), and soon, very soon, it would change into something else.

It was changing now. She must stay very still and try to hear what was in Philip's mind behind his words.

He asked her, apparently with some pique, why she had

shown no curiosity about her horoscope, and his.

She answered doubtfully, 'Your Highness seemed displeased at my daring to link them together.'

'At the readiness of your guess, perhaps. That linked you to the sorcerer, rather than myself.'

But no, it was not that, she thought. What should she say? 'Say nothing, nothing. He has not spoken yet.'

He spoke again, unwillingly. 'Yes, the stars foretold that their courses will be in conjunction.'

Again she longed to ask how, but was silent.

'And so,' he said at last, 'I have come to hope. I think you know my hope.'

Well, the last thing she had known of it was that she should be his daughter-in-law! She bit that back; and still waited.

He actually made a movement towards her; but it froze – then, impatiently, he turned away. 'My hope is not of England, as you once accused me,' came on a sudden sour note; evidently he had expected some sign from her and been disappointed; 'I have no hope nor understanding of this ungrateful, stubborn country. You seem to have it; – very well then. I would leave England to you to manage.'

'The Queen does that, sir.'

'Must you pretend for ever? We are alone. The Queen will not live for ever. She may not live very long.'

'Did Dr. Dee foretell that?'

'The Devil take you! And Dee, if he has not taken him already. The Queen knows nothing of the horoscopes, and I will not tell you what he said of her chances of a long life. The doctors could tell you of them as easily as he, if they spoke truly. But he said that you – and I – would live long.'

She could hear Philip's thoughts clearly now. He was

cautiously transmuting the base metal of his dishonourable proposals into the pure gold of matrimonial intentions. Here was alchemy indeed! Equal to Dee's, and partly due to him. The Prince of Spain was translating the prophecies by the light of his desire for her.

It should be easy to fall in love with this handsome young man who would be the master of the world. But could he master her?

'Why do you start?' asked Philip, rising and walking to the window. 'What did you see out there?'

'Nothing. A kingfisher. I saw a flash of red and green.'

'But a kingfisher is blue.'

'Then it was a woodpecker – green in the sunlight, and the flaming crest on its head.'

But it was not a bird she had seen at the window; it was her own thought, that had flashed across her vision in the form of the child that had been herself, a being not afraid to walk through the world alone, a world whose purpose it was to overcome her. And could Philip? 'God's death, no,' she almost exclaimed aloud, 'let him try all his life. He'll never be my master.'

'Come, what were you telling me?' she said aloud. 'That our lives would be long? Did Dee foretell how they would end?'

'In bed.'

'The same one?' rushed out on a spurt of laughter, but was instantly choked with the exclamation, 'If bed's so deadly, I'll never go there.'

'It's saved you from death more than once. And so have I.'

'May you never regret it,' she said tenderly, for a messenger was approaching them from the Queen, and he would have no further opportunity now to ask her if her hopes matched his. But he probably took that for granted.

He did. It was not Philip's way to ask questions.

He gave special injunctions for her safety, tactfully to Mary, commandingly to her principal lords and ministers, before he left England. It was late August by the time he went, after just over a whole hateful year in England, and nothing accomplished in it, not even the assurance that it, and Elizabeth, would be his when Mary died. Ruy Gomez, now to be created Prince of Eboli on his return, assured him of it with confident chuckles, but Philip could not feel sure.

> "*Souvent femme varie,*
> *Bien fol qui s'y fie,*"

he quoted gloomily to himself from that prince of lovers, François I of France, but not aloud, for not even to his closest friend would he admit his fear that any woman should be so variable as to throw him over.

But no woman could equal the inconstancy of the English people, so fickle and light-minded they welcomed any change for the sake of novelty; so said the Spaniards, and with some reason, on their last amazing ride in public with the Queen. She had insisted on seeing off her husband at least as far as Greenwich, though still very ill, but thank God no longer believing it to be from pregnancy. They drove through the streets together, with Cardinal Pole on her other side, in an open litter to show themselves to the crowds that were already packed close as salted herrings in a barrel with all the countrymen who had come up for St. Bartholomew Fair. And countrymen and Cockneys alike yelled themselves hoarse, waved and huzza'd and flung roses all the way before Mary's path, and ran nearly mad with joy at the sight of her after this long weary time. Laughing and weeping like prisoners suddenly set free, they thronged round the litter of the sick woman they had mocked and defied, in almost frantic desire to show her that while they hated her husband, her Church, and all that she loved, they passionately loved and sympathized with herself.

'England likes Queens,' was the Count de Feria's dry verdict as he rode behind the litter with Ruy Gomez. 'They welcome no King except as a Queen's consort. It is a Mother country.'

'If they forsake the worship of the Virgin Mary,' his friend answered, 'they will make up for it with worship of their "Virgin Princess".'

'You surely speak ironically if you call Elizabeth a virgin!'

'I speak officially, since that is what she is to the public.'

'She could hardly be anything else – in public.'

'You know the Queen has had her sent by water all the way to Greenwich, for fear that she should draw an even more rapturous greeting from the crowd. She's already the Queen of Cockney.'

'Prince Philip is mad to interfere on her behalf.' (It was always safer to talk freely when in the heart of a crowd.) 'She will be a danger to him as long as she lives, and so I warned him. But he won't listen. To think that he should be in love with one of this unstable and unruly race.' De Feria's left eyebrow curved up sharply, a dandyish trick that he liked to practise, he had had his portrait painted so; he flicked his riding-crop towards a girl who was struggling, shrieking, fighting her way with fists through the crowds in the open market of Cheapside. 'What woman in Spain would behave so? Here they want *form*.'

'Does your Lady Dormer? Aha, you think I do not know about that? You are a fine one to talk, Feria. And of constancy too.'

For the Count de Feria had fallen so deep in love with an English beauty, the Queen's lively young lady in waiting, the widow Jane Dormer, that he had broken off his engagement to the heiress cousin whose estates marched with his own at Zaffra, or Little Seville as he liked to call it. He had already gone to all the trouble and expense of procuring the Papal dispensation for marrying a cousin, but that could still be used and her estates secured to the family, if he transferred the lady to his brother. He would get it all settled in Spain, and then, when he returned to England as Philip's envoy, he would marry Jane Dormer.

He laughed a little self-consciously at his friend's chaff; he would never permit it in a true Spaniard like himself, but Ruy was Portuguese-born, somewhat nouveau-riche and, like the English, inclined to 'want form.' Which could certainly not be said of the pretty young widow riding so elegantly ahead of them. He looked at her with pride, then with sudden alarm.

Only in England could things happen like this! That mad girl down in the crowd had fought her way even through the guards, and was now hanging on to Lady Dormer's long skirts, shrieking to her for help. The guards laid hands on her to pull her away, but Jane Dormer was stopping them and speaking to the girl, she turned her horse's head away out of the procession, and the two women, together with three or four guards, were now detached from it in a huddled excited knot at the side of the road.

Feria quickly swung out of line and spurred his way through the crowd to the group. His fiancée was calling to him as he came – 'Your squire, de Valdez, we must rescue him instantly!'

The girl, still clutching frenziedly at Lady Dormer's skirts, turned towards him a wild, fair face, spattered with tears, her pale golden hair flying bedraggled about it.

De Valdez had come in secret to her father's house in Cheapside early this morning to carry her off with him, away to his home in Malaga. Her father had caught him there, and her elder brothers and the neighbours came rushing at his call and seized him and pushed him into the boiler with shouts of horrible laughter, and lighted the fire and swore that there he should boil alive, as his Prince had caused true Englishmen to burn. 'Not that they are Protestants,' stammered Mary Talbois through her frantic weeping, for even in these straits she would not betray her family, 'but they will not let me marry a Spaniard. But my Lady Dormer is going to do so, and sure she will help me, and you, sir – but, oh, sir, come now at once or it will be too late.'

It was not too late. By the time they reached the candlemaker's house, Diego de Valdez had not yet begun to boil. The guards pulled him out, dripping, mad with fury, issuing challenges to all concerned, by the duello to the death, but Feria pushed them away.

'You are lucky to be alive,' he said, 'and the Prince sails within three days, and Lady Dormer will speak with the Queen to get your love married to you within that time, and go with you to Malaga. You are luckier than I, who have to wait for *my* English bride.'

He was indeed, for it was four long years before Don

Gomez Suarez de Figueroa y Cordova, Duque de Feria, Governatore di Milano, could take the English widow Jane Dormer to become an ultra Spanish wife in his home at Little Seville.

But his squire was married to Mary Talbois the very next day. The Queen was delighted to arrange it – a happy omen, she said, sobbing, to Philip, that there should be two such happy Anglo-Spanish love-matches in his train.

'But *three*,' he said gallantly, raising her tired, puckered hand to his lips. 'Come back again?' Of course he would, almost immediately. He would look in at the Netherlands, as was essential, report to his father, and be back here again probably in less than a month.

She did not believe him; but she pretended to do so.

She did not like it when he told her that she must safeguard Elizabeth's life; but she promised to do so.

She could hardly bear it when he told her she must not allow any Act of Parliament to be introduced that would declare or imply Elizabeth's bastardy, and so disinherit her from the throne; it was what she had longed to do ever since her father had done it to herself. But this too she promised. She would have said or done anything to win him back to England and herself again.

And for his part he had to tell her yet again that he loved her; had to enter the sad embrace of her thin arms, had to say that he lived only for the moment when he could return to her. But he added somewhat hastily that she was now ill and overwrought with her loyal subjects' rapturous welcome of her, and must take some rest. And having safely despatched her at last, he went down to the river to welcome the arrival of the Princess Elizabeth by boat.

CHAPTER NINETEEN

Smiling and shining in pearl and silver, she alighted from her gaily coloured barge, apparently delighted at having been deprived of her share of the triumphal procession.

So pleasant, cool and restful, she told him her voyage had been, and commiserated with him on the heat and noise and smells of his ride through the streets; how had he liked the hotch potch of enthusiasm spiced with onions, the burr of Bartholomew Fair bumpkins bumbling through the shrill narrow vowels of the Cockney crowds? She mimicked both accents so that others near her doubled up with laughter, but Philip hardly heard her talking on; and in his silence her real self became silent also behind her chatter, aware of the urgency of what he could not yet say.

People were apt to keep a wide distance when the Prince of Spain talked with his sister-in-law; he soon had his chance to speak in a low and private voice. Yet when he took it he might have spoken loud for all to hear.

What was all this he was telling her with such strained urgency about the Troubles in the Netherlands (and when were there not?), and then again about his father clamouring for him to come and set him free to make his peace with God (and why could he not make it while at work?), and about the war with the French, who would never forgive his father for having kept their magnificent monarch François I in a Spanish prison for two years (of course they wouldn't, so why did he?), and now about the next new Pope (there was always the Pope and he was always new); the new one this spring had lasted only a few weeks, and now the Pope was that old firebrand Caraffa, who had never forgiven his father's Imperial troops for their Sack of Rome.

'But that was when you were born!' she exclaimed, 'and you are now twenty-eight.'

'But Caraffa is eighty, and to him it seems like yesterday. He was on the royal council in my great-grandfather's day, he opposed Ferdinand of Aragon as an 'Arrogant Usurper,' and so he calls all our House ever since. As for this Sack of Rome, worse even than Atilla's,—'

'Caraffa remembers that too perhaps?'

'He's mad enough to think so. He takes three hours over dinner, his "frugal meal" he calls it—'

'All Papal meals are. Granted, he drinks more than he eats.'

'Yes, and walks as he drinks, bounding up and down with a step as light and free as a young man's, while he airs his age-old grievances against us. My father never ordered the Sack, was not even there. Yet it's been held against him ever since, and even against me, an infant in the cradle, as a bad omen for my reign. And the instant this mad braggart Caraffa became Pope Paul IV, he vowed a holy war against us both, and against all Spaniards. He swears they are the spawn of Jews and Moors – that he will ally himself with Lutheran heretics, yes, and even the heathen Turks if they will come and help him drive the last Spaniard out of Italy.'

'It looks,' said Elizabeth drily, 'as though Christendom will have to find a new name for itself. Even Europe is a misnomer if Italy calls in the Turks to help fight against Spain. Will Your Most Catholic Majesty march against the Papacy and sack Rome yet again?'

'Never that!' he exclaimed in horror. 'Alva has sworn never to set foot in Rome by force. He is devout as any monk. But I shall have to send him at the head of an army to Italy if our settlements there are attacked. And they will be, if Caraffa lives. But he ought to die soon.'

'Nobody dies when they ought, least of all Popes. Decrepit old invalids are put in to fill up gaps for the moment, and when they put on the tiara they last a decade. But the saintly Marcello, welcomed by all, goes and dies almost as soon as he's elected.'

'Caraffa is full of years.'

'And his carafe is always empty. Even now that he's become Paul the Fourth, the Four Bottle Pope!'

Philip was shocked by her ribaldry. 'The man is my enemy, not the Holy Office.'

'I trust you will be able to separate them. Why do you speak of them to me?'

'To tell you that I do not know when I may return here.'

'That is not what you told the Queen.'

'I must keep her calm, as far as I can.'

'It will not calm her to suffer the tortures of suspense.' She saw his surprise at her compassion, and added, 'She suffers as I could never suffer. I have more sense, or less heart.'

'Your heart may find you out. Have you indeed so little of it – El-iz-a-beth?'

It was the first time he had called her by her name and it made a stillness on the air. Every syllable fell distinct and slow, like the four petals of a flower falling one after the other in the heavy late August evening. She had to brace herself to meet what all this time he had been bringing himself to say to her. Now it came at last, abruptly, and so direct, it could not be Philip; or was he ceasing to be Philip when with her? The words jerked themselves out of him as if against his will.

'I have two days left in England. But only this night can be made free for me. And for you. Will you give it me?'

He flung up his hand as if to ward off a blow. 'Do not answer. I did not intend to say it like that. You do not know what this means to me. This may be the only chance I ever get to prove myself to you as a lover. I have put it in your power to deny it me, but take care how you use that power. My sojourn in this country has been an insult to my manhood.' He broke off. 'Nothing comes as I would say it. You have laid a mocking spell on me that twists my words. Love is cruel as fear.'

So she was to vindicate her country's insults to his manhood, and if she did not, so much the worse for both! She was too angry to laugh, and, as he had warned her, it would not be safe. His terror lest any woman might refuse him was terrifying.

'I can well believe you did not mean to woo me with threats,' she said slowly, 'but it is plain you care nothing for my safety, after all your promises. All that you have done to guard it will go for nothing, if some spy should tell the Queen.'

'No spy shall ever get the chance. I can trust my men. They will keep guard. Can you not trust me as far as I trust my servants?'

Once before she had stood here in these rose-scented gardens on a late summer evening and watched the river shine darkly through the heavy trees and their long slanting shadows, while she talked with her brother's Irish page just before her brother died. Barnaby Fitzpatrick had loved her with a boy's love, unselfish, pure and harsh, adoring, disapproving. What love did Prince Philip offer and hope to win from her?

She drew a deep breath. 'What if I should bear a child to you?'

She saw the light leap up in his pale eyes. 'I shall not let that happen,' he said.

But it was what he wished; it would be the final vindication of himself to England and to her.

'You do not trust me?' he demanded.

'How can I? And how can you? You are young and virile.' Again she saw that dangerous light, but he lowered his eyes.

'Whatever happens I swear it shall bring you no harm. It would only precipitate our marriage. I could get a Papal annulment—'

'From *Caraffa*? Your enemy! Why even easy Pope Clement VII wouldn't do it for my father.'

'Because he feared to offend *my* father. Can you never leave politics and become human? This mockery of my marriage will end one way or other, by death if not annulment. I must have you in the end – but why not now, this night? We shall never be younger. What are you? Not woman only. Not man—'

'God forbid! Do you make me out an hermaphrodite?'

'God forbid again. Yet there is something in you that is of either sex, and of something beyond sex – a goddess maybe – but not holy.'

'No. I am that Other Woman that husbands love to worship in secret. A wedding ring is a yoke ring.'

'Not if it were with you.'

'But *I* might find it so. Could you tame a goddess – an unholy one? Queen Hecate is not for the hearth, but the woods. She turns married women into wild Maenads.'

'And men into monsters. As you will turn me if you drive me too far. I think you wish to drive me mad.'

'I think I do sometimes – Philip.'

It was the first time that she had spoken his name either, and on a note as caressing as his had been. But it was the wrong note. His eyes rested on her, heavy with suspicion.

'Your tone is sweet music,' he said, 'but it withholds the words I've sought from you. You would withhold yourself even in my arms.' The anger mounted in his voice. 'You mean to play me false. You have played with me all these weeks, months, baiting me with false hopes so as to fish safety for yourself and your accursed heretic country, which you *mean to rule*. I see it now. That is why you have kept me dangling on here in the humiliating pretence that I believed the Queen's false hopes. She and you have cheated me between you – the Tudor sisters!'

There was hysteria in his laugh. She dared not show her fear, nor soothe him too obviously. Once suspicion were awake in him it would coil and twist interminably; better to seem to ignore it than do anything to attract its attention. So she spoke stammeringly, nervously, of his plans for their meeting, discussing the difficulties of her escape from her room, as though she were thinking so hard of the practical arrangements that she had scarcely understood his outburst against her.

In whispered, hurried confusion, more convincing than any protestations of love, she told him that if it were humanly possible she would come to him that night.

CHAPTER TWENTY

She had had no intention of keeping her promise. She sat by the open window in her hot room; the tall candles melted and bent over in the heat and their flames flickered as the moths fluttered in out of the dark and danced to death around them. Her resolve began also to melt and flicker as she looked at it now from this angle, now from that. It might lead to escape and freedom for herself; it might lead to disaster and ruin for her country.

The steamy night outside showed no star. A mosquito bit her forehead. Cat Ashley tried in vain to get her to come to bed.

The night was heavy as fate, it held all the years to come in its dark womb, and she was the midwife to help bring them to birth – in what shape? That would be determined by her whim to go or not to Philip tonight. The danger to herself of going was obvious, but the danger to her country of her not going might be far greater. He would never forgive England for another affront to his sexual pride; the worst, since it came from her. His emotion was something growing in the dark; for years you might think there was nothing there, and then it would rear its white head in growth sudden as a fungus and show its poison. It was a horrid image – why a *white* head? Almost she could see it in front of her, pale as the veiled moon hovering in the murky dark outside, waiting for her, either as lover or as enemy. She had sworn no man should win her through fear. But fear of what his revenge might be quickened her senses into curiosity.

And if she did not give him reason for revenge? Then he too might become something very different from the cold implacable image, nursing its secret hate, that she had imagined just now. Already she had seen the change in him when with her – the unwonted directness of speech that sometimes cracked out of him as brutally as an explosion. His fate also hung in the balance. He and she would live out their brief day, England and Spain would go on for centuries, but the course of all might be determined by what she did tonight.

She could sit still no longer, all her nerves were jangled in an agony of indecision. With the spring of a cat, she uncoiled herself from her hunched position on the window sill, swung a cloak over her head and shoulders, and ran down to the door that had been left unlocked and unguarded as Philip had contrived.

As soon as she was moving under the sky, heavy and close as it was, she ceased to feel trapped within an ever narrowing circle of conflicting fears. She was free here, and alone. A livid forked flash split the edges of the darkness and against it the huge trees loomed over her head, but the lightning would not strike them, they would not fall on her. Nor would destruction from Philip, if she played her game well. She and England, now so utterly within the power of Spain, would make a shift to wriggle free, in spite of the wounded vanity of a thwarted young man. To hell with him, she thought and would have laughed aloud if she had not been so careful to move noiseless as a shadow. She stood for a moment gazing defiantly up at the threatening sky, and one or two drops of rain fell heavy as blood on her upturned face. She had been a fool to come. Why then, she would be wise and go.

She turned and moved as fast as she could under the blackness of the trees, half running, stumbling back towards the Palace. She hurried round a huge tree-trunk, tripped over a stick, fell forward, and was gripped by arms that held her in a furious grasp. As furiously she struggled and hit out, without a sound, then suddenly knew the man who held her was too tall for Philip. Nor was it his voice whispering in her ear.

'So you're baulked of him – or had you baulked yourself? You came away before you'd met him – what way then *were* you going. Never trust a fox-haired woman – a vixen fox.'

'Robin, you fool! I was going back to the Palace.'

'You didn't come out just to go back. What happened?'

'Nothing, I've never even met him.'

'You were going to, then?'

'What the Devil does it matter? I haven't gone.'

'And why then, why? Did you quail at the thought of his full lips – cold as a sea-anemone's, I'll swear. Or his arms, long as an octopus? They'd hold you so – and *so* – if you lay dead in his grasp.'

'Let go of me. You talk like the foul fiend.'

'You talk too loud. Come this way. It's safer.'

He led her through an undergrowth of thick shrubs as surely as if he could see in the dark; she had no notion which way they were going until through an opening in the bushes she could see the iron glimmer of the river flowing sluggishly below. 'Safer?' she demanded, 'but we are far further from the Palace!'

'And from Philip and his guards.'

'What do you know about them?'

'Only what I've spied out and guessed. I played scout tonight when I found your door was left unguarded. But you changed your mind? Say you'd changed it!'

'A hundred times. And always will. What's a woman's mind for?'

'I'll swear you never wanted to go to him. You were afraid not to.'

She did not like that. She said coolly, 'Two devoted wives, one passionately permanent mistress, among others, should recommend him as a lover.'

'If you want a lover—'

'What maid does not?' She sang under her breath, but on a note of wild hilarity,

> '"Then oh, then oh, then oh, my true love said,
>   She could not live a maid."'

'No, Robin, no! I don't want you as a lover because of a silly song.'

'Nor because of anything else?'

His caresses were moving her almost unbearably, shaken as she was already by the torment of indecision, dread, and sensual hunger that had worn the guise now of attraction, now repulsion. She *had* wanted to try Philip as a lover, and had hated the thought of it. And perhaps it would be the same with any man. She told Robin this; trembling with desire, she could yet whisper her doubt if she could ever really give herself. 'Even if I lay in your arms and played at love with you, I could never bring myself to that last surrender.' He demanded reasons, and she could find none, but said at last on a gasp, 'It may even be because my father killed my mother.'

'What has that to do with you and me? Do you think I could be cruel to *you*?'

'No. But I could to you.'

He swore that he would not listen. Love could be cruel and shot through with fear, as she herself had found it; violent death on the scaffold had prevented her final surrender to the man she had first loved. That was why she so feared it.

But it was not only fear, as she tried to tell him.

She could not bear to give herself up into the power of any other thing or being. Neither man nor magic, wine nor lust, should ever be her master. However passionately she might desire to be his mistress, she would always want far more to be her own.

He pleaded, argued, but could make no headway against it, and had to fall back defeated.

But a strategist has more than one line of attack.

Very softly, he began to chuckle. In astonished indignation she demanded why.

'I was thinking,' he said, 'what a joke it would be if you came out to go to Philip and stayed instead with me!'

She quivered and a secret smile turned up the corners of her mouth in the dark.

'And keep him waiting – all night?'

'All his life!'

'Yes, that may be.' She was shaking now with laughter. 'Poor Philip! And I told him I'd come if it were humanly possible!'

'Well he's not human, so it's not possible.'

'He said *I* was not human – a goddess, but not holy.'

'Yet men will worship you – always. As I do.'

His kisses stifled her laughter. She sank back into his arms.

Surely this would be the final surrender. But even as he swore so to himself in triumph, she was saying with cool consideration, 'But what will happen when I meet Philip again?'

'You may never meet Philip again.'

'He's promised to come back to England within a month.'

CHAPTER TWENTY-ONE

But Philip did not come back to England for nineteen months.

To Mary it was a lifetime of agonized hope; yet human lives do not last as long as their possessions, and after four hundred years her prayer book still shows the stains of her tears at the prayers for the absent, and for women labouring with child. If only Philip would come back soon, she might still bear one.

To Elizabeth his absence was a peaceful though dubious respite. She had not seen him again, even in public, before he set sail, and could have no inkling as to his state of mind towards her. That he was still very careful of her safety was clear from his express commands to the Queen and her ministers for their good treatment of her; but his reasons for it were not so clear.

She was allowed to go back to her pleasant home of Hatfield with a sumptuous escort, and all the countryside turned out to cheer her and give her such a rapturous welcome that in alarmed prudence she hid herself as much as she could behind her guards. It was a strange reversal from the time she had been brought away from Hatfield, by force of arms, through silently watching crowds afraid to show any sign of goodwill. Yet here was her return greeted like a royal progress, and Hatfield soon wearing the appearance of a rival

Court to the Queen's. One of her many visitors wrote of her as 'a jolly, liberal dame' whose hospitality equalled that of her gay and pretty mother, 'one of the most bountiful women in her time and since'; with of course the corollary, 'and nothing like so unthankful as her sister.' Elizabeth could only pray that Mary would not hear such comparisons.

Her friends were her worst enemies, she complained to her former tutor, Roger Ascham, who was there to read Greek and Italian and other languages with her; as he wrote somewhat cryptically to a colleague, 'I teach her words, and she me, things.'

To her fears he replied, 'There is no danger in walking in fields.'

But her rural retreat came to be threatened by further plots and risings in her name. Her household were questioned, some of them imprisoned, but Cat Ashley held staunchly to her declaration that it was 'as much as her place was worth' to speak anything against the Queen. Elizabeth also wrote in exalted strain to protest that 'such misty clouds should obfuscate the clear light of my truth.' She liked that new word of hers; but to Mary her flowery style was only an irritating token of her insincerity and immunity; she muttered angrily yet again that Elizabeth's 'disguised and colourable letters' were no proof of her innocence. But no proof could be found either of her guilt, and Elizabeth did not remain obfuscated for long.

Yet there were other 'misty clouds'. Her suitors were the most troublesome. The young Earl of Devon, Edward Courtenay, now in exile, bored and short of cash, kept on writing her desperately lovesick letters, which made it very awkward for her when rebels declared their renewed intention of putting him and her together on the throne. Then he died suddenly, some said suspiciously, and that it had been arranged by that useful fellow of Prince Philip's, Ruy Gomez da Silva, now the Prince of Eboli. It gave Elizabeth a cold shudder when she heard that rumour.

Philip kept his hand hidden; but no one knew how far the fingers stretched.

The Archduke of Austria proposed (through Philip) for her hand; the Crown Prince of Sweden, son of the great Gustavus Vasa, proposed to herself; she refused them both, and with possibly the greater emphasis because she feared to hear next of their premature demise.

The only suitor Philip favoured was his former choice, Philibert Emmanuel of Savoy, of whom she had complained as a lobster on account of his night and day wear of armour. But she won some respite from him after a gossip-writer had reported that he had 'been observed making love out of a window' to the Duchess of Lorraine. Elizabeth's maidenly sense of propriety declared itself outraged; she could only hope that Philip's sense of property would be as tender, for he was now known to be the Duchess's lover.

He had been enjoying a prolonged spell of violent and sometimes even vulgar dissipation in Flanders; many said, even in England, that he had done something to deserve it after his year of far too holy matrimony with Mary.

Elizabeth heard of it with the curiosity that was always the main part of her feelings towards Philip. It was odd to think of that austere, sometimes terrifying dignity of aspect changing its pale colour for a masked disguise, while rollicking in the streets of Brussels in search of adventure. 'Rollicking Death, I should think!' she exclaimed mockingly;

but she found herself frequently wondering what it would be like to encounter him in such an adventure.

But for her, everything was being very circumspect, placid, cautious and ladylike, in a world that had suddenly become too predominantly feminine for her liking.

Robert Dudley and his brothers had been sternly warned by the Queen's ministers to stay quietly at home in their country estates, nobody quite knew why, but it was rumoured that they had been attending subversive political meetings in London. In any case the Queen had no reason to like the sons of Duke Dudley, and had never appreciated Philip's curious interest in the eldest, Robert, who looked so boldly at Elizabeth. As soon as Philip left her Court she saw to it that Robert did too, and was determined he should never return to it.

'So

> *'This is the way the lady rides,*
> *Nim nim, nim nim,'*

chanted Elizabeth, and could remember a mighty voice shouting it somewhere above her head while she rocked on a vast, warm, satin knee; though that must have been before she was three years old. At least she could say King Harry VIII first taught her to ride! And as long as she rode 'nim nim' now, the road seemed quiet and fair for her.

She was invited by the Queen to Court; she rode to Whitehall through Smithfield and Old Bailey and Fleet Street with a great company of gentlemen in velvet coats, and of men in red coats, and settled at the Palace of Shene, which at once became gayer and more popular than that of the Queen's at Whitehall. But the 'lobster's' claws were still outstretched; she soon found that she had been summoned only to be pressed into marriage with him and that speedily, so that Philip should be gratified with it as *a fait accompli* when he came to England next month. Yes, it was true, he was really coming at last, and everyone could believe in it now that the reason for it was so clear and urgent; that he must at all costs draw England as his ally into the war against France.

He was now the greatest monarch in the world, for his father had carried out his long-promised abdication. Charles V had retired to his monastery and had given over to Philip all his kingdoms and the whole of his vast empire, though he had not been able to pass on the title of Emperor. That went by vote, and to the Emperor's indignation, the arrogant electors had refused to vote for his son. But the Holy Roman Empire was becoming an empty pious relic, said the cynics, neither Holy nor Roman nor an Empire.

To make up for it, and for all the scornful snubs he had received while trying to curry favour in the impudent little country of England, Philip was now, in Europe, King of Spain, Naples, Sicily, and titular (though still uncrowned) King of England, Duke of Milan, Lord of Franche Comté, Burgundy and the Low Countries; in Africa, he was the ruler of the Cape Verde Islands, Canaries, Tunis, Oran and other great ports on the Barbary Coast; in Asia, of the Philippines and Spice Islands; in America, of the gold and silver cities of Mexico and Peru and most of the West Indies.

It was, as the Emperor mumbled with a fair show of content, though still grumbling at the choice of that insignificant fellow Ferdinand as Emperor, enough to go on with.

And his abdication was 'the most impressive scene in history,' people declared; everybody wept; even the iron composure of Philip was melted, and to his annoyance was shown a tentative sympathy by his cousin, Prince William of Orange, a popular, talkative young man of whom the Emperor had lately made a great favourite. He leaned heavily and affectionately for support on William's arm throughout the proceedings, and bade him and Philip keep friends always. Charles was incapable of recognizing congenital antagonism in people, any more than in nations; he had never noticed how uncomfortable Philip always was in the company of his much younger but also easier, more frank and friendly cousin, William of Orange.

'You two dear lads will work together in carrying on my work,' said Charles as he embraced them both goodbye, with tears that he did not attempt to hide. He had had to take off and wipe his spectacles several times as he made his long, exhausting and often touchingly simple speech in farewell to mighty dignitaries of this world, which he was now leaving for a monk's narrow cell.

But he may be said to have enjoyed his abdication.

Mary longed to add the actual Crown of England to her husband's new honours. She tried to lure him back to her with hopes of his coronation; she prayed frantically for his return. Her friends tried to keep from her all the gossip about his infidelities; but once she was found tearing his portrait with her fingernails.

Yet even jealousy was not so strong as her desire to please him. In desperation she now did her utmost to force Elizabeth into the marriage with Savoy. It was the most painful thing that she could do to herself, for she knew that Elizabeth would then be living near Philip, and strongly suspected that this was his chief motive in urging on the match.

'I shall be jealous of Your Highness,' she wrote to him,

'which would be worse for me than death. Already I have begun to feel uneasy.'

Yet against her own wishes she fought like a fury to make Elizabeth obey. Elizabeth was badly frightened, but swore that she would rather die than consent. But the position now was very different from that of just three years ago, and she did not think that the country would let her die. Philip could no doubt have it arranged. But she did not think he wished her to die.

She could find out nothing from himself, for she was sent packing in disgrace back to Hatfield just before he arrived in England. There she waited, walked, rode, read and talked increasingly irritably with Ascham, looked out her jewels, tried on her best dresses, practised different ways of doing her hair, all in readiness for when Philip should send for her to come to Court. But he did not send. She was summoned on one or two occasions to meet the Queen at a Court function, but it was in Philip's absence. He spent indeed little time on functions. He was attending more to the raising of an armed force from England. As soon as he had succeeded in coercing Mary into a declaration of war against France and her present ally Pope Paul IV, he set sail again and went to war, with Philibert Emmanuel of Savoy as his Commander-in-Chief, and Robert Dudley as Master of Ordnance to the Earl of Pembroke, the leader of the English Expeditionary Force.

So now Elizabeth was quit of all three of them. She was amazed, amused, relieved, chagrined. She began to wonder if Robin Dudley's guess had been right, and that she would never meet Philip again.

That would not mean that she had done with him.

* * *

It was surely one of the oddest wars in history, and to all the Spanish explanations of it as 'a good war,' Cardinal Pole would reply, 'War is never good.' He was Mary's chief adviser and had moved from Lambeth into the royal palace so as to be in constant attendance on her. They had need of all the comfort they could give each other, now that her passionate heart and muddled mind had landed them in the worst impasse of both their careers. The crowning achievement of those careers had been their conversion of their country back to the Papacy – yet here they were at war with the Pope! Caraffa, as everybody still called Pope Paul IV, was extending his insane fury to Pole, trying to depose him from the post of Papal Legate and summon him to Rome, where he would certainly be clapped into the dungeons of the Inquisition. And in order to prevent this, the devoutly Papist Queen Mary had to prevent the Papal envoys from entering her country. The climax came when Pole was commanded to go to Rome on charges of heresy.

Elizabeth heard of it with wild and angry laughter. Of what use was it to have a good nature without good sense? Of what use to amble through life like a melancholy mule in blinkers, seeing only the right and wrong of each step ahead of him and blind to everything on either side? For this was the end of Pole's conscientious scruples.

He had refused to let himself be made Pope, so now the Pope was an old barbarian whose most frequent piece of rhetoric was 'Cut off his head! Cut off his head! Cut off his head!' In his arrogance and ignorance, his enmity to all thought, all art and learning that did not subscribe to his conception of religion, Caraffa was doing his worst to crack the unity of Christendom.

But one might say Pole had done it too in standing by and letting such a man step into power; and had helped Mary to do it by allowing her to insist on Cranmer's death by fire.

To Elizabeth that was their supreme crime in blunder.

She had good reason herself to hate the late Archbishop of Recanterbury, as she called him. He had signed the death warrant of the man she had loved when she was a very young girl, and it had been against Canon Law for him to do so, an illegal murder. He had also helped to bring her mother to execution, and had proclaimed herself a bastard, as he had done earlier with Mary. So she had as much reason as Mary to hate him.

But, though seventeen years younger, she had already begun to know that if love is blind, hate is blinder. Mary could have executed Cranmer long ago for treason and perjury; he had signed the Proclamation to make Lady Jane Grey Queen instead of the rightful Sovereign, he had supported Duke Dudley as usurper; legally he could have been hanged, drawn and quartered as soon as Mary came to the throne.

But she had kept him in order to make a martyr of a traitor. Heresy was treason against God, and therefore worse than treason against herself. Her motive was admirable, the result deplorable. Even when it came to the trial for heresy, she threw away all her cards. For Cranmer gave them all into her hands. He had made his supreme recantation, had put Mary and her injured, falsely divorced mother in the right for ever; had declared Elizabeth finally illegitimate, and Protestantism a crime. He had said it all, all that Mary could ever wish – that he had sinned against England as well as against God; against King Henry VIII as well as against Queen Katherine of

Aragon; he had confessed that he was the cause and author of their divorce, and that that divorce was the 'seed-plot of all the troubles in this country,' of heretics, and the violent deaths of good men; of the slaughter of so many souls and bodies.

Yes, he had said 'the souls,' and proclaimed 'the souls of the dead I have defrauded.' Could any man say more to blast himself and his cause for ever?

So Mary won it all – and threw it away. Hate is blind. She could have kept Cranmer alive as an example to all the world of a shameful turncoat, a self-confessed liar and perjurer who had damned his own cause for ever. But she hated him to the death, so to death he must go. But all that he had said had been said in the hope of escaping death; for he had been 'so afraid, he wished to creep into a mouse-hole.' Then he found the mouse-hole stopped; and that he had not saved himself by his recantation, not by so much as a faggot, not even gained a hanging instead of a burning. But a mouse can turn, even a 'Mumpsy-mouse,' as Elizabeth as a child had called him. He had recanted, and all for nothing; very well then, he might just as well re-recant.

He did, in the hour of death, before his judges and executioners and all the populace who were expecting to hear his abject confession yet again. Instead, they heard him call the Pope Antichrist, and say that he had only acknowledged him 'for fear of death, and to save my life if it might be.'

They rushed to hush it up, they hurried him to the flames to stifle his words. But he thrust his right hand first into the fire and called out that it should suffer first because it had written his lying confession. And so his shrinking, terrified flesh gave the strongest testimony of all against Mary.

'She has cut her own throat,' said Elizabeth as she walked

in the fields round Hatfield with Roger Ascham, where there was no danger, for no one was near them. He noted that she hated her sister for her bungling more than for her cruelty. And Cranmer for his cowardice more than for his treachery.

'God never meant the poor mouse for a martyr,' he said gently.

'No. And he could write. Those collects of his, their prose is like the clear music of flutes. He should have stayed a Cambridge don, and it was my father's fault, not his, that he did not.'

'He could stand up even to your dread father, when it came to prose.' Ascham chuckled and stole a glance at his Princess. 'He knew the King did not write the King's English as well as himself, and calmly showed it in his comments on King Henry's corrections of the Bible translation.'

'Did he dare to be critical of my father?'

'Critical? He was barely civil. "This is superfluous," he wrote in the margin. And – "This obscures the sense," and further – "I perceive no good cause why these words should be put in here". Should I dare to write as much to Your Grace?'

'Get out, you devil. I know what you are at – that unlucky word, "obfuscate". Yes, it's true that Cranmer had the courage of a scholar. And Mary a warm heart. And Pole integrity. All good people by nature. Yet look at the Devil's brew they've broiled between them. No one can be everything. I suppose it is too much to ask for a grain of common sense among all these martyrs and saints – yes, and a lunatic who sits on the Papal throne and jangles the keys of St. Peter. They are all of 'em tearing England to pieces.'

'How would you save her, Madam?'

'How? By a touch, not a clutch on the bridle; by a bit, not a spur; by a care-free laugh, by the appearance of ease and confidence in security, even when the reality were never more absent. And when the gulf yawns indeed beneath our feet, to cry "Farewell to such miseries, and to hell with melancholy!" Or as you would say, Master Tutor, "*Valeant ista amara; ad Tartara eat melancholia.*"'

CHAPTER TWENTY-TWO

Charles V's taste for public ceremonies had been somewhat curbed since he had become a monk, though he still insisted on hearing all the news and telling his son's ministers what he thought about it.

'Is Philip in Paris?' he demanded when Philibert Emmanuel of Savoy won a resounding victory at St. Quentin. If not, why not? If Philip, in immediate consequence of it, had ordered his Commander-in-Chief to march direct on Paris, then by now all France would have been at his feet.

Instead of which, he let the war drag on, until even Calais, English for over two hundred years, was lost to England; and Spain had to make a humiliating peace with her implacable enemy the old Pope Paul IV, whom his own countrymen still swore at as 'Caramba! Caraffa!!' The Duke of Alva had to apologize publicly to this old ruffian who had declared war on them, for the crime of having impiously defeated his troops; for Caraffa had sworn that 'sooner than surrender this point I would see the whole world perish; not so much for my own sake as for the honour of Jesus Christ.'

So Alva had surrendered the point, and in return Caraffa had asked him to dinner. The result of the war was that the troops in Italy had died by thousands of the pox; that the prosperous commercial city of Naples was ruined financially, though it remained under Spanish rule; and the Turkish pirate fleet, that heathen devil raised by the Pope, sacked the Calabrian coast and carried off Italian Christians to be Moslem slaves.

It was a severe penance for both conquerors and conquered. But the only penance done by Caraffa, who had caused it all, was to execute two of his favourite nephews and to fill the Inquisition prisons with so many suspected heretics that everyone went in terror of spies and secret police.

All this would have been saved if Philip had marched on Paris directly after his great victory at St. Quentin.

What he had done was to note that it had taken place on the day of St. Lawrence's martyrdom, and, to his remorseful grief, that the beautiful old Church and cloister of St. Lawrence in the city had been sacked, defiled and destroyed. Yet again, it was 'not his fault,' any more than the Sack of Rome had been his father's. But yet again the weight of unwilling guilt settled on Philip's soul. He longed to win a victory unstained by sacrilege; a victory for God, and over himself and his sinful lusts. He found a new hope in his boyhood's vision of a nun's face in the black of the night, as he had stood at a window looking out at the storm that raged along the jagged mountains of the Guadarramas; it had been the face of a nun who 'prayed for suffering.' He too would show the courage of a true soldier of Christ by praying for it, and by building a temple in praise of it; he would dedicate it to St. Lawrence.

He would build it high up to dominate the rugged leonine mountains that he loved; it should be his palace, and also a monastery, and a royal tomb.

And it should be in the shape of a gridiron. For it was on

that instrument that St. Lawrence was burnt in martyrdom. It would be called the Escorial; and it was there that Philip proposed to live eventually until such time as he should come to die and be buried in a superb vault under the Palace, together with all the bodies of his kingly ancestors that he could collect, and all those of his successors in the years to come.

The father's necrophily was challenged by the son's. Philip was taking long views about his obsequies; Charles would show what he could do about his own funeral. He ordered an impressive rehearsal for it in his mountain monastery at Yuste, and watched it from a gallery; some said he even helped to ring the bells for it.

It was an unlucky omen, for Charles had too much gusto for life to wish himself dead; he had only wished to see what it would look like. But in due consequence, some said, he died in good earnest a month later. He had already bequeathed his vast empire to Philip; he now had only one final heirloom to send him, the blood-stained scourge with which he had sought to expiate his sins in these last years.

Philip received the grisly relic at the same time that he heard his wife Mary was very ill, probably dying. She had never recovered, they said, from the blow of the loss of Calais; her letters still besought him to come to her, if only to bid her farewell. He read them, he remembered her, he thought of Calais and her possible reproaches, he looked at his father's scourge, he did not go. It was all too much. After all, he was only just thirty, he was not yet halfway to death, however much he might plan for it, and draw gridirons for the design of the Palace-tomb of the Escorial. Besides, he was very busy.

He sent instead his faithful Count de Feria, who would be

glad to see his pretty English bride-to-be, Jane Dormer, again, and gave him many messages for the Queen – and some for the Princess Elizabeth.

And the matter of first importance in Feria's mission was to ensure that Queen Mary should acknowledge her sister as the undoubted heir to the throne. Feria found her ministers and confessors already hard at work on that, and hard it was to win the Queen's consent, for she was still passionately against it. When they told her it would prevent civil war in England, she still said it would be wrong, since she believed Elizabeth to be Mark Smeaton's daughter; when Feria told her how much Philip wished it, she wept bitterly, for she wondered if this were because Philip would then marry Elizabeth, when she lay in her grave.

She knew now that she was approaching it. The faces of her doctors told her so; and the fewer and fewer faces of her friends. Only her dear Jane Dormer stayed constantly by her, trying to warm her with her fierce affection, to stifle her indignant sobs at 'those rats – *rats*!'

Where were all the other faces, where had they all gone? Why, to Elizabeth of course, to worship the rising sun, now that Mary's dim star was setting.

At Hatfield Elizabeth waited safely away, but not too far away, from London; seemingly passive but preparing her forces, secretly mustering from a distance what armed bands she could raise in case of revolt against her. There she received more and more of Mary's servants who came to swear that they were devoted only to Elizabeth's service. Their changed loyalty reassured her, but a shudder shot through her relief.

'Shall *I* be deserted on my death-bed by my formerly faithful friends?' she asked, and answered herself quickly,

'No, only by those *formally* faithful!' For she must joke, or choke, she said; suspense had her by the throat. Mary was almost certainly dying; but no one could tell what move the Roman Catholic leaders might make at her death.

Cardinal Pole could head a formidable resistance against an anti–Papal accession; he was not only the Archbishop of Canterbury, but of the blood royal, and more royal than her own. The Archbishop of York, Nicholas Heath, was Mary's Lord Chancellor and firmly committed to the supremacy of the Pope. Two Archbishops would be alarming adversaries, with all the Bishops on the Bench behind them. But the Archbishop of York was an amenable man. Elizabeth had been at pains to make friends with him lately, and now he actually invited Cecil to his house, and showed himself most reasonable, a trifle more loyal to the Tudors than to the Pope.

An ally greater than Cecil dealt with the Archbishop of Canterbury.

Reginald Pole would soon be faced with his final chance of action, the chance to strike a blow in deadly earnest for his Church, the Church of the woman he most nearly loved, and of his country as he had known it when he most loved it. The action would be in a form more repugnant than any he had yet had to consider. He would have to head an armed revolution against the young female claimant to the throne, and to lead England into civil war all over again. 'War is never good,' he had said. This action would belie him. And his whole nature would be belied by the appalling possibility that the revolution might compel him to take the throne himself.

But this time he did not have to refuse.

* * *

1558 was a full year for deaths. The Emperor's came in the last week of September, at one end of the scale of greatness; and at the other end came that of a shivering, wretched ghost, whom most people believed to have died long ago, if they remembered him at all.

This was Geoffrey Pole, Reginald's younger brother, who just twenty years before, when under torture, had betrayed all his family to the butchery and undying enmity of Henry VIII. He had tried in his remorse to kill himself, but lacked the nerve even for that. Now he sought out his brother the Cardinal and begged his forgiveness, so that his death, which he felt to be approaching, might come to him as a friend and not an enemy.

He found an ill old man who looked at him with hollow eyes above his resplendent robes. 'You may account me of equal guilt with yourself,' Reginald Pole told him. 'This scarlet bears the stain of our mother's blood. My ordination as Cardinal condemned her to the scaffold.'

'You did what you thought right,' stammered the younger brother.

'And you, what you knew to be wrong. Yet the result was the same. A righteous Nero – do you think that title consoles me?'

Then, for the poor wretch was sobbing, Reginald bent over him and blessed him with his absolution and said he believed that God would forgive them both, and that soon now they would see their mother's smiling spirit again, twirling a sprig of honeysuckle between her fingers.

He did not know if he believed what he had said. But since Mary's illness he had felt (or hoped) that there was little time now left to him; and in that time there was only one thing left he wished to do, and that was to give comfort where he could. He wished he could have given more of it to Mary. If he could have either supported or withstood her more firmly, if he could have led the country truly to the Church, or herself to mercy, she would not now be so wretched in her last illness, crying out that her whole life had been a tragic failure. But so it had been; and so his own would be. For he had begun to believe that he would not have to make the final decision, whether or not to fight Elizabeth. Once again the decision would be made for him, in accordance with his wish, perhaps his will. He had no will to live and fight.

Elizabeth would triumph. Yet he and Mary had aimed at least as high, or higher. Why then had they failed, and failed each other? He had planted fig-trees in the gardens of Lambeth Palace, to grow for centuries to come, and that would be his most notable achievement.

The Queen died before dawn on the morning of the 17th of November, and the Cardinal's household determined to keep it from him, as he was then lying dangerously ill; but a stupid servant let him know of it. He said nothing for some time, and then he spoke quietly to a friend, of her and himself. Their fates, he said, had been akin, and so were their natures. He then fell silent again, 'but,' his friend wrote later, 'though his spirit was great, the blow had entered into his flesh,' and he died just twelve hours after her.

In death as in life they were close together. Both had wished deeply to do only what was right; but she had lacked wisdom; and he, vigour. Her vision was clouded by passion, while his remained clear to distinguish evil from good; but he had the sloth, and despair of his own judgment, to let evil pass for good. So she became known in England as 'Bloody Mary';

and he might well have said to his country the dying words of another Cardinal, one that lived only in the imagination of a poet, 'And now I pray thee, let me be put by and never thought of.'

Nobody was thinking of Pole or of Mary in that autumn sunrise on the 17th of November, as the men of the new reign rode through woods that were burning gold and red up over the high ground to the Palace of Hatfield, to tell the only thing that now mattered about Mary – that she was dead, and Elizabeth was Queen.

But she was not in the Palace; she had walked abroad early this morning, the servants said; no doubt she was somewhere in the Great Park. They found her sitting under an oak tree, reading, with a red-and-white straw summer garden hat on her head to guard her complexion from the strangely hot autumnal sun. She stood up at their approach, and all the branches above her seemed to be lifting their arms like flames. She heard their news, that the 'old Queen' was dead, that she had nominated her sister as her successor; she took from Sir William Cecil's hand the ring that Queen Mary had bequeathed in token of this now undoubted fact.

She stood beneath the mighty oak that their ancestors had worshipped; she looked at all the men's faces before her, at Cecil's, neatly chiselled and cautious, the face of a born lawyer, and behind his the face of Robin Dudley, newly returned from the wars, handsome, eager and ardent, and behind them many others of hopeful Englishmen kneeling on the dead damp leaves to do her homage as their Queen. She too fell upon her knees, and spoke in an ancient tongue, not used for many centuries in the common speech of men, 'A

Domino factum est istud, et est mirabile in oculis nostris.'

But every man there understood what she said; 'It is the work of the Lord and it is marvellous in our eyes.'

Suddenly she rose and sprang towards them; in a flash she was transformed from the priestess to a creature of the woods with the dappled sunlight glinting on her hair, for her hat had fallen off and Robin Dudley, catching it, flung it up among the branches of the oak, shouting, 'You are Queen Elizabeth, you are our Queen!' And she had seized him by one hand and Cecil by the other, crying, 'I am your Queen, and you, Robin, are my Master of Horse, and you, Cecil, are my Secretary of State. Laugh man, laugh, all England will be laughing now!'

And so they were – laughing to see her ride in state all dressed in sparkling white, over roads strewn with flowers, to London to be Queen; and when they told her, tiresomely, that some old man in the cheering shouting crowds had turned aside to weep, she would not listen to any trouble-making but said happily, 'I'll warrant you, it is for joy.'

She knew well that many must regret the old order and 'poor Queen Mary' who had done her best – and worst – to bring the country back to it, but of what use was it to her, or help to them, to think of that now?

Poor Mary – even Elizabeth could feel that, now that she at last was safe from her. She looked at her lying dead, so much calmer and more at peace than ever she could be in life. 'She had a wintry life,' she said; 'her spring was nipped in the bud.'

So had Elizabeth's own been nipped, but not too late, like Mary's, to bear hope of summer.

And now high summer shone on her, now in the late autumn of 1558, though nearly all her onlookers prophesied darkly that it was unlikely she would outlast the winter, and that her little hour of triumph would melt with the frost and snow. The bookmakers of bets throughout Europe gave her six months at most to sit on her shakily balanced throne. Only a speedy alliance with a strong European Power could possibly make her safe. She knew of these gloomy forebodings, but they did not dim one spark of the glory of her present moment.

Its climax was reached when the procession brought her in the triumph of a reigning Queen to her royal Palace – fortress of the Tower, its great guns thundering out their welcome at her approach. She looked up at those dread walls and remembered the most despairing hour of her life when she had entered them, less than five years ago, by the Traitors' Gate, and never thought to come out except to her execution. She turned to all those around her who were thinking of the same thing, and bound them to her by her masterly simplicity.

'Some,' she said, 'have fallen from being Princes in this land to be prisoners in this place. I have been raised from being a prisoner in this place to be Prince of this land.'

She spoke too of God's justice and mercy, but it was her frankness in speaking of the dramatic contrast in her fate that struck them, and gave them belief in her. As the Protestant exiles were proclaiming in joy throughout Europe, 'The Lord has caused a new star to arise!'

But she would countenance no sudden changes in religion, no hard and fast rules 'making bold with God Almighty,' she said, intruding 'as many subtle scannings of the blessed will, as lawyers do with human testaments!'

* * *

That went for both sides of the religious fence, and nobody was yet able to discover on which side of it she stood.

The Count de Feria made a determined effort to do so at his very first meeting with her as Queen. It took place at the gorgeous ceremony of welcome to the new Sovereign at Somerset House, with all her lords and ladies and foreign envoys thronging round her – no moment, obviously, for any discussion of politics or religion. She was speaking now to one, now to another, in Latin, French, Italian, and most often in the 'mere English' that came with the same homely direct ring from her curved red lips as it had done from her father's terrifyingly straight-cut mouth. Her supple figure in the white dress made her look very tall, her usually pale cheeks were flushed (or were they rouged?) her eyes wide and shining; but in the excitement of her new triumph she bore herself as one who had been Queen from birth. Feria's quizzical black eyebrows arched in recognition of this. The grandee of Spain, with the diamond Order of the Golden Fleece around his neck, advanced with some difficulty through the crowd towards her.

She saw him, smiled in welcome, and at once everyone made way for him, and she took off her glove for him to kiss her hand. The correct compliments passed between them; she was delighted to receive her dear brother's Ambassador; and he was there only in order to let her dear brother know how he could serve her.

But he added unexpectedly, perhaps even to himself in the stress of such a moment, that her brother had told him to ask her to be very careful about religious matters, as they were what chiefly concerned him. She had to answer it, and on the instant.

At once a hush fell on the gossiping multitude. Here was an ultimatum with a vengeance! At the Queen's very first public appearance, before she had been given any time to hold her first Parliament, or even consult with her private ministers, she was being called upon, before a host of witnesses, to proclaim what her intentions were with regard to the religion, and therefore the policy, of her future reign.

Would she proclaim herself Protestant or Papist? If she defied the wishes of the Very Catholic King of Spain and the Netherlands, and of rather more than half the world besides, and denied the supremacy of Rome, then she would almost certainly lose the Crown, which was still only hovering above her head.

If on the other hand she plumped for appeasement, and told the Spanish Ambassador that she and her realm would be truly Roman Catholic, then she would throw to the wolves all those who had stood by her so staunchly through the long-seeming years of Queen Mary's reign; who had believed in her, hoped for her, prayed for her; and risked their fortunes and a horrible slow death in doing so.

Which then would she, could she, do? It was a fearful predicament to face, after years of disgrace, imprisonment, and fear of death, in the first moment of her power; which might prove her last, if she answered wrongly.

Yet in all the vast assembly she alone seemed unperturbed. Her lips were still smiling, her hand made only a slight movement, and that was to still Lord Robert Dudley, who had made a quick step towards her. But her light calm eyes never turned from the inquisitorial gaze of the dogged little Spaniard, though they opened a shade wider in surprise at his raising such a question in the midst of this purely ceremonial occasion. And she answered gravely, 'It would indeed be bad of me to forget God, who has been so good to me.'

Well, there was nothing he could say to *that*, everybody agreed in whispered chuckles, and he in silent fury. Her answer was too simple to be straightforward. He would write to Philip that it had been 'equivocal'. But he had to keep on good terms with her, and do his best to further his master's suit in marriage to her.

That also was still equivocal; although everybody in Spain and the Netherlands knew of it. The Venetian Ambassador had stated clearly that the 'whole Spanish Court is full of the King's intention to have her for himself.' Yet Philip had given Feria no free hand with regard to it; and though he knew perfectly well that it was what Philip wanted, he also knew – and perhaps so did Elizabeth – that it was the hardest thing in the world to get Philip to do a thing just because he wanted it. A hundred other reasons had to be found for it, conscientious, pious, and if possible self-sacrificing.

At the present moment Feria had to recognize that he had made a blunder, even rather an impolite one. He hastily spoke of other matters; he tried to arrange another interview. The Queen most graciously promised it, and that she would send two of her Council to summon him when it was convenient. *Which* two, he asked quickly, hoping to find easy channels of communication; and found they would be Sir William Cecil, whom he regarded as the trickiest time-server in the country, and fat old Parry, who had been her secret aid and abettor ever since the bad old days of her disgraceful affair with Lord Thomas Seymour. Certainly she was sticking to her old friends, however shady, with a vengeance.

In the meantime he decided not to pursue the vexed question of religion.

The Bishops, however, were not so prudent. Bishop White preached what many called 'a black sermon' at the funeral of Queen Mary, comparing her successor most unfavourably with her, but admitting that 'a living dog was better than a dead lion'. He was arrested as he came down the pulpit stairs, and seized the opportunity to threaten the new Queen with excommunication, and to glorify himself on his approaching martyrdom. Elizabeth told him she did not care a rush for his threats, and would give him no chance to gratify his hopes, for his only martyrdom would be a short period of house-arrest.

But after that she felt it wiser to forbid all sermons, whether Papist or Protestant, for the time being. She had quite enough on her hands, she said, in preparing for her Coronation, and, she might have added, in fending off her suitors.

CHAPTER TWENTY-THREE

It might seem impossible for a young woman as vain as Elizabeth to have too many wooers, especially when her vanity had had to be curbed and concealed all through the years of its most natural expression. She had been repressing it ever since her first love affair at barely fifteen had brought her imprisonment, shame, and the death of her lover; and she had done so with a self-control which amounted to heroism. Until she was twenty she dressed as plainly as was possible for anyone who was not a nun; she dragged her hair straight, wore no jewels at all, and chose only the soberest and dullest of colours. The end of the ultra-Protestant régime of her young brother and his ministers had brought some respite, since Queen Mary had liked her ladies to make a fine show in dress, and her young sister had been delighted to follow suit; but in behaviour it had been necessary to be more circumspect than ever.

She had been well aware of the malicious gossip circulated by the Venetian Ambassadors concerning her Spanish brother-in-law's particular care for her safety and succession to Queen Mary's throne; she had had to work her hardest to prevent Mary sharing their suspicions that the true cause lay in her attraction for him. And she had not been really successful; the thing had been a race between her and Mary's death; she was fortunate to have won.

Now, on the instant, she was free. There was no woman to stand in her way, no one in England to order her about, no one anywhere to whom she had to give obedience. She was twenty-five last September, but for the first time since her early adolescence she was able, without fear of her life, to behave like a girl. The result was staggering to everybody, sometimes even to herself.

The pale young woman of doubtful position and reputation, with her anxious eyes and compressed lips, who had had nervously to watch her every word and look in public, was instantly transformed to an outrageous coquette, of a gaiety so headlong that it would pay no heed to what others thought, or said, or wrote to their royal masters. She cared not a rap for any of them – let them say what they would and to hell with them! She would now do and speak, look and wear, what she pleased.

Her hair suddenly bubbled up into a myriad of curls; her skirts spread like peacocks' tails, her ruffs like transparent wings. She painted her face; once she wore a light green wig of spun silk. Jewels worth a province sparkled on her neck and breast and on the long fingers that she liked to show off; if one or other of them came in token of love or homage from the King of Spain or some lesser royal lover, she was so much the surer to display the finger that bore it.

She was no longer the well-behaved young lady, she was indeed, said some, no lady at all. She was preposterous, said Feria, she was behaving abominably, she put him quite out of countenance, and also her own ministers. Sir William Cecil, the most discreet of men – and if serving under four such different reigns as Edward's, Jane's (though for rather less than its nine days) Mary's and Elizabeth's, did not prove a man's discretion, then what did? – was evidently in agony as to what she would say or do next. He was about thirteen years older than she, but seemed more than two or three generations. Not that Feria liked Cecil, but at least he was not as irresponsible and imprudent as all the other young people who clustered so thickly about the Court that Feria could never get a proper chance of speaking quietly to the Queen. He wrote to his King that when he tried to send her a message they 'all fly from me as though I were the Devil.'

He complained to the Queen too, and told her he really ought to be given apartments within the Palace; it was due, he said, to his position of honour as the most important of the foreign Ambassadors. She exclaimed, 'What, have they not given you a lodging? My people shall learn how you are to be treated. You shall occupy my own chamber, and I will give you my key!' Then, at Feria's startled look, she made a complete volte-face and declared that on second thoughts it would be improper for them to be under the same roof as they were both unmarried, and he might become her suitor.

He was shocked at such flippancy and the insult to his affianced lady. But Elizabeth could not bear his Countess, an opinionated young woman so conceited as to believe that Edward VI had had a boyish passion for her, and so cruel as to have encouraged Queen Mary to burn heretics.

There were indeed few women that she did like, now that at last she was free of them; certainly not Cecil's learned blue-stocking of a second wife, who had been Mildred Coke; and still less Robin Dudley's little white doe rabbit, Amy Robsart, married to him in his boyhood; but at least Amy had the sense and inclination to keep quietly down in the country. And she was useful in preventing Robin from swelling the already overpowering army of suppliants for her hand in marriage.

For there were as many English suitors as foreign, and all the more obstreperous because they were in her presence, and each other's. Once or twice they actually came to blows in front of her, and she had to pretend not to notice; and there were still more occasions when the elderly Earl of Arundel, now 'very smart and clean,' as Feria sardonically observed, or the young Duke of Norfolk, or the elegant dilettante Sir William Pickering, laid his hand on his sword at sight of some new upstart who dared make pretensions towards the Queen.

If the quarrelsome English were the more immediately troublesome, the absent foreign suitors were the more dangerous. Some of them refused to remain absent; the coloured sails of their ships advanced up the Thames in more and more embassies that needed to be handled with the greatest tact to avoid a foreign entanglement or, worse, antagonism. Lesser lights such as the faithful Savoy's were being dimmed by offers from the Crown Prince of Sweden, from the King of Denmark, who wore a crimson velvet heart pierced with an arrow to proclaim his love for her; also from his handsome brother, the Duke of Holstein, who came in person and was enthusiastically encouraged by her. Germany and Italy entered the chase, a brace of Hapsburg Archdukes and about a score of other suitors, more or less eligible. The bookmakers on the Continent were as busy taking bets on the Queen's lovers as on her chances of survival, and the stakes ran furiously high.

Elizabeth's head could remain cool in spite of her flighty tongue, but even she began to find it tiring to go on finding fresh excuses for not marrying one after another. She would marry no man she had not seen, she said – but then it would cause offence to invite a suitor to her Court and find she did not like him. And she would not trust to portraits, for she could well remember her father's fury when Holbein's charming picture of Ann of Cleves had led him into marriage with her. Unfortunately – or perhaps fortunately from that point of view – there were no painters like Holbein now, for all the portraits of herself made her look a fright.

She did not want to marry a foreigner, as that would take her out of England; nor a subject, as that would make him her sovereign. Though indeed, she asserted, she was at perfect liberty to do so if she chose, 'as my father did – several times'.

The one man she would really like to marry was the Pope. Or the ancient Marquess of Winchester, so she told him, and he regretted that he was not a bachelor and fifty years younger.

The strangest and most subterranean hint at proposal came from Henri II of France, who put out a feeler to let Elizabeth know how much he would like to have her for his wife, if only his own, Catherine de Medici, were conveniently dead.

It almost sounded as though he had access to the secret poison cupboard that his Florentine bride was popularly supposed to have brought over to France as part of her Medici dowry. If so, the plump pug-faced young woman had shown restraint in not using it on her husband's *maîtresse en titre*, Diane de Poictiers, who had ousted her, all her married life, both from Henri II's affections and from her position as Queen.

And now Elizabeth might be given her chance to oust the Medici. Her prompt response to the hint was that if Henri had such a flattering regard for her, he should show it by at once giving Calais back to the English. But naturally these dark suggestions were only whispered (in church, somewhat inappropriately) between the Ambassadors, and were never mentioned in the very long, elaborately affectionate letters from the French King to 'Madame ma bonne sœur' of England, accompanied by an occasional diamond trinket. Elizabeth had at least enough discretion not to send any present in return – but that was a discretion that came naturally to her, especially in the present bankrupt state of the Exchequer. She actually cut down the numbers of the royal household to about half of what it had been in Mary's reign; this showed great courage, as it made for unpopularity – but not with the poorer classes. From the first she made it abundantly clear that to her they were the most important part of the kingdom.

'She is very much wedded to the people and thinks as they do,' wrote Feria to his master in high dudgeon, for he had done his best to make her admit that she owed her crown, and indeed her very life, to Philip; but she had flouted this in the most casual way. It had been nothing of the sort, she had told him ungratefully; she owed her crown to her people alone. No foreigner could have given it to her; it was the free gift of her people's love. And yet, he wrote, 'she seems incomparably more feared than her sister, and gives her orders and has her way as absolutely as her father did.' In short, she was a baffling tangle of contradictions, and Feria was being driven nearly mad by her. And by Philip.

For nothing could be more tangled and contradictory, more tortuous, cryptic, elusive than the mass of directions, instructions, hints and allusions in King Philip's letters to him. They wound themselves through page after page, and, worse still, in and out of the pages, on to the margins. Feria had to ask the King's secretary to leave wider margins for the notes added in the royal hand, for Philip had taken to adding even to his additions, in fact actually 'crossing' them, and Feria found himself getting cross-eyed in his efforts to read them.

He showed his exasperation to the King himself. Why could he not come out into the open and admit that he wanted to marry Elizabeth? Feria even suggested that it would be a good move if he reminded her how jealous Queen Mary had been of her husband's affection for her. Philip was deeply shocked by this. Not in any way should Feria remind her of those horrible scandalous suspicions, nor anyone else, nor himself. He wished never to hear of them again.

Feria cocked an already highly arched eyebrow at such violent protestations; he could almost see that portentous nether lip of the Hapsburgs thrust out over the page as Philip wrote them in his own hand. No doubt they bore witness to His Majesty's good taste as a gentleman, but he thought the gentleman really did protest too much when he declared that there was no fleshly desire in his thoughts of this marriage; that he was indeed undertaking it in the purest spirit of martyrdom, since 'it is difficult for me to reconcile my conscience to it; and it would not look well for me to marry her unless she were a true Catholic... I nevertheless cannot lose sight of the enormous importance of such a match to Christianity and the preservation of religion.' To ensure that England 'should not relapse into its former errors, which would cause to our neighbouring dominions serious dangers and difficulties' (he meant the Netherlands of course, as Feria well understood, where heresy was a growing danger and difficulty under the encouragement of their cheerful, garrulous young Prince, William of Orange) – to ensure this, wrote Philip, 'I am resolved to render this service to God, and offer to marry the Queen of England.'

There followed a multitude of conditions to make it 'evident and manifest that I am serving the Lord in marrying her.'

> *'Was ever woman in this humour woo'd?*
> *Was ever woman in this humour won?'*

Feria had been on the point of sending in his resignation when the letter arrived. But now at last he had a definite proposal to make, and resolved to make it in his own best manner, thanking heaven that Elizabeth need never know how Philip had propounded it.

He went to her, pluming himself in confidence of her awe-struck acceptance of the most magnificent prize that could possibly fall to her in the marriage market. Why, Philip was the master of the world. She had only to do as she was bid, about religion, and a few other matters, and save her poor little country – now all but ruined, lately defeated in the war with France, sought after as an ally only because her odd position as an island made her a precarious point of balance between the greater Powers. Now England would be allied to an empire on which the sun never set, owning dominion over every quarter of the globe – Europe, Africa, Asia and the new-found America – its mighty navies flying the flag of Castile on the Atlantic, Pacific and Indian oceans.

But Elizabeth was not in the least awe-struck. She did not even seem surprised; or if so, only because she had not received the proposal before. There was certainly an amused suggestion in her manner that, in spite of His Majesty's previous hints on the subject, he had been a long time in coming to the point.

She too must take time to think things over and consult her advisers, particularly her Parliament, without whom nothing could be settled. She spoke of gratitude and respect for Philip very prettily but rather perfunctorily; she might have been discussing just any of the odd dozen or so of proposals that she had had to consider lately.

Feria found himself burning with exasperated desire to tell her that even the fortune-tellers, most cautious of prophets, did not give her more than a year to reign.

But he could hint it. If she did not keep Philip's powerful support the Pope would certainly excommunicate her; Mary Queen of Scots would enforce her claim to the English throne, and her father-in-law the King of France would back that claim, send a French army to join the Scots, and invade England.

Elizabeth gave her thanks to Spain and the Netherlands; but tiresomely insisted on playing the mere woman, almost the little woman, whose marriage was her whole life, and must be given time to know her own mind. On a tenderer note she asked him earnestly, but with a charming diffident hesitation, to tell her dear brother 'that if she should ever marry, she would prefer him to all men.'

That cheered him a good deal as he took his leave; it was only afterwards that he wondered if he had not heard her say much the same thing to others.

He would have been appalled if he had heard her first remark to Cecil after the interview: 'What compensation should I claim in the marriage articles for the Lord of the Netherlands' nether lip?'

* * *

Now at last she knew. Philip was prepared to forgive her past behaviour to him; her chief problem now was to see how far and for how long she could make him continue to forgive her future behaviour. As long as she could keep him, and everyone else, in uncertainty, then he would go on protecting her in the hope of winning her consent; and her enemies would be afraid to attack her while they still hoped for her refusal. Nor was she the only one to lose or gain, and she showed Feria she knew it well. The Lord of the Netherlands needed the commercial aid of England and could not afford to lose it. The two were playing a tricky game of alliance and bluff with each other, and the bookmakers might well have laid a fresh series of bets as to which of them would win. But their odds would certainly have been very long against the young woman of twenty-five, half heretic, half bastard, who hoped to stake her wits against all the powers temporal and spiritual of the world that had prevailed till now.

Twenty-five? She seemed a raw lass of fifteen or less to the sophisticated Spanish Ambassadors, who did their best to 'keep her pleasant and in good humour,' as Feria pathetically protested, and then spoilt the effect by bursting out that the country 'has fallen into the hands of a daughter of the Devil.' And even his suave episcopal confrère, the Bishop de Quadra, who had lately come over to help him in the most intricate piece of work that ever an Ambassador had to tackle, even the Bishop followed suit when he exclaimed, 'What a pretty business it is to have to treat with this woman? I think she must have a hundred thousand devils in her body, for all that she is for ever telling me that she yearns to be a nun and to pass her time in a cell, praying!'

Was it in sheer devilry? Nine-tenths of it was, no doubt,

and in sheer delight at watching the frustrated fury in the swarthy, usually smooth, impassive faces, so supremely self-contained and indifferent, of her Spanish Ambassadors. Feria, angrily impatient of all others' points of view, de Quadra, quietly and slyly cynical about them – there was certainly a pleasure in flicking them into a startled awareness of another country, another outlook, another breed of womanhood, than in their own. She was playing for high stakes, but she could not help playing showily, in a bravado of defiance.

But one-tenth of what she admitted was true. At the very outset of her reign and of her high-flushed triumph in arriving at it, she sometimes found it baffling to keep it all up. She was the young Queen of a Court of arrogant men, native and foreign, whose advantage it was, as well as their pleasure, to make love to her. As it was to her advantage and pleasure to pretend to believe in it. But she was no fool nor a guileless maid. She had begun to see that whomsoever she married would land her in terrible difficulties. She saw also that her feints at marriage, and the hopes of it that she held out, could be an integral part of her policy. They were her moves in an intricate game where any false step on her part might mean the loss of her throne and the ruin of her country. Very well then, let it be a game, a pretence at passion, an absurd, sometimes sentimental, but always artificial comedy, in which she would act her part with the best of them, and with more pleasure than most. But an actor has only to play the same part over and over again until he learns a new one, and she had to act a different one every day, sometimes every moment.

For anyone strung on fine wires, as she was by nature, and had been for many years by danger, it was sometimes very tiring. It was in such moments that she sighed at the difficulty of preserving order among her turbulent nobles, knew that she had to go on attracting them to her Court in order to keep them out of mischief, and to maintain its splendour, but sometimes wished she could tell the lot of them to go to the Devil.

And then it was that she talked wistfully of the old ways of worship with Feria; or when de Quadra's softly cushioned hand administered a gently episcopal pat, while sitting beside her in the royal barge as they glided quietly down the Thames, that she could admit, and believe, that one part of her wished only to be a nun.

Even then she could laugh secretly at herself, knowing that this was but another thread in the airy web of diplomacy that she would always have to spin around her, and enjoy spinning.

She did not always enjoy it. Once she herself broke through it, when ill in bed with a feverish cold; the doctors called it the new disease or 'Influence.' She had hoped for a few hours in which to sneeze and shiver in solitude, but Feria had insisted on an interview, duly chaperoned, in order to demand her answer to a question she had forgotten. He had asked it six days ago, he exclaimed, and still he had received no answer.

'And God made the world in six days,' she snapped, 'but you cannot expect lesser folk to follow such an example.'

He did not reply to this blasphemy. He glanced at her ladies, who discreetly understood only English, and assured her that their talk would be strictly confidential and that she could speak candidly. At that moment she could not speak at all because of coughing, so he told her that Philip was very uneasy about her attitude to religion; he must know, and at once, if she intended to become the Head of the Church in England.

She sneezed furiously in answer, but a 'No' struggled through the explosion.

Then, if not in name, did she intend to become its Head in actual fact?

It was too much. Her hands were burning with fever and the desire to box his prominent ears, to slap his indignant, self-righteous face. She burst out that all this was waste of breath. Since Philip thought she was a heretic, she could not marry him, so of what use to go on talking about it?

He stared aghast at her; she sneezed and, he believed, swore. He hurried to reassure her; he did not believe she was really heretical, nor did King Philip. There was a muffled mutter, as she blew her nose, that she did not care a tinker's curse what either of them thought, but before his horrified hearing could make sure of it, she emerged from her handkerchief sufficiently to say clearly that the King of Spain seemed to care a deal more for his Church than for her.

So that was it! The inordinately vain young woman was expecting protestations of passion. Feria promptly gave them. But she paid no heed to them, denied that she would ever be Head of the Church, but declared that all the same she was not going to let tithes and Peter's Pence go out of the country, and that she couldn't bear Bishops.

Her servants came and told him it was supper time, which it was not; he left her with the sad reproach 'that she was not the Elizabeth he knew.'

But she was, the next time he saw her; she was well again, gay and laughing, too much so for Feria, who feared uneasily she might be laughing, not only at him, but at his

Very Catholic Majesty the King of Spain himself. It would be his duty to warn his King in secrecy of this possibility; and of one even more shocking, that Elizabeth might refuse his proposal. In fact she had actually said 'she could not marry him.'

He reproached her for her harsh words at their last meeting; did she mean what she had then said? She asked back, how should she know what she had meant?

'I had a cold,' she added airily.

Such insouciance was suicidal. He warned her that she might keep Philip waiting too long for her answer. She was putting him to a torture of suspense; if he found he could not bear it—

'You mean,' she interrupted, 'that he cannot bear any indecision except his own.'

This was too true to answer.

But suddenly she veered to another breeze. She smiled into his smooth plump face that had looked a shade less self-satisfied of late, and whispered, 'Have patience; and teach it to your master. Remind him of Cesare Borgia, who said he would 'eat the artichoke leaf by leaf.' I have many leaves to eat in this tough artichoke of my kingdom before I can savour the heart.'

His eyes goggled sympathetically. He began to speak a few beautifully rounded Latin platitudes on the heart, the impetuous lover (Philip), the hesitating maiden (herself). She heard them all before he spoke them, and already she seemed to be sitting in a mantilla at the wedding, trying to blush, and confident only that the Spaniards would admire her auburn hair. At the third or fourth reference to her hotly impatient wooer, she choked on what the scandalized Feria took at first instant for a hoot of laughter, but it was at once wafted away on a regretful sigh. Ah yes, she said softly, they were both young. But he was a King, and she a Queen.

'The King would wish me to answer him as a Queen. And I am not yet crowned.'

CHAPTER TWENTY-FOUR

One thing at a time, she had said. Whatever might come later from all the dangers and difficulties that beset her, she would make her Coronation a show to be remembered for generations to come. Those who were not yet born should tell their children, 'Ah, but you never heard my grandfather tell of the Crowning of Queen Bess!' That at least would be secure and true to the heart of her new reign, however brief the gamblers said it would be.

But she too was a gambler, and would take on the longest odds against herself. She believed that she would keep her power; that she would truckle to no man, be he friend or foe, wooer or counsellor, as to how she, a mere woman, should use it. Her strongest desire was of no lover in her arms, nor infant at her breast, but, as she said herself, 'to do some act that will make my fame spread abroad in my lifetime, and, after, occasion memorial for ever.'

Nor should it be only for vainglory. She promised that to herself, even while she gave the order to keep all the imports of scarlet silk in the country, because she wanted every scrap of it for her Coronation. Everything was to be red everywhere for that sunrise of hope and splendour, and if it snowed, then the warm colour would show up all the better.

It did snow at times, and the foul weather made deep mud,

but sand and gravel were thrown down before the procession; and nobody minded the cold and wet in this Crowning Hour.

She herself was all in cloth of gold with jewels on her red-gold head that sparkled brighter than the frost. Sitting in an open chariot on a raised pile that was covered to the ground with gold brocade, escorted by a procession of a thousand glittering horsemen, she was a figure of as unearthly magnificence as any golden image of the Blessed Virgin, or indeed of any heathen goddess from the distant Indies or Cathay. Yet this shining apparition, borne on high through the uproarious clamour of worship in the streets, was also one of the crowd. Her eyes were bright with joy at their welcome, she laughed at what they called to her and what they said to each other – an old man told his neighbour, 'I remember old King Harry VIII,' and she turned and smiled at him with intimate friendliness; she looked now at this one and now at that, so that each felt that he or she had alone caught her eye; she even stopped the procession to speak to some, or, rather, they stopped the procession. Again and again they broke through the barriers and even through the ranks of her guards, and she would not let them be repulsed. She gathered into her arms simple winter nosegays that poor women and little ragged boys threw into her chariot; at the end of the ride to Westminster she was still holding a branch of rosemary that a beggar woman had given her in Fleet Street.

The Spanish and Italian Ambassadors took pleasure in agreeing that her free and easy behaviour 'exceeded the bounds of gravity and decorum,' but it was her Coronation, not theirs – in fact, Feria was so annoyed with her that he pretended to be ill in order to avoid attending it. But he had a good look out of his window, noting in disgust that her new

Master of the Horse, Lord Robert Dudley, rode just behind her chariot on a huge charger, leading her white horse draped in cloth of gold.

'That was an easy bit of jobbery,' he snorted to his friend, the Bishop de Quadra; 'the moment Queen Mary's dead, young Dudley rides to Hatfield on a snow-white stallion, shows off his skill in managing it, and gets himself made Master of the Horse within the hour. And for what reason, I ask you, *what*?'

The Bishop, a plump soft elderly man like a well-padded purple cushion, gazed wistfully after the superb figure of the young adventurer that towered over all around him, and replied more sympathetically, 'His beauty, stature, and florid youth recommend him.'

The Bishop was painfully conscious of his lack of all three qualities. He had some time ago arrived in England after a ghastly wintry crossing, during which his only comfort had been that the English Earl of Arundel, one of the many aspirants to Elizabeth's hand, had been even more seasick than himself, and had indeed cried like a child until their horrid little bobbing vessel had at last bounced them both into port.

Even now the Bishop could not quite believe himself on terra firma; he believed it less every time he met the new Queen of this misty portion of it. He had brought her a priceless ring as a present from his master, King Philip, and she had pocketed it very readily – or rather, wore it on her finger – with a charming smile and expressions of gratitude, but apparently no recognition of its significance.

In the Spanish Court everyone knew the King's intention to marry the Queen of England; but here, in this strange country, which seemed to be entirely given over to raw, new, showy, ignorant young people, they did not seem to think the King of Spain's intentions half as important as those of the Queen of England. Even his superior, the Count de Feria, was not at all reassuring; he kept swearing at the Sovereign they now had to deal with as a 'Medea,' a 'Jezebel,' a 'she-devil' of so many tricks and wiles that there was no knowing where to catch a hold of her.

'Look at her now,' Feria was spluttering as the gorgeous cortège spun itself out beneath their window in an unending glittering ribbon; 'do you see what she is aiming at? The *common people,* the crowds, the apprentices, even the beggars, and their wives, that is the audience she is playing to. She cares nothing for the rest of them – or for us. She is making a new religion for them, she is playing at being a goddess. Think of the Easter processions in my own dear town of Seville – well, it is yours too – think of the image of the Holy Virgin all in gold encrusted with jewels, carried shoulder-high through the streets, with the children singing her praises, and the crowds shouting applause to her, and all the Brotherhoods of the Inquisition following her in their Caps of Invisibility three feet high, with slits for their invisible, ubiquitous, anonymous eyes – think of them carrying her into our vast cathedral, the oldest and largest Gothic cathedral of Europe, adorned with barbaric gold from our new Indies, singing and shouting and dancing, they carry her image, swaying and glittering in the sunlight, into the dark cave of her mysterious worship, the worship of the Mother of God, the Mother of all this queerly mingled world of ours, and as such, they give her honour.

'And this young woman, begotten of God knows whom, of

the son of a Welsh adventurer who made himself King, some say, of a strolling base-born musician, say others – this smart young lass who has a charming appearance and is of a sharp wit, but *has no prudence* – this bright insolent girl, a heathen or all but, is setting herself up to be worshipped like the Virgin herself. For it is that which she is posing as – a Virgin Queen – the rival of the Virgin Mary, to supplant her in the affections and veneration of this God-forsaken people.'

De Feria spoke as one inspired, and so he was, with fury, as he twirled his upturned moustaches. He was longing to return to his 'Little Seville', and might soon have to do so. But the Bishop de Quadra could not welcome any move that would entail another sea voyage during the winter months; he seemed positively to enjoy this spectacle of an impudent, imprudent, cocksure young woman, upheld as a goddess by the ignorant vulgar, with one of her showy lovers *(sic)* in flamboyant attendance; he murmured gentle allusions to her transit as that of Atalanta, who would not pause in her race for glory, no, not even for golden apples (this apparently because she had given him no due recognition of the importance of King Philip's ring) – no, he said, he liked the girl's spirit, and the resplendent show that she was making.

Gentlemen pensioners in crimson damask surrounded Elizabeth, their gilt battle-axes gleaming dully through a light fall of snow; an army of footmen in crimson velvet marched around her, showing 'E.R.' for Elizabeth Regina studded in massive silver on their breasts and backs; pages in crimson satin followed her on their gorgeously caparisoned horses. She had left the Tower for a familiar City now transformed into a fairyland; the windows and wooden barriers before the houses, all the way from Fenchurch Street to Cheapside, fluttered with draperies, with banners and streamers of brilliant silks and cloth of gold. Trumpets sounded, choir boys sang, the City aldermen presented her with a thousand gold marks in a crimson satin purse; and in a quick impromptu speech she promised that for her part, 'for the safety and quietness of you all, I will not spare if need be to spend my blood. God thank you all.'

A mighty roar went up from those who heard her 'loving answer,' and it was shuttled down through the further crowds who could see only her spontaneous gestures and 'merry countenance'. Their cheers swung into a tune, catching up in ragged shouts the song that a boy was singing to her of their

> *'true hearts, which love thee from their root.'*
> – *'True hearts'* – *'skip for joy'* – *'thy happy name'* –
> – *'thy triumph now that ruleth all the game'* –

echoed back to her from thousands of lusty throats.

Another echo followed them in her mind, from her little brother Edward's Coronation when they had sung to him,

> *'Sing up, heart, sing up, heart, sing no more down,*
> *But joy in King Edward that weareth the crown,'*

and she, a child of thirteen, had wondered if that would ever happen to herself. It was happening now; and all these true hearts round her were singing up and up with hers.

There were pageants all along the route; historic or mythological figures greeted her at every street corner.

Under a flowery arch at the upper end of Gracechurch Street, two actors dressed as her grandparents sat in two vast roses, red and white, for the Houses of Lancaster and York, and from them a stem twined up into a second stage, where in another rose, striped red and white, sat the representative of her father, all red and gold between his enormous padded sleeves; and beside him, shown for the first time since she had been beheaded at her husband's command, was a lady of remarkable likeness to her mother, Ann Bullen – a thin white face under an old-fashioned coif like a church window, slant eyes as black as sloes, and long white hands. It was the only moment in the procession when Elizabeth had no appropriate comment to make.

But she made up for it at the Little Conduit in Cheapside where an old man came out of a cave towards her with a scythe and an hour-glass. She lifted her face towards a gleam of sun that shot down on her through the dark blue snow clouds, and exclaimed in delight, 'Time! And time has brought me here!'

Philip had once told her that he and Time together would be a match for any man; but now, in a sudden light of confidence, she felt that she and Time would be a match for Philip. Time should be more prompt at her command, for she stood in the sunlight where his hand moved on the dial, and Philip in the shadow where Time's hand stood still.

Time's daughter, Truth, stepped forward to give her a Bible, and she kissed it and thanked the City for this present of 'the lively Oracles of God.'

At St. Paul's, the head boy of Colet's school spoke in eulogy of her as an example of Plato's philosopher-monarch, and she capped it impromptu in Latin at least equal to his own. The eight Beatitudes (all very pretty children) pranced before her at the entry to Soper's Lane and told her she had been blessed, among other qualities, with meekness and mildness, a speech it was as well the Spanish Ambassadors did not hear. The old gate of Ludgate was more fantastically decked than any maypole; and in Fleet Street, Deborah sat enthroned, 'the judge and restorer of the House of Israel,' to show what a woman ruler could do in spite of Mr. John Knox's shrill 'First Blast of the Trumpet against the Monstrous Regiment of Women,' which he had blown in open publication some months before.

But neither the Presbyterian's sour maledictions, nor on the other hand the old Pope's angry threats of excommunication, could cloud the glory of the Coronation Service the next day, though in some eyes its rites were maimed. But Westminster Abbey had been made 'all glorious within' by Henry VIII's entire collection of tapestries, some of them from Raphael's designs, and of such biblical subjects as the stories from Genesis and the Acts of the Apostles, but others of the secular campaigns of Caesar and Pompey, since it was a pity to leave any out.

The dreamlike scenes, that would last for centuries, glowed and wavered in the draught behind the glory of this present moment. Queen Elizabeth, followed by her peeresses, walked in through the great doorway over a spread purple-blue cloth which the crowd outside cut away bit by bit, to keep the pieces as souvenirs. A little dark Italian writer, hungrily seeking employment in this strange country, feasted his eyes on the procession of noble ladies who all seemed to him tall, fair and beautiful; they trailed their long coloured robes behind them and held their proud heads high under their coronets as they paced slowly past him out of the raw northern daylight into the glimmering richness of the Abbey.

Four earls marched before them, carrying naked swords, one without any point, to signify Ireland, so somebody told the little foreigner, 'because it had never been conquered'; but others said it was because it was Curtana, the Sword of Peace and Mercy. Another sword represented France; but as even Calais had now been won back from England, the sword should surely have been more pointless even than that of Ireland. And why did the Sword of Justice, and its scabbard loaded with pearls, have to be redeemed from the altar for the price of a hundred silver shillings – was that the price of justice in this country? It was all rather confusing to the Italian visitor. Earls, Marquesses, Kings of Arms, which were which? The orb was carried by the Marquess of Winchester; and one of the sceptres by the Earl of Arundel, who had long ago recovered from his seasickness, but still looked as though he might cry at any minute. This, they said, was from sheer vainglorious excitement because he was made Lord High Steward at the Coronation and believed it to be a sign that his young Queen returned his passion for her. There were also two other sceptres, one of them signifying France, as usual; and three crowns, one of them carried just behind the Queen by the Earl Marshal, the young Duke of Norfolk. He was the only Duke left; all the others had lost their heads. How long would young Norfolk keep his? He did not look as though it were much help to him.

And there was as sad a lack of Bishops as of Dukes. There were no Archbishops, armoured in white and gold; no crimson Cardinals.

Oglethorpe of Carlisle, not really important, was the only Bishop who could be got to crown the suspected heretic; and he had had to borrow the robes of 'bloody Bishop Bonner' for the occasion, at the very last minute. He was in a twitter of nervous agitation, especially when Sir William Cecil, the new Secretary of State, passed notes to him from the Queen during the Service, telling him to read the Gospel and Epistle aloud in English as well as Latin.

Some asked behind their hands what business had Cecil, a layman, servant only of the State, in this sacred service; some feared that the Service was not sufficiently Roman Catholic; others, that it was too much so. It was Catholic in form, but did not commit the English Church to Rome, nor promise what course it would take in the future. Elizabeth herself was acutely aware of the anomaly, and of how quickly it might grow into complete division; the exiled Protestant zealots, now swarming back into the country, were pressing hard upon her with their demands that she should lead a revolution to overthrow all the forms of the Church and convert England by force to extreme Calvinism. Force she would not use, least of all for an aim she detested. Her aim was to have simplicity in religious intention, and a wise toleration. If people worked together for God and their fellow-men, it would bring a truer unity, peace and concord than any dialectic. But no one yet dreamed toleration possible, since religion also meant politics.

She must hold the uneasy balance of her reign by favour, and she alone could do it, because she was the Prince the people needed in this hour. Already ballads were being hawked on broadsheets in the streets to tell how wretched England had been under Mary, dulled by fear, disillusion and despair; and how through it all the only hope lay in the refrain that

'We *wished* for our *Elizabeth*.'

She too had recognized in her triumphal progress through the City that the crowds, for all their jollity and friendliness, had acclaimed her almost as a goddess. She must keep and increase that worship; it would lighten dreary thoughts, restore their confidence in their country and make it great.

The sacerdotal robe of gold was placed upon her, in the same ritual that consecrates a Bishop, and she was dedicated to God and to her people, to whom she had just promised, if need be, to spend her blood. The need might well arise; Philip of Spain still bore the title of King of England, and would till the day he died. He might well try to make it good by force of arms, if and when other means should fail him. But her life, even in this hour of glory, was not dear to her. She now, to herself, promised more; that she would at need spend her happiness. That promise was not made so easily; standing in the stiff archaic gold that might have sheathed a Byzantine priest, she felt that she was decked for sacrifice.

Then her spirit soared as she knew that her life was now indeed hallowed in this most ancient rite of 'the Sacring,' by the love she would give her people. They had been depressed, down-trodden, driven to fight for a foreign Power, and defeated; returned dismayed and forlorn, with nothing to hope for in a world where the old faiths and hopes had become meaningless to many, and a mere excuse for cruelty. They felt that God no longer cared for them, and no man would do so.

Now she had come, and she would care. Once the Sovereign had been a Priest; once he had been a God; but a ruler in Macedon long ago had known more truly when he said, 'kingship is a glorified servitude.' She was here to serve her countrymen; they were her charge, for God had charged her with them. This was the meaning in the heart of these long hours of ceremonial; and no hope of her own happiness, as it might be in the person of her Master of the Horse riding so jauntily behind her in the procession, could compete with this charge that had been laid upon her, and the joy of loving that it would bring her.

No one guessed then at that private hallowing of herself; human as it was, rather than pious, it was too much for her tense nerves; she had to break away from it in mockery, and shocked her ladies who changed her robes after her 'Sacring,' by telling them that the holy oil was 'nothing but nasty grease and stank.'

And as for being their 'undoubted Queen,' as the Bishop of Carlisle had presented her to her subjects, she knew well how many there were to doubt her title; but that was one of the many things one did not say, even in the sudden reactions of flippancy which so often helped her to keep her balance.

Yet it was that moment of her Election and Recognition as 'undoubted Queen' that was the most significant for her. For when she had to mount the tribune and be shown to all the people in the Abbey – North, South, East and West in turn – to ask if they were willing to do their Homage and Service to her as their Liege Lord, she was following the old tradition that a monarch did not reign by hereditary right alone, but was chosen freely by the people.

She owed her crown, she had told Feria, to the will of the people. Now they spoke that will with one voice; they acclaimed their wish for her as Queen in shouts of 'Yea! Yea! Yea!' so tremendous that they drowned the blare of trumpets and peal of bells that proclaimed it to the world outside. It sounded as though the world were coming to an end; and so indeed it was, for better or for worse, for joy or sorrow, the old world, the old ways of worship that Queen Mary had tried to bring back to England, were gone for good or ill, now that this new young Queen had been crowned.

She came into the outside world again, the orb and sceptre in her hands glittering in the wintry light of day, and on her head the great ruby of the Black Prince, which Henry V had worn in his helmet at Agincourt.

She smiled and talked to everyone near her, to the delight of the English and disapproval of the graver Latin observers; she changed her dress again and sat down to a banquet in Westminster Hall at which everybody was dressed in red, and drank red wine in the flickering light of the torches and great log fires. The old world of chivalry came back into the hall when the Queen's Champion, Sir Edward Dymoke, rode into the midst of it on a black charger draped with cloth of gold, and flung down his mailed glove in challenge to fight to the death any who wished to dispute the titles of his most worthy Empress. Nobody wished to do so, and the Queen drank his health in a gold cup worth two hundred crowns, which she presented to him. She sat all through the banquet, which had begun at three in the afternoon and lasted for ten hours; and at one o'clock next morning she went to bed for a week.

POSTLUDE:

THE KING AND QUEEN

Feria stood before his King in Flanders. He had finished his account of his mission in England; that at least was something. Ambassadors were sometimes struck dumb with awe when first confronted with Philip's pale and icy majesty. This was by no means Feria's first meeting; he had known him well (*how* well he suddenly doubted); had always stood up to him in his letters; and the King had never shown displeasure. But could his face ever show anything? It seemed to have crystallized still more of late.

The dark and angry little man who confronted the slighter figure of his King had to remind himself that it was through no fault of his own that he had failed in his mission; to console himself that at all events he had for ever shaken the dust or rather the mud of England off his Spanish-leathered shoes. He squared his broad shoulders and twirled up his aggressive black moustaches. No blue-blooded hidalgo from 'Little Seville' should let himself be overawed by a half-Flemish King who tried to seem more Spanish than all Spain, but gave himself away by the plodding industry of a German clerk. His glance slid down to the gold-inlaid desk at which Philip was reckoned to sit frequently for about sixteen hours a day.

He noted with disapproval that it was covered with the architects' plans for the new palace-monastery-tomb of the Escorial – a fantastic idea, and where was the money to come from, with the Exchequer in its present state? There was too much of this mountain-monastery business. The King had ordered the whole of Spain to collect alms for the building of a great new church at Montserrat near Barcelona, probably all because his father had visited it nine times and said there was a '*je ne sais quoi*' about the place. Armies of workmen would have to scramble two thousand feet up an almost inaccessible mountain with sacks of cement and loads of iron on their backs; Feria resented the expense of effort even more than that of money. Philip was behind the times. Mountains were holy only because they had been the refuge of the past, against the heathen Moors. Now, on the sea-board, lay the future of Catholic Spain.

He thought hard for an instant, then abandoned thought, and his words broke out as explosively as a bubble from a frog's mouth.

'Piety should be practical – and patriotic. All the good workmen in Spain should now be in the dockyards, preparing an armada for the conquest of heretic England.'

He urged Philip to this heroic master-stroke with a few well-placed pinpricks, insinuating the petty details that had revolted him of late in England. Their climate they could not help, poor, sodden, half-drowned devils. Their manners they had learned too late to learn, half civilized as they had been while Spain was leading Europe and discovering America. But their tastes! His eyes goggled, his mouth burst open, as he told Philip how their new young 'Virgin' Queen liked English beer, which Philip loathed; her own was 'so strong as there is no man able to drink it,' and went by such low, uncouth names as 'double-double' and 'hum and huff'.

That, he assured himself, should cure His High Austerity of wishing to feast with the tall girl who looked like a white and gold lily.

'Beer for Bess,' he rubbed it in, was the slogan of the new reign – how different from the life of their late Queen!

He spoke in terms of praise, but tones of scorn, of Elizabeth's extraordinary gift for the unconventional and impromptu – the very gift which Philip would regard as vulgar and ridiculous.

She had stopped a formal procession to call up to a sick friend at a window and ask after his health – oh yes, it was always 'his'; she had no women friends.

She had chaffed her dignified old ex-jailer, Sir Henry Bedingfeld, a devoted adherent to Queen Mary of blessed memory, by telling him that when she wanted any prisoners guarded with extra strictness she would put them in his charge.

She had no dignity, no propriety. Feria could not bring himself to repeat the jokes and innuendoes she had made to himself. But he repeated a good many.

He broke off suddenly. The King's face showed no sign of interest; he had not answered. He frequently did not answer. But Feria felt that a change of subject might be advisable.

So he congratulated him on the recent betrothal he had made for his young son, Don Carlos, with the eldest daughter of Henri II of France. It was a firm step forward, this matrimonial alliance with France, in the project of subduing England; Feria gave it his unqualified approval. And Isabel de Valois, a lovely and gentle girl of sixteen, barely two years older than her prospective bridegroom, would be an added grace, an easily malleable tool for the Court of Spain. She would also make a true man of the eager boy who, said Feria with a spruce smile, was already reputed to be madly in love with her portrait.

The King made a slight movement, but only to bow politely. His servant's thoughts began to course wildly. Could there after all be some truth in the stories he had heard? Did the King really hate his odd, outspoken, backward, yet sometimes precocious son and heir? Philip, like all the Spaniards that he emulated, was respectable. Carlos gave no sign of ever being so. He was vulgar, violent, rude and uncontrolled. But everyone said that since his betrothal he was a changed creature, quiet and modest, walking as in an enchanted dream with the miniature of the dark grave-eyed girl who was to be his bride; when he thought himself alone he kissed it, talked to it, promised it that now he would be good and gentle and worthy of her love.

Just such an idyll had been Philip's own first marriage in his boyhood; Feria wondered if he should suggest this. No flicker of expression passed over the impassive face before him, yet Feria could have sworn that at that moment the King shared his thought. So why not say it? But he did not.

He shot back to the vexed question of England, and answered it in arrogant confidence. The country, once conquered, would be re-converted with ease. The English would always worship as their rulers and their interests demanded. His spies' statistics had proved that only one per cent. of the population were even now really Protestant – and they were only negligible artisans in sedentary jobs that gave time for conceit, such as tailors and cobblers.

At last there was a break in the mask; the faint eyebrows had arched themselves slightly. 'In my father's day,' said the low, even voice, 'a petty cobbler led the revolt of the Communidades in Majorca which slaughtered the patrician families and held out against the Emperor for over a year.'

'And then was conquered only by a dirty Flemish trick,' Feria longed to add, but even he did not dare. He found himself hovering, clinging on with his Spanish-leathered toes to the marble floor, while he desperately propounded that

England was only heretic because of her Queen, who had to be one, or else declare herself a bastard with no legitimate claim to the throne.

It was no use. He found himself dismissed, and with no idea as to what was the King's decision – if any.

Philip himself could not have told then what it was. He needed time to think it over, alone, at his desk. Time, he had said, was on his side. But on which side of him? He knew, to his torment, that he had two sides, and could never be sure on which stood Time. He thought of the rocky peaks in the rare luminous air of Castile, where the castle homes of his boyhood had been built long ago – Segovia, Toledo, Avila of the eighty towers. There his spirit lived, and longed to draw to its end on earth, as his father's had done on the mountain top of Yuste. But his body had to stay now on this soggy plain of Flanders, where his father had blamed him for inaction. Surely that released spirit could not *now* think it better to have marched on Paris than to have planned the Escorial?

He looked down at the designs for the soaring edifice of austere granite that should rise in harmony with the surrounding rocks and pines, but in an urgency of pure spirit. Majesty would be shown as sacred; above the temple a spire would point to the sky, crowned with an orb to signify the power of this world, but on top of the orb would tower a gold cross. He held up the design in his hands, but he was not looking at it now; his gesture was that of offering it to another. He was holding it in self-justification to his father. This was his answer to the Emperor's accusation.

Action meant grasping, seeking for oneself, and therefore ignoble. Self sacrifice, suffering in devotion, was the purest form of action, perhaps the only true form of it. His eyes turned, as so often, to the crucifix on the wall. God the Son had shown the way. In contrast, God the Father had made the world; and, in doing so, a mistake.

'Let me alone,' he had once prayed when a boy, 'for I am not better than my father,'

But it might be that Christ would wish him, too, to prove the contrary.

Not in life, but in death, lay the answer to life. He had known it even when he was still a boy. He knew it better now. What good, even from the view of this world, came out of all this busy planning and self-seeking? He had tried to marry his wife's young sister, a bastard heretic with flaming hair, but eyes as cold as the sea when she looked at him. He had lusted after her while his wife was still alive and tortured by her jealousy of them. And still she had not consented to marry him. God had not only denied him, but cruelly humiliated him through this white witch, this false goddess who now sat on the precarious throne of England. In her arrogance she preened and plumed herself there like a peacock, ignoring the fact that it was he who had placed her there, that but for him she might well be dead. Better dead, since she lived only to flout him; to ignore, even mock his conscientious scruples as those of a fussy little man – yes, that was how Feria had shown that she regarded him – a little man at the mercy of a woman's whim.

Yet again England had wounded him in a personal matter that struck at his masculine pride. It was of no use now to look at his plans for the Escorial, to think of death, the leveller, who made all men equal, even in stature, in the grave. God had used this woman as a sign, to show him that not only must he turn from his longing for her quick, lithe body, her flashes of speech and laughter, all the bright blazing life of her, but that he must turn against her. Her power was for evil; that was now clear from her use of it over himself. Therefore he must withstand it; he must take action, and quickly, hateful as that was to him. Soon she would be boasting throughout Europe that she had refused his offer of marriage.

Philip did not tell himself that at all costs he must forestall that insult; that he must prove to the world that he had jilted 'that jilt, the Lady Elizabeth,' before Elizabeth had jilted him. But he began to see how it could be done. How also, in compensation for his lost false love, God might reward him with a true and docile wife, tender as the opening rosebuds, comparable only with his own first bride, when he had tasted rapture (but for how brief a moment!) in his boyhood.

He thought of his fourteen-year-old son, of Carlos's pathetic belief that when he was married he would be a man, whom no one would dare to scold or order about any more. But how fit was his son to bear the excitements and responsibilities of such early marriage? They might not lessen but increase his abnormal tendencies. It would be terrible to think of a young girl in the power of a crude, savage adolescent.

Philip had already thought of it, but felt that he could not say it; he could not accuse his son, show that he doubted the sanity of his heir. Whatever happened, he would never do that. So he had taken no action; had let matters take their course; had allowed his counsellors to hurry on the betrothal for the sake of the political alliance.

But he could now see another way to secure that alliance, a way that was outrageous to him, contrary to his whole nature – but necessary.

The clock his father had made ticked on. The sky outside

darkened into the Netherlandish night, then grew pale in a watery dawn. Time stepped past at King Philip's side, and his thoughts dragged after it, drawing him slowly towards the only impetuous decision he ever made.

It fell like a thunderbolt on Europe – and on Carlos. The King of Spain proposed to marry his son's prospective bride.

People were shocked, horrified, amused. The King of Spain had chosen an odd way to restore himself to his full stature in his own sight, by behaving like a disappointed lover in a violent fit of pique. Everybody knew now that Elizabeth must have refused him, or that he knew she was going to, since here he was rushing off, without a word of warning, to marry his son's betrothed bride. 'Rushing off' – it was inconceivable in connection with Philip; yet it was true. His dislike of action, his deep-seated fear of ridicule, had led him to the most ridiculous action of his life.

To his son, it was also the worst. The young Prince's burst of frustrated rage was dreadful to see and hear. He uttered such threats against his father, who he declared had always hated him, and now had stolen his wife from him, that people said he really must be mad, and unsafe to be at large.

But the Spanish and French politicians were jubilant. The two countries, after generations of enmity, would now be in the closest possible alliance. With the King of Spain as son-in-law to the King of France, Europe would be united as one Power against the heretics. Nothing now could prevent the invasion of England, to depose Elizabeth and set Mary Queen of Scots on the throne. The French and Scots armies were all ready to march down on London from the North, while the Spanish flotillas would attack the East coast from Flanders across the Narrow Seas.

Spain's greatest soldier, the Duke of Alva, sat at work in Antwerp with maps before him of English harbours, particularly in East Anglia. The Dutch bargees jeeringly called the barge's mooring-post a 'dukdalf' after him, he was so long and thin and wooden; but he was a mooring-post in grim earnest for the Spanish armadas that were thronging to his command.

And his spies came as thick and fast, to tell him how broken were the English armies, how weak their navies and rotten their ships, how frantically busy all their dockyards. Let them build ships night and day, they could not build them in time.

The bookmakers in Europe had given the new young Queen six months at most to keep her throne, and the days were running out.

If you enjoyed *Elizabeth and the Prince of Spain*,
read on to find out about more books
by Margaret Irwin . . .

To discover more great fiction and to
place an order visit our website at
www.allisonandbusby.com
or call us on
020 7580 1080

YOUNG BESS

Growing up in the shadow of her mother, the infamous Anne Boleyn, young Princess Elizabeth has learnt to be continuously on the watch for the political games played out around her. It is never certain when one might rise in, or precariously fall out of, royal favour.

When her distant father, Henry VIII, dies, the future brightens for Elizabeth. She is able to set up a home with Henry's last wife, Catherine Parr, who now has a new husband, Tom Seymour. Tom, however, is playing a risky game. Marrying a widowed queen is one thing; flirting with the king's daughter and second in line to the throne is another. As the adolescent Elizabeth finds herself dangerously attracted to him, tragedy looms ahead for her and the kingdom . . .

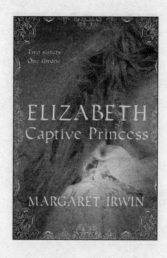

July, 1553. Sibling rivalry has never been more turbulent and perilous than between the daughters of King Henry VIII. Queen Mary Tudor has just won possession of the throne, but her younger half-sister – the beautiful and vivacious Princess Elizabeth – holds the hearts of the people. Knowing this, Mary banishes her sibling to a country retreat, determined to keep her as far away from court life as possible.

But Mary's health is fading fast and her power beginning to crumble. The people of England are crying out for a new monarch and it seems, at last, they may have their wish and crown their beloved Bess as Queen. In these treacherous times, when all about her lies secrecy and deception, Elizabeth must rely on her faith and courage if she is to rise to fulfil her destiny.

THE GALLIARD

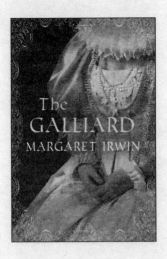

The young and trusting Mary, Queen of Scots, is sailing home to her kingdom after years in exile. The danger from her cousin, the English Queen, has not lessened since she first departed. Religious divides threaten to tear the nation apart and, across the border, Elizabeth keenly watches this new threat to her throne.

Amid the furious turmoil and uncertainty in her Scottish kingdom, Mary finds she has one loyal servant – James Hepburn, Earl of Bothwell, a 'glorious, rash and hazardous young man' known to all as the Galliard. In Bothwell's courage and love for her, Mary finds serenity, and though fate works against them, no force can conquer their spirit.